# CURTSIES & CONSPIRACIES

FINISHING SCHOOL BOOK THE SECOND

# GAIL CARRIGER

Little, Brown and Company
New York  Boston

Little, Brown and Company

Hachette Book Group
1290 Avenue of the Americas, New York, NY 10104
Visit our website at lb-teens.com

Little, Brown and Company is a division of Hachette Book Group, Inc.
The Little, Brown name and logo are trademarks of Hachette Book Group, Inc.

The publisher is not responsible for websites (or their content) that are not owned by the publisher.

First Paperback Edition: October 2014
First published in hardcover in November 2013 by Little, Brown and Company

Library of Congress Cataloging-in-Publication Data

Carriger, Gail.
    Curtsies & conspiracies / Gail Carriger.—First edition.
        pages cm.—(Finishing school; book the second)
    Summary: In her alternate England of 1851, fifteen-year-old Sophronia tries to uncover who is behind a plot to control a prototype that has the potential to alter human and supernatural travel, and to learn what role Mademoiselle Geraldine's academy for young spies plays in the affair.
    ISBN 978-0-316-19011-4 (hc)—ISBN 978-0-316-19020-6 (pb)
    [1. Boarding schools—Fiction. 2. Schools—Fiction. 3. Etiquette—Fiction. 4. Espionage—Fiction. 5. Robots—Fiction. 6. Great Britain—History—George VI, 1936–1952—Fiction. 7. Science fiction.] I. Title. II. Title: Curtsies and conspiracies.
    PZ7.C23455Cur 2013
    [Fic]—dc23

                                                                            2012048520

10 9 8 7 6 5 4 3

RRD-C

Printed in the United States of America

## DANGEROUS PUDDINGS

Miss Temminnick. Miss Plumleigh-Teignmott. With me, please, ladies."

Sophronia glanced up from her household sums. She was glad of the distraction. She was convinced she s miscalculating the purchase of the three most deadly flower angements. *Does one need four fully grown foxgloves for deco-ng a dinner table for six guests? Or is it six foxgloves to kill four y grown guests?*

Unfortunately, what Sophronia saw when she looked up did fill her with confidence. Lady Linette stood at the front of class wearing an austere expression that clashed with her ious yellow curls and a bonnet covered with drooping silk s. She was wearing a good deal of face paint and a purple-jade plaid dress of immense proportions. It was neither her ression nor her location at the front of the class that made hronia nervous. It was the fact that she was present in *this* class, for this was Sister Mathilde Herschel-Teape's lesson on domestic accounting. Sophronia and her age-group were to go to Lady Linette *after* tea, for drawing room music and subversive petits fours.

"This decade, Miss Temminnick!"

Dimity was already standing next to Lady Linette. Sophronia's friend gestured her forward with a hand hidden to one side of her skirt. Ordinarily, it was Dimity daydreaming and Sophronia having to chivy *her* along.

Sophronia leapt to her feet. "Apologies, Lady Linette. I wa so very absorbed. Foxglove quantities can be most illuminating

"Very good, Miss Temminnick. An excuse couched in tern of academic interest. Nevertheless, we must be away."

For most of Sophronia's six-month sojourn at Mademoise Geraldine's Finishing Academy for Young Ladies of Quali lessons had *never* been interrupted. Not even when flywaym attacked. Young ladies of quality stayed *in* class in times strife. Certainly no student had been removed from one tea er's purview by another teacher. That was quite rude!

Then over the last month, starting with the dratted Monic every one of Sophronia's fellows had systematically been tal away by Lady Linette in just such a manner. They retur traumatized and silent. All Sophronia's skills, many of th learned at Mademoiselle Geraldine's, had been put to figur this out. To no avail. Even her particular friends, Sidheag Agatha, wouldn't explain what had happened when Lady Line absconded with them.

Sister Mattie was unperturbed by the interruption, sitt placidly in her mock-religious attire behind a wide desk rounded by potted plants and bottles of deadly poison (or tea concentrate, one never knew which). Sister Mattie was a bit of a mystery; her preference for a simulated nun's habit—wide-skirted and to the current fashion, with a wimple partly configured like a bonnet—remained unexplained. The girls saw her as a nice sort of mystery and one of the more benign teachers, so they mostly respected her eccentric choice of dress.

Sophronia's fellow students were looking on with wide eyes. Sidheag and Agatha tensed sympathetically. Monique and Preshea sat with arms crossed and ill-contained delight on their faces.

Sophronia wended her way through the plush chairs and rolltop writing desks to the front, where she curtsied before Lady Linette. It was a perfectly executed curtsy, not too deep, with a slight tilt to her head but not enough to seem obsequious.

Sister Mattie said kindly, "I shouldn't worry, Miss Temminnick. I'm certain you'll do very well."

"Follow me, please, ladies," snapped Lady Linette.

"Good luck!" Agatha said quietly. Agatha rarely spoke, so it had to be something serious.

Sophronia sidled up next to Dimity. The hallway was hardly big enough to accommodate two ladies in full day gowns side by side. Their multiple skirts smushed together. Neither minded the wrinkles as they linked arms for comfort. Mademoiselle Geraldine's Finishing Academy was housed in a massive airship that looked like three dirigibles crammed together. Its corridors twisted and turned in a noodlelike manner. Sometimes the passageways led up stairs or out onto balconies. Most of the time, they simply got darker, lit by gas lamps that looked like upside-down parasols. Whatever attire the corridors had been designed to accommodate, proper lady's dress was not one of them.

Lady Linette led them toward the upper squeak decks. These open-air decks sat under the massive balloons that kept the academy afloat and adrift over Dartmoor. It was an odd place to be headed at this time of day. Dimity's hand on Sophronia's arm tightened.

The two girls swung to flatten themselves against the wall, like a hinged gate, so a maid mechanical could roll past. Its face was a mosaic of gears instead of the metal masks worn by most menials. It had a white pinafore over its conical body and gave the impression of busy superciliousness.

If the students had been alone, the maid would have whistled the alarm upon encountering them, but Dimity and Sophronia were in the company of Lady Linette. All the models, from buttlinger to footmech to clangermaid, had protocols that instructed them to ignore students in the company of teachers. Most of the hallways were laid down with a single track upon which the school's many servants trundled, performing the myriad of menial tasks needed to keep a ladies' seminary running smoothly. Sophronia had once seen a footmech model carrying a whole stack of doilies, some of them quite deadly, from Sister Mattie to Professor Lefoux. In her parents' country estate, such an important task would never have been entrusted to a mechanical, but here steam-powered staff far outnumbered human.

Sophronia had thought, after six months, that she had most of the school mapped. But as they walked from the midship student section, which housed classrooms and sleeping quarters, to the rear recreation area, they entered a place she'd never seen before. While the massive dining hall and exercise facilities above the warehouse and propeller engine areas were familiar to her, Sophronia and Dimity were being taken farther up.

"I didn't know there were rooms *above* the dining hall," said Sophronia to Lady Linette.

Lady Linette was not going to give in to Sophronia's hunt for information. She ignored the comment and quickened her pace.

Sophronia and Dimity bounced in order to keep up—they had not yet had lessons on rapid walking in full skirts, though both of them were admirable gliders at a more leisurely pace.

This section of the ship smelled of old candle wax, chalk powder, and pickled onions. The mechanical track was not oiled properly and there was dust in the corner grippers. The walls were hung with paintings of disapproving elderly females and framed feats of crochet.

Finally, Lady Linette stopped in front of a door. The sign read ASSESSMENT CHAMBER ONE: ENTER AT RISK. It reminded Sophronia a little of the record room. She didn't say anything about that, though. The record room infiltrators of several months ago had never been caught. Sophronia wanted to keep it that way.

Underneath the sign someone had scrawled in white paint NO MUFFINS FOR YOU! Underneath that, it said NOR GALOSHES, NEITHER, in what Sophronia knew was not proper grammar.

"Miss Temminnick." Lady Linette gestured. "If you would?"

Sophronia stepped into the room alone. Lady Linette closed the door behind her.

Sophronia's attention was entirely taken by the huge mechanical thingamabob in front of her. It looked very like the difference engine she had seen last summer when her family visited the Crystal Palace. This one, however, was not being used for sums. It was rigged and draped with objects—fabric hung at the back, paintings dangled, and a few pots and pans drooped uncertainly to one side.

Sophronia frowned. *Didn't Vieve once describe something like this to me? What did she call it? Oh, yes, an oddgob machine.*

Next to the oddgob, positioned to operate a crank, was a mechanical designed to accompany the apparatus.

Sophronia faced both, hands crossed lightly at her waist, a position that Lady Linette encouraged her girls to assume whenever at a loss for action. "The crossed hands denote modesty and religious devotion. The placement draws attention to the narrowness of one's waist. Bow your head slightly and you can still observe through the lashes, which is becoming. This exposes the back of the neck, an indication of vulnerability." Sophronia's shoulders tended to hunch, a habit Mademoiselle Geraldine was trying desperately to break. "We can't have you tensing up like an orangutan!" she chided. "Do orangutans tense?" Dimity had whispered. Dimity, of course, crossed her hands divinely.

Sophronia worked to relax her shoulders.

Neither the machine nor the mechanical seemed to care, for nothing happened even when her posture was perfect.

Sophronia said, "Good afternoon. I believe you are waiting for me?"

With a puff of steam, the mechanical whirred to life. "Six-month. Review. Debut upmark," it said, clicking as a metal tape fed through its voice box.

Not knowing what else to do, Sophronia said, "Yes?"

"Begin," ordered the mechanical, and with that, it reached out one clawlike appendage and began to crank the oddgob.

An oil painting flipped over from the top of the engine and dropped down, dangling from conveyer chains. It depicted a girl in a blue dinner dress, decades out of style, that embarrassing nightgown look. The subject was pretty, with cornflowers in her hair, enjoying an evening gathering.

The mechanical continued cranking, and the painting was jerked away. A hatch opened, and a full tea service on a silver tray rolled forth.

"Serve," ordered the mechanical.

Sophronia stepped forward, feeling silly. The service was for four. The tea in the pot was cold. She hesitated. Ordinarily, she would have dumped the contents into the receptacle and sent it back with sharp words to the cook. *Do I act as I would in real life? Or am I to pretend to serve the tea regardless?*

The mechanical was still whirring, indicating that she had only a set amount of time to decide.

Sophronia served. She did as etiquette demanded, pouring her own cup first and then the others. With no one to ask if they wanted sugar or if they would prefer lemon, she only checked to ascertain both were provided. The sugar pot was half full. There were four slices of dry lemon. Like the tea, they had been sitting for some time. She opened the top of the pot and checked the leaf. Top quality. As was the tea set—Wedgwood blue, or a very good imitation. She sniffed the pot, the milk, and the cups. They all smelled as they should, although one of the cups might have boasted a slight lavender odor. There was a plate of three petits fours dusted with sugar. Sophronia poked each gently on the side with a glove-covered fingertip. She was unsurprised to find that one of them was fake, no doubt from Mademoiselle Geraldine's personal collection. The headmistress had a mad passion for fake pastries. The other two appeared to be real. They both smelled of bitter almond. Sophronia raised up her Depraved Lens of Crispy Magnification, a present on her fifteenth birthday from Dimity's brother, Pillover. It was essentially a high-powered monocle on a stick, but useful enough to keep at all times hanging from a chatelaine at her waist. The sugar on the top of one of the cakes looked odd.

The tray was whisked away.

Next, a string of dangling hair ribbons paraded before her, pinned like wet hose to a stretch of twine. Sophronia's dress today was a pale-yellow-and-blue ruffled monstrosity her mother insisted would *do*, even though it had been worn three seasons already, by three older sisters. Sophronia's absence from the Temminnick household was combined with an absence from Temminnick expenses. She hadn't had a new gown in ages. One of the ribbons was cream and blue in a similar shade to her outfit, so Sophronia unclipped it. Because her hair was covered—as it should be—by a respectable bonnet, she tied the ribbon about her neck in the complex knot of a Bunson's boy. Bunson and Lacroix's Boys' Polytechnique was an evil genius training academy, sort of a sibling school to Mademoiselle Geraldine's. If one thought of those siblings as hostile and estranged.

The ribbons were taken away, and the oddgob machine presented Sophronia with a new selection: a letter opener, a pair of ornate lady's sewing scissors, a large fan, a crumpet, two handkerchiefs, and some white kid gloves. Sophronia felt she was on firmer ground at last. These were tools of great and fateful weight when applied properly. She chose the scissors and one of the handkerchiefs. The other options were removed.

Next came a slate upon which had been written the phrase SEND HELP IMMEDIATELY. In front of it, on a wooden board, lay a piece of parchment with ink and quill, an embroidery hoop with needle and thread, and a bag of raspberry fizzy sweets. Sophronia chose the sweets, cracked one open with the aid of her scissors, and dumped out the fizz. She used the needle from the embroidery to prick her finger, smeared the blood on the inside of the broken sweet, and popped it back inside the little sack. Then she cut off a bit of the ribbon tied about her neck and used that to secure the bag.

The remaining items disappeared into the oddgob, and the mechanical stopped cranking.

Sophronia stepped back and let out a sigh.

Her stomach rumbled, informing her that a good deal of time had passed. She had been given longer to contemplate each test than she realized. A bang sounded at the door. When she opened it, a maid mechanical sat there, bearing a tray of food. Sophronia took it gratefully, and the maid trundled off without ceremony. Sophronia closed the door with her foot and, in the absence of chairs, balanced the tray precariously on one section of the oddgob.

She assessed the food. Nothing smelled of almonds. Nevertheless, she avoided the leg of mutton in glistening currant jelly sauce and the Bakewell pudding and ate only the plain boiled potatoes and broccoli. Better to assume everything was still a test until Lady Linette returned to tell her otherwise. Sad, because she loved Bakewell. When nothing else happened, Sophronia put the tray down and examined the oddgob while it was not waggling things autocratically in front of her.

It was a fascinating apparatus. She wondered if Vieve knew of its existence at the school. Genevieve Lefoux was a dear friend, a mercurial ten-year-old with a propensity for dressing like a boy and a habit of inventing gadgetry. If Vieve didn't know of the oddgob, she would want to, and she was certain to ask all sorts of questions. Sophronia took mental notes in anticipation of conversations to come. When tired of that, she used the scissors to extract a small part from the machine. It was a crystalline valve, faceted, and awfully familiar in shape and style. It looked like a smaller version of the prototype Monique had tried to steal last year. This valve appeared to have been only propped in, so Sophronia was certain that removing it would make no difference to the function of the oddgob. When they'd first discovered the prototype valve last year, Vieve had prattled on about point-to-point transmissions. A revelatory breakthrough indeed, since the telegraph machine had recently proved a dismal failure. If this was a new version of that same prototype, Vieve would want to see it.

The door behind Sophronia creaked open, and she hastily

stashed the mini-prototype up her sleeve, where the pagoda style allowed for secret pockets.

"Miss Temminnick, have you finished?" Lady Linette asked.

"Isn't everyone finished at the same time? The oddgob cycle seems to be prescribed," replied Sophronia.

"Now, now, manners."

Sophronia curtsied apologetically, although she did feel as if she had been abandoned for longer than necessary.

"I had to assess Miss Plumleigh-Teignmott first. Technically, she was admitted ahead of you. If you'll recall, you went for tea with Mademoiselle Geraldine before you were formally allowed into the school."

Sophronia recalled it quite vividly, as a matter of fact. All those fake cakes.

"Now for your report." Lady Linette removed something round and mechanical from her reticule and shook it violently. Was she mad?

Nothing happened.

"They said it was working. Oh, bother." Frustrated, Lady Linette marched over to the oddgob and jerked a few cranks and switches on the underside of the mechanical's carapace. In response, the mechanical turned a smaller, hidden crank at the back, well out of human reach. On the far end of the oddgob, a massive roller ratcheted down, dipped into a pan of ink, and rolled across a series of letters. These then beat down in a sequential blur onto a taut piece of parchment. A large pink blotter rocked back and forth across the finished text.

Sophronia was impressed. She hadn't noticed that the odd-gob contained a printing press.

Something rattled in the machine and then whined.

"Stop that," said Lady Linette to the oddgob, shaking the mysterious object in her hand at it again.

*Oh, dear, perhaps the mini-prototype was vital,* thought Sophronia.

The oddgob whined louder and began to shake.

"Stop cranking," Lady Linette instructed the mechanical, shaking the object harder. "Miss Temminnick, I think we had better make haste." The teacher gestured for Sophronia to precede her from the room.

Too late, however, for the oddgob exploded with a terrific bang. Hair ribbons fluttered up into the air, the tea service shattered, the fake tea cake bounced like a rubber ball, and ink squirted out from the printing press.

Sophronia and Lady Linette flattened themselves on the floor, heedless of crushed dresses and flipped petticoats.

"My goodness," said Lady Linette into the resulting silence. "What did you do?" She stood and walked to the oddgob, now tilted to one side as if it had a limp.

"Me? Nothing at all!" insisted Sophronia, sitting up.

Lady Linette tutted as she brushed ink spatter off her well-powdered cheek with a handkerchief. "Where's the new valve gone?"

"What valve?" Sophronia blinked wide, confused eyes at her.

Lady Linette gave her a long look. "Probably rolled free during the explosion. I told Professor Lefoux it wasn't tight enough in the cradle. And I said it wouldn't work properly regardless." Sophronia didn't say anything. "I wish we could have tested it on a less valuable machine. Never mind, we've got your results." Lady Linette waved the oddgob's printed paper.

Sophronia stood and innocently offered her teacher the additional handkerchief she'd acquired during the test. Lady Linette took it absently, then paused, pondering. She did not apply it to the remains of the ink on her face, instead handing it back with a little smile.

"Oh, very good, Miss Temminnick. Very good indeed!" She examined the printed sheet. Closely.

"Let us begin your review. The painting, time period?"

"Eighteen fourteen, by attire," said Sophronia. "Give or take a year. Evening party."

"Dress color?"

"Blue on the central subject, green and cream on those in the background."

"Bonnet style and decoration?"

*Trick question!* "None of the ladies were wearing hats. The subject had cornflowers in her hair. As I said, it was an evening party."

Lady Linette arched an eyebrow over her spectacles. "And have you any additional thoughts?"

Sophronia straightened. "A great many."

"About the painting, Miss Temminnick. Don't be coy."

Sophronia forbore mentioning that Lady Linette had said only yesterday that there was always time for coyness in young ladies of quality. "The painting was well executed, but the artist was probably poor."

Lady Linette looked nonplussed. "Why do you say that?"

"No expensive pigments, like red and gold, were used. Either that, or the painter feared toxicity. He did not sign it. There were approximately twelve people in the image." Sophronia paused delicately for effect. "And one cat. The wallpaper was striped, and the garden through the window had a Roman feel."

Lady Linette nodded, dislodging her spectacles. She reseated them on her nose with a sniff of annoyance. Lady Linette always dressed younger than she was. Spectacles, under such circumstances, might be considered a fate worse than knitwear.

"Moving on to the tea service, Miss Temminnick. The tea was cold. Why did you still serve it?"

Sophronia nibbled her lip. It was another habit her teachers were trying to eliminate. "If you must draw attention to the lips, a small lick is superior. It is too academic to nibble" was Lady Linette's customary admonishment. "It's all very well to be an intellectual, but one shouldn't let others see. That's embarrassing" was Mademoiselle Geraldine's opinion.

Sophronia stopped nibbling. "I did consider dumping it entirely, but I thought the oddgob indicated I was to be evaluated on the *act* of serving. Had there been other people present, I would have sent it back."

"Milk first, the lower-class way?"

"But necessary if the cups were lined with an acid-based poison. The milk would curdle or discolor. Also, one of the cups smelled of lavender."

Lady Linette said, unguardedly, "It did?"

"Yes. I don't know of any poisons with that smell, but it might be used to cover over another scent or, of course, it might have been your cup, Lady Linette."

"My cup?"

"You *always* smell of lavender."

"The tea cakes?"

"One was fake. Of the other two, both smelled of bitter almond—one because it was an almond cake, I believe. The other was powdered in cyanide." Sophronia had been saddened by the cyanide lesson with Sister Mattie. For the rest of her life—unless she learned to bake—almond cake was right out. There was no surefire way to guarantee lack of cyanide in any almond-smelling confection.

"Moving on to the ribbons."

Sophronia explained, "I selected the one that matched my outfit and tied it in a Bunson's knot."

"There's a piece missing."

Sophronia grinned. "I must beg your patience in that matter, my lady."

Her teacher was taken aback but continued. "Why the Bunson's knot?"

Sophronia parroted a recent article she'd translated from the Parisian fashion papers. Vieve, of all people, had given it to her. Vieve might dress like a newspaper boy, but she took an interest in current styles, particularly hats. This article had delighted the young girl. "It has a pleasing military feel. I read recently that the juxtaposition and power of masculine elements can inspire confidence in the wearer, and the accompanying aura of authority is never a bad thing," Sophronia paraphrased.

Lady Linette looked impressed. This was not part of any lesson. "And *do* you feel more confident and authoritative, Miss Temminnick?"

Sophronia touched the ribbon. "Actually, I do."

Lady Linette nodded. "It would be a good style for you to pursue. I suggest you encourage your mother to have at least one new dress made up with military detailing." She gave Sophronia a pitying look.

Sophronia blushed. She and Dimity did their best to make over her dresses. But her older ones had such a narrow silhouette, and with skirts getting progressively wider, there wasn't much they could do. It was impossible to add volume to a dress. And this was a finishing school—everyone *noticed* such things. Still, if Lady Linette thought more masculine fashions might suit her, perhaps gold tassels and epaulets were in order. Dimity would be over the moon.

Lady Linette interrupted her reverie. "You chose the sewing scissors and one of the handkerchiefs from the next test. Why?"

"We have not completed knife training with Captain Niall, so I wasn't confident in the letter opener, but I know I can work scissors to my advantage, and it is always good to have an extra handkerchief."

"Why not the fan or the gloves?"

"White kid is impractical for a lady of covert activities. We have not had any fan training yet."

"The crumpet?"

"Oh, no, I'm not worthy."

"Lastly, we had you send a coded message. Give it to me."

Sophronia presented her with the bag of sweets tied with the bit of ribbon.

Lady Linette nodded her approval. "Ribbon used to indicate character of the sender. Nice touch, Miss Temminnick. You made use of the scissors from the previous selection." She opened the bag and poured out the contents, including the one carefully broken sweet with the blood inside.

Lady Linette sniffed it and examined the stain. "Show me your hand."

Sophronia removed one glove to display the finger she had pricked.

"You would have had to set up the code ahead of time. Nevertheless, an innovative method of getting a message across, and virtually untraceable, particularly as your recipient can eat the sweet." Lady Linette looked down once more at the printed paper, then produced a stick of graphite and made some notes at the bottom.

Sophronia could feel her shoulders tensing and fought to keep them down. *Were my choices correct? Do they want the expected route, or is it better if I did something out of the ordinary? Will they send me down?* Sophronia was in ever-greater fear that her sojourn at Mademoiselle Geraldine's might come to a premature end. Only half a year ago she had resisted finishing school with every fiber of her being, until she realized Mademoiselle Geraldine's offered no ordinary education. Now she dreaded the possibility of returning home to her former life.

Lady Linette said, "Everyone's results are given together. You will receive your final marks in front of your peers."

Sophronia's heart sank. This explained the pale faces of the other girls—anticipated trauma. Agatha, in particular, hated public exposure.

"However, my initial assessment is that your capacities are suited to our institution. You are overly independent. I suggest focused study in social congregation and deportment. Groups, Miss Temminnick, are your weakness. Generally speaking, most *lone* intelligencers are men, not women. We ladies must learn to manipulate society."

Sophronia could feel herself flushing. It was a fair assessment, but she did not like criticism. She knew she was good. Better than many of the other girls of her age-group. True, Sidheag could beat her in physical combat, Dimity and Preshea were more ladylike, and Monique was better at social graces, but Sophronia was the best at espionage. Nevertheless, she held her tongue and stared at her hands, forcing herself not to clasp them tightly. Lady Linette had only said that *most* lone intelligencers were male. Perhaps once in a while there was room for a female.

"Thank you, Miss Temminnick. You are dismissed."

Sophronia bobbed a curtsy. It was just shy of being too high and too brief and thus rude. But before Lady Linette could comment, Sophronia swept from the room in a manner so grand that no teacher at Mademoiselle Geraldine's would critique the action.

## THE 2ND TEST

# RESULTS DISORIENTATED

S ophronia found Dimity waiting in the hallway. Her friend's face was white and her lower lip trembled.

"Oh, Sophronia," she cried. "Wasn't that *perfectly* ghastly?"

*She's getting more and more dramatic,* thought Sophronia. *Overexposure to Mademoiselle Geraldine.* "It certainly was odd." Sophronia's gift for understatement was almost as good as Dimity's gift for overstatement.

"I poured the cold tea," admitted Dimity. "Did you?"

Sophronia nodded.

"Oh, good, I thought you might. You're usually right about these things."

"Not always."

Dimity was crestfallen. "Oh, dear. Your assessment wasn't wholly positive?"

"Not by half!"

Dimity brightened. "Really? Neither was mine. That's good, then. Perhaps I won't fail."

"I thought you *wanted* to be sent down. I thought you wanted to be put into a *real* finishing school, to become an ordinary lady with a respectable parliamentary husband and no concerns beyond planning the next dinner party."

"I did. I mean, I do. But Mummy would be so very disappointed, and I would have to leave you. And Sidheag. And Bumbersnoot."

Sophronia could only agree with Dimity's logic. "True."

"Speaking of which, I must talk with you about this letter I received." Dimity flashed a suspiciously embossed missive.

Sophronia grabbed for it.

Dimity was faster. "No, you can't see it until we are with the others."

Sophronia stuck her tongue out but waited obligingly until after luncheon. Due to the presence of Monique and Preshea in the drawing room, Agatha and Sidheag joined Sophronia and Dimity in their private room for a gossip.

Both embarrassed and excited, Dimity produced the letter. "It's from Lord Dingleproops!"

"Dimity," objected Agatha, "should you be getting private correspondences from an unattached gentleman friend?"

"No, but this is the first. I didn't write to him! And it can't be that bad; our families *are* acquainted."

Agatha was properly concerned. "Has he permission to court you?" Agatha Woosmoss was small, round, and red-headed, with a freckled face that wore a perpetual expression of distressed confusion, not unlike that of a damp cat.

Dimity flushed even redder. "No, but I'm certain he would."

Sidheag was reading the hastily scrawled note. "It's worse than simply a letter. He wants to meet with you, in private and secretly!"

"Dimity!" Sophronia said. "Why didn't you tell me?"

Dimity was truculent. "Because I knew you'd be all Sophronia-ish about it. That's why. It's not *that* bad, is it? He probably only wants to chat a bit about the weather or something."

Sidheag, still in possession of the shocking missive, said, "Since it says here that he intends to come to you on this airship, it can't be *that* banal." Sidheag Maccon was an overly tall young woman, almost of an age with Sophronia. She had a long, proud face and a general attitude of indifference to both manners and dress that drove their teachers to distraction.

Sophronia was having none of it. "Dimity, he'd have to steal an airdinghy and then try to find us. I've no idea where we are over Dartmoor, do you? I'm sure he doesn't. Besides, I don't think Bunson's has airdinghies. The whole idea is foolhardy."

Dimity liked Lord Dingleproops rather more than she ought and was disposed to think well of him. "It must be important, then, mustn't it? Perhaps it's a declaration!"

"Oh, Dimity, really!" said Agatha.

Sophronia added, "You're only just fourteen, and he's what, sixteen?"

Dimity protested, "My birthday was weeks ago!"

Sidheag, the blunt one, said, "He isn't even holding yet. He can't declare without his parents' permission." Sidheag could be quite crass, the result of having been raised by men, or Scots, or soldiers, or werewolves, or all four. Since she was also

Lady Kingair, her crassness would have been an accepted eccentricity—in a much older aristocrat. In a fourteen-year-old, such vulgarity was as odd and uncomfortable as last season's hat.

Sophronia took the missive out of Sidheag's hand and examined it. It was under the Earl of Dingleproops's heading, which gave it a certain weight. But she did wonder what the son was doing with his father's stationery. Probably using it to write angry letters to poor tradesmen in his father's name and torture decent young ladies like Dimity.

"He wants to meet with you on the back squeak deck in a week and a half?"

Dimity nodded. "Isn't that romantic?"

Agatha protested. "You're not *going*?"

"Of course I'm going! He will have come all this way."

"It'll all end in tears," foretold Sidheag morosely.

Sophronia said nothing further; Dimity could be awfully stubborn. Privately, Sophronia vowed to follow Dimity. Lord Dingleproops was up to something.

They were made to wait until the end of the week for their test assessments. At long last, after supper, instead of the customary parlor games and card counting, their age-group was separated from the others. Agatha looked like she might faint, or cry, or palpitate, or all three—which would be a real feat. Preshea—small, dark, and unreasonably lovely—looked like she intended to kill someone. But then, Preshea always looked that way. Dimity's round porcelain face was set. Monique, having been through this before, swept her skirts behind her with an air of determination. Sidheag loped along as though she hadn't a care in the aether. Sidheag could be irritating like that.

Sophronia wondered how she herself was showing tension. Not at all, to those who did not look at her shoulders. She would have been surprised by how impressed Lady Linette was with this accomplishment. Lady Linette had also been impressed when Sophronia ate only the vegetables from the meal provided after the exam. Sophronia was the only student to have considered that the test might include the meal. Even Monique, who should have known better, had eaten seven bites of her meat and all her pudding.

Lady Linette led them to her own teaching quarters. These were decorated as if a boudoir had procreated with the set of *She Stoops to Conquer*. There were red curtains, a good deal of gold, and chaise longues instead of chairs. Several fluffy cats with funny scrunched-up faces and possessive attitudes to hassocks lounged about.

Lady Linette left the six girls there.

They sat in expectant silence. Agatha stared at her feet. Sidheag slouched. Both knew better but were regressing into bad habits out of anxiety.

Professor Lefoux entered the room.

An almost audible groan met the appearance of this, the harshest of their teachers.

Professor Lefoux was not so much a battle-ax as a pair of pinking cutters—sharp, toothy, and uneven in temper but very useful. They hadn't any lessons with her yet. Rumor had it she was deemed too fierce for the younger girls. Tall and bony, with a stiff face and hair scraped back into a bun, she *looked* mean. She also had a French accent, which hundreds of years of animosity had trained nice young Englishwomen to suspect as evil.

Professor Lefoux did not bother to explain her presence. "Monique de Pelouse, your assessment is not really one of six months, as you have now been in attendance at this school for four years and eight months. Nevertheless, due to your attempted theft of the crystalline valve prototype last year and your regression in status as a result of that failure, you are undergoing public review along with the others of your rank."

Monique sat silent, her gaze straight forward, her attitude one of superiority rather than penance.

"Your marks are as expected. You are a fair intelligencer but prone to lack of creativity, which could get you killed. You are ladylike but favor overt manipulation, which could get you ostracized. Given your age, it is the recommendation of the staff that you marry with no second attempt at finishing."

Monique looked, for the first time in Sophronia's miserable association with the girl, as if she might genuinely cry. Sophronia had seen her fake-cry on several occasions, but never had an honest tear come from those pretty blue eyes. The blonde said, "How could you? Why, I ought to have my father refuse funding. I shall report you to my *special friend* for this."

Sophronia perked up. She knew Monique had an advocate on staff, but this was the first time the girl had admitted it publicly.

Professor Lefoux interrupted any further tirade. "Silence, young lady. You are to remain a student here until your coming-out ball and will conduct yourself as such. You will do very well for yourself in society, but it is the formal assessment of this institution that even with retraining, you could not exceed your personality. You are *not* to be made an agent."

*Am I seeing things,* wondered Sophronia, *or is that a smile on Professor Lefoux's face?*

Monique rose as though she might storm from the room.

"Sit down, Miss Pelouse!" ordered Professor Lefoux. "You are required to witness all the assessments."

Monique resumed her seat, almost trembling.

"Preshea Buss." Preshea's dark eyes were wide, and her normally crafty face was carefully blank.

"You are adept at social manipulation but too apt to trade on your looks for assistance. You underestimate intelligence, even your own. Improve your execution, or you will be good only for marriage without covert orders."

Preshea protested, "But I've been here less than a year!" She spoke precisely and sharply, as though each word were being murdered by her mouth.

"Which is why we tell you this *now*."

"What if I *want* to get married?" grumbled Preshea under her breath to Agatha.

"I thought that was one of the ways to finish," Sophronia whispered to Dimity.

"It is, but to be dismissed into marriage without covert orders is dishonorable."

"Miss Temminnick, Miss Plumleigh-Teignmott, if you would like to include the rest of the class in your discussion?" Professor Lefoux's ire was turned abruptly on them.

Dimity and Sophronia looked up. "Sorry, Professor," they singsonged in tandem.

Professor Lefoux glared but clearly wished to continue. "Agatha Woosmoss," she barked.

Agatha's bottom lip wobbled.

"Very poor marks indeed. Have you been paying any attention at all in your lessons? You are hereby put on probationary status for six months. You must improve both covert and social aspects of training. Your father is a great patron of our institution, but we cannot play favorites with a weak component."

Agatha began to cry, fishing about for a handkerchief. As usual, she had misplaced hers. Sophronia passed her a spare, wincing in sympathy.

Professor Lefoux continued. "Sidheag Maccon, Lady Kingair."

Sidheag looked directly at the teacher, like a soldier facing execution. The girl's unique yellow eyes were wary.

"You chose all the weapons and showed excellent use of them, even the fan. However, your social skills are middling, and your dress and posture have entirely failed to improve. We understand your background is unusual and that your expectations are different from those of other students. We are sending you into Scottish society, but you will be presented at court eventually. A woman of your rank will need all skills, not only the ones you find interesting. You too are on probation, and your *father* has been informed of this."

Sidheag looked more worried than Sophronia had ever seen her. Her so-called father, Lord Maccon, was really her great-great-great-grandfather and Alpha werewolf of the Kingair Castle pack. Sidheag always spoke of him with a fond irreverence. Now Sophronia could tell from her friend's expression that he could also be fierce.

Professor Lefoux moved on to Dimity. "Miss Plumleigh-Teignmott."

Dimity's face was ashen.

"Your marks are fair, although not as we would have hoped given your lineage. Your reluctance to pursue subterfuge does you a disservice when it is rooted in laziness. Your good humor may work in your favor if you can harness it for information gathering and not simply gossip. Concentrate on combat and solo reconnaissance. You must build your character, Miss Plumleigh-Teignmott. Flibbertigibbets are only good if they have a solid foundation."

Dimity looked humbled but relieved. She clearly had thought she too would be placed on probation.

Professor Lefoux turned to Sophronia.

"Miss Temminnick, you are in receipt of the highest marks we have ever given in a six-month review. Your mind seems designed for espionage. Nevertheless, you veer away from perfect in matters of etiquette. Do not let these marks go to your head; there are many girls at this school who are better than you. Our biggest concern is what you get up to when we are not watching. Because, if nothing else, this test has told us you are probably spying on us, as well as everyone around you."

All the other girls in the room, even Dimity, turned to stare at Sophronia.

In that moment, Sophronia knew they hated her. And because she was exactly as Professor Lefoux had said, one small part of her wondered if her assessment had been inflated for precisely that reason: to challenge her by pitting her against her fellow students.

"Oh, Sophronia," hissed Dimity, "couldn't you have faked it a little?" Dimity hadn't a vengeful bone in her body, but even she could be manipulated.

Sophronia looked out from under her eyelashes at the others. Agatha was no longer holding back tears. Sidheag wore a small smile of discomfort. Preshea and Monique were openly hostile.

"Good luck," said Professor Lefoux to them all, almost cheerfully, before walking swiftly from the room.

Everyone began talking in hushed tones. Everyone, that is, except Sophronia. And no one talked to her, just *about* her.

"Isn't she Miss High and Snobby now?" hissed Monique.

"Bet she thinks the sun rises out of her tea in the morning," added Preshea in her sharp, clipped voice.

"Highest marks ever. Isn't that something? We witnessed history," said Sidheag, her yellow eyes cold.

"I can't believe I'm on probation. Papa will kill me," said Agatha, possibly not exaggerating. One never knew with parents who sent their daughters to Mademoiselle Geraldine's.

Sophronia tried out tactics in her head. Just now, she had nothing to say that wouldn't sound falsely modest. Even if she told them her suspicion that she was being set up, she'd sound defensive. She would have to hope that Agatha and Sidheag would figure it out on their own. She felt certain, however, that she could count on Dimity.

Sophronia cocked her head to one side to look at her best friend.

Dimity looked away and said something sympathetic to Agatha.

Sophronia bit her lip and stared at her hands. She had thought Dimity would stay loyal, just a little bit.

The girls continued to ignore her all that day. It made for lonely classes and an uncomfortable evening meal. Sophronia tried not to let it affect her. They should recover from their resentment if she did nothing to aggravate them. But every time she performed a task well or answered a question correctly during lessons, she could feel the dislike. Several days saw no change to this pattern, and even Dimity still wasn't talking to her, which was particularly awkward, as they shared a bedroom. Sophronia was both annoyed and hurt. She stopped having an appetite at dinner and started filching the occasional roll for later. She even contemplated not following Dimity when the girl crept out of quarters for her assignation with Lord Dingleproops. But since Sophronia figured that the letter was some kind of cruel joke and that the boy wouldn't show up, she simply couldn't let her friend walk into heartbreak alone. So when Dimity snuck out of quarters, having changed at bedtime into her best evening dress rather than a nightgown, Sophronia followed.

Dimity used a series of evasion and climbing techniques to get around the ship. She held perfectly still and flattened herself against walls so mechanicals patrolling the hallways slid right by. It made getting around after hours very slow, and there was always a risk of discovery whenever a maid rolled into sight. Dimity was better at it than Sophronia had thought, which made her proud. After all, Sophronia had taught Dimity every-thing she knew on the subject.

Sophronia stayed out of sight, tracking her friend effortlessly, knowing Dimity was headed to the back squeak deck. Sophronia had it easier. She used a small grappling rope knotted at stages for climbing, her own personal invention. It was unde-manding to creep along the same level, but up and down could be a challenge on an airship hull. Sophronia had scavenged rope from the sooties and asked Vieve to build her a hook and the emission hurlie. The hurlie was a kind of turtle-shaped device that clipped to Sophronia's wrist. Vieve was fond of things that clipped to wrists. Once Sophronia flipped the catch at the turtle's tail, a spring-loaded release mechanism allowed her to fling the turtle's shell, with the grapple underneath, and the rope followed behind. Best of all, Sophronia didn't have to use the ladder from Lady Linette's balcony every time she wanted to visit the sooties.

Instead of climbing up onto the deck after Dimity, Sophronia continued edging around to the very back of the ship. She reeled in her grappling hook and hung off the side, looking into the skies, hunting for an airdinghy. Above her, the squeak deck was abandoned under its great balloon, except for Dimity. Dimity's view was obstructed by the smokestacks, mast, and propel-ler, but Sophronia could see around and between them. The school floated with the breeze, so the air around them felt still and windless.

Hours seemed to pass, and Sophronia was convinced that the letter was a hoax. Then she saw it, coming up from below—an airdinghy. There was someone crewing it, but she could make out nothing from her vantage point but its sail and four balloons.

Above, Dimity's silhouette came to the rails and looked out, but she could not see what Sophronia saw.

Sophronia wondered how Lord Dingleproops intended to board without setting off any of the school's alarms. The back was the safest choice, since teachers and staff slept in the forward section and students in the middle, but there were mechanicals everywhere. Several had protocols that had them do nothing but look for shapes in the sky and set off alarms in teachers' bedrooms when they saw something.

Fearlessly, the airdinghy rose up until it was almost level with Sophronia. She heard Dimity give a glad little cry of welcome. When Sophronia could finally see into the gondola, there were two men, not the one boy Dimity expected. Sophronia had met Lord Dingleproops once at a party; he was a reedy, chinless, redheaded blighter, and while tall and strapping, he was not bulky. Both of these men were bulky. There was certainly something wrong.

As the airdinghy rose higher, Sophronia squinted, trying to make out more of the figures in the dark. Then she realized what was off about them. No top hats. No gentleman would ever meet a lady without appropriate headgear, even if that meeting was a joke. Whoever these men were, they were not noblemen. Plus, Lord Dingleproops was a member of the Pistons, a social club. A Piston's top hat was his marker, his sign of status; to travel without it was unthinkable.

Sophronia was not prepared to mount a defense, but she didn't want anything to happen to Dimity. She threw her bread roll from dinner at the men. It hit one in the head but didn't appear to do any permanent damage, even though it was a very hard roll. The man swore and looked up at her.

Sophronia cursed herself. All she had done was attract their attention, and one of them now pointed a pistol at her. Banking on the fact that he wouldn't want to fire because of the noise, she wrapped one arm tightly about the railing that was her current anchor and pointed her hurlie at the airdinghy. She ejected the grapple toward one of the four balloons. The grapple sailed over, but on the pull back she felt the barb catch and tear through the fabric.

The airdinghy lurched to one side.

The man guiding the dinghy yelled. The other shot his pistol at Sophronia, who swung out and to one side, avoiding the bullet.

Above them, Dimity said, "What's going on? Lord Dingleproops, is that you? Was that gunfire? You'll wake the teachers!"

Sophronia shot her grapple again, catching another one of the balloons and gashing it open. Two ripped balloons was more than the airdinghy could manage, and it began to spin and sink, gaining speed as it went. The men inside were now more concerned with their own safety than with Sophronia or Dimity.

Dimity squeaked in alarm, calling, "Wait, come back!" But her imagined suitor was gone.

Sophronia yelled up to her, "That wasn't Lord Dingleproops."

Dimity was annoyed enough to actually speak with her. "Sophronia? What are you doing following me?"

"Keeping you safe."

"By sabotaging my assignation?"

"I don't know what they wanted, but they weren't Pistons. No top hats."

Clearly, Dimity preferred to believe in her own romantic visions than to see reason. "Oh, Sophronia, he was probably in disguise! Must you ruin everything?"

Sophronia couldn't think of anything to say. Since she hadn't determined what the strange men wanted with Dimity, she could hardly argue that she had protected Dimity from some sinister unknown. Perhaps one of them *had* been Lord Dingleproops, but she doubted it. Lord Dingleproops was the type to disguise himself, certainly, but he would dress up as a jester and still wear his top hat. Those men had been after Dimity, and they weren't lordlings; Sophronia would stake her reputation on it.

As Sophronia climbed back to quarters, she reflected that perhaps it was best if Dimity didn't believe that someone was after her, at least for the time being. Sophronia simply would have to keep an eye on her, whether she liked it or not. Of course, the question remained: who were they and what did they want with Dimity?

## DIAMONDS FROM SOOTIES

G iven that all her female friends were aloof and noncommunicative, Sophronia took refuge in the boiler room. There, fire and smoke turned scurrying workers into creatures of shadow, and boys not much older than Sophronia worked to keep the steam engines running and the airship afloat. Among these sooties, Soap stood out as the tallest, boldest, and shadowiest. Sophronia would have sworn he'd grown a foot in the months she'd known him. She was no petite lady herself, but Soap's lean, muscled form towered over her, his wide face made all the more handsome by its perpetual smile.

"I hear you did particularly well, miss." Phineas B. Crow—Soap for short, sootie by profession—attempted to look serious by concentrating on Bumbersnoot, but he couldn't hide his inherent cheekiness. He also couldn't hide the fact that he didn't care one whistle for her high marks.

"Soap, I wish I had access to your sources of information."

"You do, miss. Through me, a'course!" This comment was accompanied by a flash of glee from his dark eyes. "Here you go, Bumbersnoot." Sophronia's mechanimal was snuffling about in black dust, his clockwork tail *tick-tock*ing back and forth in excitement. He expressed his delight at the small bits of coal Soap dropped from above by eating them. Little puffs of smoke made his floppy leather ears flap.

"Didn't bring Miss Sidheag south with you this time?" Soap prodded gently.

Sophronia gave him a look.

"What, even *her*? You'd think she'd grog to the fact that you'd been pickled."

"Not Sidheag. Takes everything at face value, that girl. It's one of the reasons she didn't do well. . . ." Sophronia trailed off, realizing what Soap had said. "*Even you* figured out I've been set up?"

Soap took offense. He stopped feeding Bumbersnoot. "Even me? I've been around this here school long enough to pick up a few tricks."

The mechanimal's tail slowed to a steady *tick-tock, tick-tock*.

Sophronia looked at her friend: his buoyant demeanor, his skin so dark it was often difficult to tell where he began and the soot left off. "Are you happy here, Soap?"

"Why, miss, what a question." Soap's ready smile faded slightly.

Bumbersnoot, ignored, puffed steam at them, as if to say, *What about me? No one asks if I'm happy. You know what would make me happy? More coal. Yoo-hoo, down here. You, with the*

*coal!* There was, of course, a pile of coal nearby, but Bumbersnoot wasn't too bright. He was only a simple mechanimal, with very basic protocols.

"I mean, are you happy as a sootie?"

"Suits me well enough, miss. Decent hours. They let me get away with fooling about a bit. Not a bad life. Both my parents were slaves. Or that's what I've been told. Never knew 'em myself."

"You're quite smart, you know?"

Soap raised his eyebrows.

Sophronia took out a little book from her reticule. It was an early primer, meant for young children. She'd been teaching Soap to read lately. They used what bits of time they had and the light from one of the boilers. "I don't mean book learning, but smart in other ways."

Soap began to follow where the conversation was headed. "Your school don't train them like me," he said, "even if they took boys."

"Bunson's?"

"I ain't got the brain for science, miss. Only other stuff. Naw, leave me here; it'll do for now."

"But . . ."

"Now, miss, just because you ain't got any projects to work on, don't be casting them pretty peepers my way."

"Projects? What do you mean, *projects*?" Sometimes Sophronia couldn't understand a word that came out of Soap's mouth. She got the meaning underneath, mostly. How could she not, when his own "pretty peepers" twinkled at her something terrible? *Flirt.*

"Miss Sidheag and them others you collect. Them as needs a little help to make it through. Them's your projects. I ain't interested. Course, if you wanted to make me somewhat else..." He trailed off and waggled his brows suggestively.

Sophronia cocked her head and lifted the primer. "You sure you aren't a project?"

"Aw, miss, reading's one thing, but I can't be a gentleman, and that seems part and parcel of that secretive work of yours."

"Doesn't have to be."

Soap was not to be persuaded. If Sophronia were to make an intelligencer of him, she'd have to do it without his knowing. "Well, I appreciate your sources; that's all I'm saying," she said.

Soap smiled, a flash of white teeth. "Speaking of which..." His eye had been caught by someone coming up behind Sophronia.

She whirled around to see a purposeful newsboy silhouette walking straight across the boiler room, like a delivery lad.

The engineering chamber was a mere hum of activity at night, unlike the crashing cacophony of daytime. Most of the sooties and greasers were asleep, and all of the officers, but the boilers always had to be tended. The flickering orange glow from the burning coal turned the cavernous room into a waltz of light. Sophronia adored it. Sooties trotted about, but none of them moved straight across the open space between boilers— they stopped to feed them. Only one person moved with such directness—Genevieve Lefoux.

"What ho?" said the scamp, dimpling up at them. Vieve was from above stairs; she belonged to Professor Lefoux, as much as she might be said to belong to anyone. But she was rather cat-like about the situation. She never sat for lessons, and went wherever she pleased at whatever hour. Since she liked engines, much of her time was spent in the boiler room.

After the customary pleasantries, Vieve said in a sprightly manner, "Hear my aunt got you good, Sophronia."

Sophronia cast the primer up at the ceiling in a gesture of appeal to higher powers. "You, too? Isn't my business secret at all?"

"Well, I might have read the report. You made them allover sticky with the highest six-month marks *ever*. Good on you, Miss Poofy Skirts."

"You turning against me, too?"

"Oh, I'm not miffed. Amused you had to go up against the brunt of Aunt's charms."

"She's a dragon, your aunt."

"Sing that! Now, about—oof!" Vieve stumbled as a sootie hurtled into her, knocking her over.

"Hey!" he yelled as Vieve bounced upright. "Watch it there, runt!"

Sophronia pulled her shoulders back. "You watch it, you turbot!"

The boy snorted at her. "Oh, mighty Uptop, what could you do to me?"

Soap stepped in when it looked like Sophronia might actually launch herself at the boy. "Run along now."

Strong from shoveling coal most of his life, Soap loomed over the smaller sootie. The boy scuttled off.

Sophronia sputtered. "Why, that turnip! Who does he think he is? Vieve, are you well?"

Vieve dimpled at her. "Don't concern yourself, miss. I'm not easily damaged."

Soap said to Sophronia, "Now, miss, don't go causing a ruckus in my domain, please."

Sophronia stopped vibrating. "Oh, dear. I am sorry. This thing with everyone angry at me has rather put my nerves on edge." Sophronia hoped Soap couldn't see how hurt she was by the ostracism. Soap's eyes were so direct, she rather thought he might see into her heart better than anyone.

Soap shook his head at her sympathetically. "Still, miss."

Sophronia agreed with the reprimand. She should have minded her manners, even with a sootie. Especially with a sootie. "Who was that unpleasant creature?" She thought she knew most of the boiler room staff by sight, if not by name.

"Don't know," admitted Soap, embarrassed.

"Don't know? But you know *all* the sooties!" Soap was like the unofficial mayor of boilers.

"That's just it. We've taken on double numbers this week. Double! Some pretty dubious types, too. Second Assistant Fireman should have checked their characters better, if you ask me. Us old guard been trying to get most of them assigned to forward engine and propeller, but they don't need that many when we're drifting. So we've got 'em all mucking about here."

Sophronia looked around. "Have you taken on extra coal, too?"

Soap nodded.

"I didn't feel us go low to meet the supply train."

"Early yesterday morning, miss."

Vieve added, "They brought it in from Bristol special."

Sophronia said, "I take it you're thinking what I'm thinking."

"Someone plans to take this ship on a very long trip." Soap pulled out a wooden pipe, lit it up with a wick from a nearby boiler, and puffed.

Sophronia wrinkled her nose. *Revolting habit.* She schooled her expression when he looked at her, but he must have caught her distaste.

He took the pipe out of his mouth, looked at it as though it had done something offensive, and then tapped it out into a coal heap and tucked it away.

*And he thinks he's not a gentleman!* Sophronia smiled—a wide grin with no artifice to it.

Soap looked a little overwhelmed by the power of her approval. Sophronia was, as yet, unaware of the effect of her smile on boys.

Vieve watched this back-and-forth with interested green eyes.

Sophronia continued their conversation. "Leaving the moor, do you think?"

Soap nodded. "A certain."

"What else do you know?" Sophronia asked.

Soap shook his head. "Simply that, miss. I have tried, but them powers upstairs are keeping this one close."

They both looked to the ten-year-old girl dressed as a boy. Vieve had crouched down to play with Bumbersnoot. She shrugged. "You got more than me. No one's talked in my hearing."

"Lady Linette! She didn't give us our assessments. Perhaps she was called away to deal with this?" Sophronia mused.

"Which direction are we headed now, Soap?" Vieve asked.

Soap wandered over to a hatch in the floor of one corner of the massive room and stuck his head out of it. A few minutes later he returned. Soap always looked as though he didn't quite have control of his limbs, like a goat. But like a goat, he was sure-footed and powerful, despite appearances.

"Toward Swiffle-on-Exe, I'm thinking."

Sophronia was impressed. This was a skill she hadn't known Soap possessed. One stretch of heath looked much the same as another to her.

"Boilers will be needing water?" suggested Vieve. "For the journey?" Swiffle-on-Exe was a riverside town.

"I wonder if Bunson's has a mission for us?" offered Sophronia. Bunson and Lacroix's Boys' Polytechnique was near Swiffle-on-Exe and the primary reason people visited.

"After Monique bungled the prototype retrieval? I doubt it," muttered Vieve. "Things haven't been roses between the schools since. Bunson's won't forgive Geraldine's for nearly losing the only working device."

Sophronia's instincts took over. "How do you know that?"

"My aunt used to communicate regularly with a professor there."

"Algonquin Shrimpdittle?"

"Yes, how...?"

"When we infiltrated Bunson's last year, you used his name to get us past the porter."

"You remember?" Vieve was impressed.

"It's what I *do*."

"Highest marks ever, right." Vieve gave Sophronia a suspicious look. "Did you hold back during that test?"

Sophronia avoided her question by asking one in reply. "Did you know about the oddgob?"

Vieve nodded.

"Oh." Sophronia was disappointed. "And I took such careful mental notes for you. Did you know it had a component part that looked a great deal like the prototype?"

Vieve frowned. "Not possible. Why would the oddgob need a crystalline valve frequensor? That valve is for wireless communication, nothing to do with oddgobbery."

Sophronia shrugged and fished the item in question out of her reticule. She handed it to Vieve, experiencing some relief at no longer having it on her person. "Here, I stole it for you. Why don't you tell me what it's for?"

"Aw, Sophronia, how thoughtful. You brought me a present!" Vieve examined the mini-prototype for a moment. Soap and Sophronia watched her for signs of intrigue. "Amazing they let it fall into your hands, when they made such a fuss over it only last year."

Sophronia nodded. "Unless it's no longer a prototype and already in production and distribution. Technology does move awful fast these days."

Vieve dimpled again. "I know, isn't it grand?" She pocketed

the valve, only then realizing Sophronia had neatly avoided her earlier question. "So, *did* you hold back during that test?"

"Maybe a little," Sophronia admitted.

Soap grinned. "That's my girl."

Sophronia glared at him. He was getting familiar.

"You are, miss." He continued to grin.

"I'm my *own* girl, thank you very much."

"Sometimes. Sometimes you're mine, or Miss Dimity's, or even Vieve's."

Vieve was too young to follow this line of reasoning, but she was bound to agree with Soap if the conversation nettled Sophronia.

This one certainly did. In fact, Sophronia was finding it most flustering. She did not like being flustered, and she did not like that it was Soap doing the flustering. She wasn't quite sure what this meant, so she resorted to orders. "Stop it, Soap."

"For now, miss. You tell me when you want this conversation to continue."

"Oh, really!"

But Soap, who certainly could be a gentleman when he tried, left the subject at that and moved the discussion delicately on to the latest boiler room excitement: the sooties had adopted a kitten.


Sophronia visited the boiler room regularly for the next few nights. Things remained uncomfortable in class and chambers.

Dimity was barely passing polite, and the other girls ignored Sophronia.

Of course, Bumbersnoot tried his best, but a mechanimal hadn't much conversation and wasn't really interested in speculating as to what might be afloat. Sophronia refused to volunteer any information to the others. The possibility of a visit to Swiffle-on-Exe and Bunson's—which meant young gentlemen— would have her compatriots in ecstasies of delighted anticipation. So Sophronia held on to the news out of spite. She didn't try to warn Dimity that someone might be after her. Dimity would take it as a pathetic excuse for interference. Without knowing the motive behind that mystery attack, Sophronia had no way to make her case. She'd no idea how lonely such a decision could be. So she escaped to see Soap, and occasionally Vieve, most evenings. It was a risk. She might get caught, but it was better than the pointed silences.

Then one morning at breakfast, Mademoiselle Geraldine made an official announcement.

Mademoiselle Geraldine was a source of amusement to the students. She was, supposedly, the headmistress. She thought her school was a real finishing school and had no idea about the espionage side of things. This was an ongoing covert operation lesson for the students—all the girls had to participate in keeping their headmistress in the dark. She always addressed them at breakfast with such concerns and inanities as might be important were they attending an actual ladies' seminary. And, upon occasion, she was given something of substance to say by Lady Linette.

Over a light repast of giblet pie, boiled whiting, brawn, cold roast capon, and broiled haddock together with tea, brown bread, and sweet butter—the teachers did not approve of a heavy breakfast—Mademoiselle Geraldine informed them that they were headed to Swiffle-on-Exe for a brief stopover and that they could expect company once they arrived. The headmistress did not look pleased. Mademoiselle Geraldine might boast the rinsed red hair, loud voice, and well-upholstered figure of a former opera singer, but she took deportment *seriously*. Whoever their passenger was going to be, Mademoiselle Geraldine did *not* approve.

Accordingly, they arrived at the outskirts of Swiffle-on-Exe the next evening after dark. Instead of taking up their customary mooring point, off a goat path west of town, they went south and put down lines near the banks of the Exe.

The girls were all atwitter over this shift in tradition. Only Sophronia knew it was because they must take on boiler water. When everyone else was asleep, she crept out of quarters. It was dangerously busy in the hallway; the tracks were screaming with maid mechanicals, bustling to and fro carrying extra linens and washbasins. Sophronia had to flatten herself behind doors and inch along the walls at a pace so slow they wouldn't register her. She decided not to visit the sooties, who would be too busy, and instead headed out onto a midlevel balcony. She leaned over the railing to watch as the airship sank down and nested, nose first, over the river, rustling the willow trees along the bank. Eventually, the front section, which housed the teachers' residence and engineering, bridged the water.

With a belch of smoke out the stacks and a loud rumbling, a huge articulated metal pipe ejected from the lower front of the hull. Standing on a midlevel deck, Sophronia was in good position to observe under the light of a half-moon.

The pipe was massive. Near its end was a set of four small inflated balloons. These rested atop the river and held the pipe, presumably, at exactly the correct angle. Round steps collapsed out like flower petals as the pipe telescoped down. Sooties in the boiler room must have been cranking up a storm to create suction, for with a slurping noise the pipe shuddered and began to take on water. It looked as though the airship were drinking up the river through a flute.

This task complete, sooties, tiny figures below her, ran down the finger keys of the flute. There were a few joyful whoops and splashes. Mortified, Sophronia realized they were bare. Having left their soot-covered clothes above, they were taking this as a rare opportunity to bathe. The water must have been freezing, but they looked to be having a rollicking good time. Sophronia supposed Soap was among them, but she couldn't distinguish individuals and wasn't certain she should. Nevertheless, she was so taken with the spectacle she nearly fell over the railing. There might have been some small part of her that wished for Vieve's binoculars.

The next morning, the airship was back in its regular visiting position, hovering over a hill west of town. The hodgepodge of buildings and mixed architecture that made up Bunson's school was in view down the path. Sophronia blushed to think upon what she had seen the night before, and regretted not having Dimity to share it with.

When Sophronia entered the communal parlor wearing a carriage dress because she could not do up the back of her day gowns by herself, Dimity was in huddle with Sidheag. Sophronia walked over to their group with an open expression, but the girls stopped talking and only smiled back. Fake, unfriendly, cutting smiles of the kind Lady Linette had made them perfect over the course of six lessons. Sophronia sighed. *Still not forgiven? But I have such interesting things to tell.*

Then, before breakfast commenced, Mademoiselle Geraldine made a most shocking announcement, one that clearly distressed her.

"Ladies," she said. "We will be taking a trip. A great trip."

A collective gasp met this statement. The girls stopped reaching for crumpets and jam and looked up expectantly.

Sophronia sat back in her seat and looked at Monique out of the corner of her eye. Monique's genuine surprise suggested she hadn't known. Monique had an advocate among the teachers, and yet she hadn't been told? The girl's expression changed from shock to annoyance. *Oh, ho, she thinks she should have been told. Very interesting.*

"You knew." Dimity was giving Sophronia an exasperated look.

*Well, at least she's talking to me.* Sophronia nodded.

"Of course she knew! She's the best, remember? Better than any of us," Preshea interfered.

Dimity looked away, flushing.

"We are going to..." Mademoiselle Geraldine made an expansive gesture and left a pregnant pause, her stage training in action. "...London!"

Squeals of delight met *that*. Every girl wanted to go to London, even the ones who had been already. The shopping alone!

Sophronia's dining table erupted into hushed exclamations.

"Think of it, town in March!"

"Directly before the Season. All the new gloves will be in!"

"I must write to Mummy and Daddy immediately to ask for an increase in my allowance."

"Will there be balls? Oh, I do hope there will be balls!"

"There *must* be balls."

Sophronia nodded to herself. That explained all the extra fuel. But their school *never* left the moor. The fact that Mademoiselle Geraldine's was actually a massive airship was supposed to be secret. No one would believe it was a real finishing school if they knew it bobbed about shamelessly midair. Sophronia's mind jumped to the problem of staying covert. *Can we avoid populated areas all the way to London?* She ought to be excited. She'd rarely had an opportunity to visit the capital. But what fun could she have in London if all her girlfriends were angry at her? It was hardly as though she and *Soap* could go tripping about Regent Street cooing over lace tucks.

Mademoiselle Geraldine called for silence. It took a while. "Now, now, ladies. Ladies! There will be plenty of time to talk among yourselves later. It will take us four days to get there. Classes will, of course, continue." The headmistress took a deep breath, straining her stays alarmingly. "And that is not all!"

The girls quieted in anticipation of more delicious news.

"We will be joined by *company* on this excursion." Mademoiselle Geraldine waved at the back of the room. The girls turned in their seats.

The dining hall doors opened and in walked...boys.

Mademoiselle Geraldine's young ladies did not squeal at this, although it was certainly an even more squeal-worthy moment. Their training took over and not a peep was to be heard. But there *was* the faint sucking hiss of multiple indrawn breaths, like helium escaping the big balloons.

Again, Dimity turned to Sophronia, as if she could not help herself. "Did you know about *this?*"

"Dimity!" reprimanded Preshea.

Sophronia had not known, but she wasn't about to tell Dimity *that*. She merely tightened her lips.

"Oh, Sophronia!"

There were some ten young men in all and one teacher. The teacher was a boyish-faced blond gentleman, wearing a seriously scholarly expression.

Sophronia recognized a few of the boys. Dimity's younger brother, Pillover, gave their table a glum nod from under the brim of his oversized bowler. There was the infamous Lord Dingleproops who, outrageously, tipped his hat at them. Dimity blushed and then stuck her nose in the air. Next to Lord Dingleproops walked a pale, dark-haired boy wearing a little kohl about his eyes and possessing a certain sullen restlessness. Sophronia and he had once danced together but had never been properly introduced. She'd had to cut him unkindly at the time, abandoning him alone in the middle of a dance. There had been prototypes and cheese pies to deal with, but he would probably never forgive her.

He caught her staring and held her gaze in a forward manner. Then he lowered long eyelashes, ridiculously long for a boy, and gave her a small smile.

*I know that trick. We learned it our first week here.* Sophronia lowered her own lashes at him and glared. Some traitorous part of her was thinking, *At least he doesn't resent me for that dance.*

The boy's smile became genuine and he gave her a little nod.

"Great," muttered Sophronia. "We got us Pistons on board."

"What's wrong with Pistons, Miss Know-It-All?" Monique asked, driven to break her silence. "They come from some of the finest families in England."

"And some of the wealthiest," added Preshea, emphasizing the *t* at the end of the word like a bullet.

Agatha said to Dimity, "Imagine Lord Dingleproops tilting his hat at you! After what he did!"

Monique narrowed in on this. "What did he do?"

Dimity said, "Ask Sophronia, why don't you?"

"Oh, it can't be *that* important."

Mademoiselle Geraldine interrupted further discussion. "Please welcome Mr. Algonquin Shrimpdittle and a selection of the top-ranked students from Bunson and Lacroix's Boys' Polytechnique. They will be joining us for the journey to London. I'm convinced you will make them welcome. Don't fuss; you will get the opportunity to socialize after tea."

The silence that met that remark practically wobbled with excitement, like aspic jelly.

"The young gentlemen will be joining you for some of your

lessons. I expect you all to behave and conduct yourselves like the ladies of *qualit-tay* I know you are!"

Another thrilled gasp met this. Mademoiselle Geraldine narrowed her eyes at Lady Linette, as though this were all her idea, and continued, "Now, don't you desire to know *why* we are headed into London?"

Truth be told, most of the girls had entirely forgotten that there need *be* a reason. Sophronia was interested to hear what excuse had been given to Mademoiselle Geraldine. Almost as interested as she was in the truth behind their trip. She turned her gaze away from the boys, now lined up at the front of the room. The abominable dark-haired one was staring at her.

"Henri Giffard is scheduled to float, from France, in the very first transcontinental dirigible!"

This was of little consequence. After all, they spent all day every day floating about in an overlarge dirigible. Sophronia waited to be impressed.

"And he has said he will do it in under an hour using *aether* currents."

This was met with pure shock. Even some of the boys looked surprised.

Float *inside* the aetherosphere? Inside the currents that swirled above the air itself? Unheard of!

"Those with the scientific know-how"—Mademoiselle Geraldine gestured at Professors Shrimpdittle and Lefoux—"tell me that he is most likely to succeed due to some exciting new valve technology. It is deemed that such a monumental historical occurrence is worth uprooting our entire establishment to witness in person."

Sophronia was caught up in the metaphor of *uprooting* a floating school.

"And now, if you gentlemen will take a seat," the headmistress continued, gesturing to an unoccupied table laid with a damask tablecloth and fine china, "we can get on to breakfast at last."

# THE 4TH TEST

## FLIRTING WITH CONSPIRACIES

T he first aether-borne dirigible flight, and we get to witness it! Do you realize, if Giffard's calculations are correct, this could halve float times? Can you believe it? We could get all the way to Scotland in four days! I wonder how he is handling aether-current monitoring. Can you imagine being that high up?"

Sophronia was not as impressed as Vieve thought she should be. "It is still faster by sleeper train."

"Yes, but this is floating. Floating! Using aether currents! The possibilities are endless. It's so exciting!" Vieve bounced up and down on Sophronia's bed.

The young inventor had stopped by for a visit after breakfast. Sophronia had no idea where the scamp ate, but clearly it was within earshot of the assembly.

"As you're here, do you think you could help me dress?" she asked.

"You're dressed already," protested Vieve.

"In something nicer?"

"Not you, too!"

"Well, everyone is putting on her best because of the visitors. I don't want to be known as *that girl in the carriage dress*."

Vieve sighed. "Oh, very well." The ten-year-old eschewed female clothing herself, but she had the French eye for apparel on others, and opinions to go with it. She mooched over to Sophronia's wardrobe and selected a dark blue-and-green plaid, two seasons old, with a narrow skirt.

"This one," she pronounced with all the authority of youth.

"Really?"

"It complements your eyes."

"If you say so."

"With the straw shepherdess bonnet." Vieve was always very assured on the subject of hats. Not to be trifled with.

"Well, you'll have to help me put it on. Dimity still isn't speaking to me."

"More fool, her. You know what's happening."

"Not now; everyone is as up on things as I." This irritated Sophronia.

Vieve dimpled. "Ah, but you'll never guess what I heard."

Sophronia brightened. "Oh?"

"One of the teachers is required in London."

Sophronia was struck, yet again, by how old Vieve always sounded and acted. One would never have guessed from her speech that she was ten. From her actions, occasionally, yes. She did bounce.

"Which one? Your aunt?"

Vieve shrugged.

"Really, Vieve."

"Now, now, Sophronia, I told you something interesting, didn't I? I can't do all the work." The girl got distracted. "What *is* Bumbersnoot up to?"

Bumbersnoot had snuffled over to one side of the room and latched onto a froufrou that had fallen into the corner by the bed. He was dragging it out into the center of the floor and not swallowing it into his tiny boiler.

Sophronia looked at her pet. "He wants to come along."

"What?"

Sophronia indicated the floof in Bumbersnoot's mouth with her head. Her hands were busy pinning on the shepherdess hat.

Vieve crouched down and gently extracted the bit of cloth from the mechanimal. It turned out to be a complex sort of sling, heavily decorated with lace, ruffles, and tassels. Vieve, being mechanically minded, realized it was designed for Bumbersnoot to wear. It covered most of the mechanimal and made him look like a reticule—if a reticule were to be designed with a metal dog head. If anyone asked, Sophronia was prone to explaining that her handbag was the latest fashion out of Italy, and she couldn't fathom how a person of taste didn't also own one.

"Dimity and I made it for him after Petunia's ball. The idea worked so well there. Everyone thought he was some fancy new accessory. This way I can take him to classes with me. He likes to get out and about on occasion, don't you, Bumbersnoot?"

Vieve's eyebrows were raised almost into her dark hair.

Bumbersnoot was, technically, illegal. Not only were students of Mademoiselle Geraldine's not permitted pets, but unregistered mechanimals were forbidden throughout the British Empire.

"Lesson five five four," said Sophronia. "Sometimes it is best to hide a suspicious item in plain sight."

"How do you keep him from smoking or steaming unexpectedly?"

Sophronia completed her toilette and turned to look at Bumbersnoot. Vieve had fastened the sling about him using the various ribbons tied into bows. "He has to behave, or he gets brought back to the room. Usually, he's pretty good. Speaking of which, I'd better get to class."

"What do you have?"

"Lady Linette's lesson on hive society."

"Then there will be boys with you."

"As opposed to? I thought they were joining us for all our classes."

Vieve shook her head, green eyes twinkling. "Oh, no, no. Bunson's doesn't fraternize with supernaturals."

"So they won't be in lessons with Captain Niall or Professor Braithwope?"

Vieve nodded and handed her Bumbersnoot.

"Oh, I don't know," hedged Sophronia, "with boys running around. Is it wise to bring him?"

"He wants to go," insisted Vieve.

Bumbersnoot flapped an ear.

"Very well. Remember, Bumbersnoot, don't move." Sophronia slung the mechanimal over her shoulder so that he dangled near her waist, looking for all the world like the oddest and most eccentric bag any lady of means had ever carried.

In class, Dimity, Sidheag, and Agatha noticed the addition of Bumbersnoot to Sophronia's attire but said nothing. Sophronia only carried the mechanimal when she thought she might *need* him. Although what defined *needing* such a ridiculous creature was anyone's guess. They would assume this was simply another moment when Sophronia knew more than they and intended to show them up.

*As if I would do that in front of boys!* Sophronia plonked Bumbersnoot down ostentatiously among the other reticules.

Lady Linette's etiquette class was augmented by four boys, including Lord Dingleproops and his dark-haired friend.

Lady Linette began. "Welcome, ladies and gentlemen. Today's class is entitled 'Faking It with Fangs.' We will go over proper introductions within a hive environment. Please pair off."

With six girls, Sophronia and Agatha were left out of the first round. Monique made straight for Lord Dingleproops, cutting Dimity off. Preshea chose the dark-haired boy. They made a fetching pair, of a kind in coloring, pleasing proportions, and sulky temperament. Yet, despite Preshea's uncontested loveliness, the dark-haired boy kept glancing at Sophronia. Which, while complimentary, also gave her an undeniable feeling of smugness. It wasn't often a boy preferred her over Preshea.

Lady Linette continued, "Queens outrank all other vampires, despite whatever landed title they might hold. Always go to the queen first in any social situation and allow one of her hive-bound vampires to introduce you. After the queen come her hive members, then any roves who may be present. All of these will be men, some landed. Drones—humans indentured to hive or rove—are classed as household staff, with a few exceptions."

One of the boys said snidely, "Are you purposefully leaving out the fact that drones are also the vampires' primary food source?"

Lady Linette snapped, "One doesn't discuss such utilitarian things openly! For today's practice, the gentlemen will pretend to be hive vampires. Begin!"

Sophronia and Agatha introduced themselves to each other. Agatha was as shy and as nervous as if Sophronia were a real vampire. The mere presence of four young men among them had her aflutter. Poor Agatha was generally overset by anything new, from the advent of a birthday scarf—How to wear it? What to match it with?—to boys wandering willy-nilly into classes.

"So unpredictable," Agatha whispered.

*The scarf*, wondered Sophronia, *or the boys?*

Conversation was allowed to continue for some ten minutes while Lady Linette mingled and made adjustments—to stance, to subject matter, to flirting, to lack of flirting, to eyelash use. She corrected both girls and boys. Sophronia realized, for the first time, that vampires had just as many rules to follow as women in society. Possibly more.

"Pardon me, Lady Linette?"

"Yes, Miss Temminnick?"

"Can rove vampires safely visit a hive? I thought they had to stay in their own territory."

"Roves can visit for short lengths of time. Think logically, Miss Temminnick. Roves must have an alliance with a vampire queen because only a queen can breed new vampires. Since roves have drones, and drones work for the right to try to become a vampire, they must maintain an alliance with a queen. In exchange for drone metamorphosis, roves perform duties for the queen that the males of her hive cannot. Roves, for example, have much longer tethers and greater mobility."

Sophronia decided tether length was something to bother Professor Braithwope about. She found the idea of vampire territories intriguing, but there was very little written on the subject. Since vampires perceived tethers as a weakness, this was probably by design. They did *love* controlling information.

Lady Linette clapped her hands. "Rotate, please. Lady Kingair and Miss Plumleigh-Teignmott, you pair out for this round."

Preshea made her way to Lord Dingleproops. The young man was clearly charmed by the girl's precise petty prettiness. Dimity looked disgruntled—she had her embossed missive clutched in one hand and clearly wished to ask Lord Dingleproops about it.

The dark-haired boy made his way across the room to Sophronia, despite the fact that Monique had moved to intercept him. He avoided her with consummate adroitness.

"We meet again, Miss Temminnick."

"To be perfectly correct, *sir*, we have never properly met at all."

He gave a little half smile. "Of course, one must always be correct."

"Oh, haven't you heard, sir?" Monique said. "Sophronia is *always* correct."

"Is that your given name, Sophronia? Pretty."

"Sophronia Temminnick. And it most certainly isn't pretty. It's a mouthful. Now, shall we do this properly? Lady Linette is watching."

"Whatever you like, Ria."

"Miss Temminnick to you," hissed Sophronia.

The boy smiled wider. His eyes were a very nice shade of blue. "No, I prefer Ria." He grasped her hand. His thumb made its way inside the top of her glove to caress her wrist. *Scandalous.*

Sophronia jerked away. "Stop that." Her heart was racing. *Undoubtedly in anger.*

Lady Linette was upon them. "Show me."

The dark-haired boy—*I still don't know his name, pox upon him*—stopped smiling and made a very neat bow to Sophronia, as though he were encountering her at a hive house door.

Lady Linette did not look inspired.

Sophronia executed a near-perfect curtsy in reply, perhaps a little brief.

Lady Linette called her out. "Why so curt, Miss Temminnick?"

"We haven't been introduced. I wouldn't want him to get ideas."

"You wish to discourage the hive? Did I say we were practicing ways to dissuade a vampire's interest?"

"You did not direct us to focus on encouragement or dissuading."

"Very well, proceed."

The dark-haired boy said, "How do you do? My name is Mersey, Felix Mersey."

Lady Linette interrupted him. "Family names only, young man. What kind of lady do you take her for?"

Felix smiled that quirky half smile. "The best kind, of course."

Lady Linette was shocked. "Mr. Mersey!"

Lord Dingleproops said, from where he partnered a self-satisfied Preshea, "Actually, my lady, he's a Golborne."

Lady Linette was impressed. "Son of the viscount?"

The four boys in the class laughed.

Felix Mersey said softly, "Golborne is a *duchy*, my lady."

"And Felix here is the eldest," added Lord Dingleproops.

Lady Linette looked even more impressed, for that meant that Mersey was a landed title, his father's second holding.

Sophronia narrowed her eyes. *Heir to a duke, is he? No wonder he's so arrogant.* The entirety of Monique's attention swung in their direction. Felix Mersey outranked everyone else in the room. *Monique's two years older than him, at the very least. She should be looking for someone her own age!*

"We call him Felix. Doesn't hold with titles, do you, Viscount?"

"A luxury only the titled can afford, I'm sure," said Sophronia.

"Don't worry, Ria," a molasses voice whispered near her ear. "You will call me Felix, regardless."

A fan snapped down between them. "None of *that*! No vampire would ever be so intimate!" Lady Linette did not hold with obvious flirting. Flirting, yes, but not *obvious* flirting.

Felix said, pertly, "I object to having to portray a vampire. It is beneath me."

Lady Linette rolled her eyes and clapped for everyone's attention. "Now, gentlemen, I understand that Bunson's predisposition is against any contact with vampires, but the fact is they pervade high society, and you will have to fraternize with them eventually. It is always better to be prepared. And what better way to understand the enemy than to pretend to be one?"

This mollified Felix. Sophronia wondered at the strength of his dislike. With Professor Braithwope, who was a dear, as her primary model, Sophronia was rather more in favor of vampires than against. She'd been raised relatively progressive. She didn't think her father had any business dealings with vampires or werewolves, but she was tolerably certain he wouldn't be against such a thing.

"How do you do, Lord Mersey?"

"It is a very great pleasure to make your acquaintance at last, Miss Temminnick. Amusing reticule you have." Felix gestured to where Bumbersnoot sat, discarded among the other accessories on Lady Linette's mantelpiece.

"Oh, yes, indeed. A gift from a friend, Italian design. How do you feel about the weather? One might expect rain soon, might one not?"

Lady Linette interrupted, "Weather is only safe with a male vampire. Never discuss the weather with a queen. Since she cannot leave her hive house, this is considered a rude reminder of her loss of freedom. Lord Mersey, how would a vampire respond?"

"Rain, in your glorious presence, Miss Temminnick? I hardly think it should dare."

Lady Linette interjected. "No, no, too much flattery. Only roves would be so aggressive. Miss Temminnick, a rebuttal, if you would?"

Sophronia said, "And how are you enjoying your sojourn on board our ship?"

Lady Linette said, "Nicely played, except, of course, no vampire except Professor Braithwope floats. We are pretending that Lord Mersey is a hive-bound vampire. Let us say, instead, that you are both visiting Vauxhall Gardens of an evening."

Felix's eyes twinkled at her. "I'm finding myself quite enchanted with . . . gardens, at the moment."

Sophronia persisted. "Have you ever visited Vauxhall before?"

"Indeed, but I find this a whole *new* kind of garden experience, now that I have met you."

Sophronia stepped away from the impossible boy with a glare. "Lady Linette, Lord Mersey is not speaking by the rules. Either for vampires or regular gentlemen."

"Well, Miss Temminnick, you are using only standard niceties. Examine your subject and tailor your remarks to his taste."

Given permission, Sophronia took in Felix Golborne, Viscount Mersey, from head to toe. "The mark is of average height and slender build. He is a man of means, but not overly interested in fashion. His hair is a little long. The mark has a slightly sullen expression denoting chronic ennui. Peculiarities include kohl about the eyes, fake gears sewn to the waistcoat, and a top hat with a brass ribbon." She pointed to the hat where it sat atop an articulated bronze hat rack. "In short, an average hive-bound toff with a few eccentricities."

Felix looked remarkably nonplussed under this string of observations. "You wound me."

Lady Linette was delighted. "Note, however, the expense of the haircut? It takes a great deal of money to acquire a look of not having spent any at all. The precise fit and cut of the waistcoat? That is *next* season's color. We have here a vampire of more than considerable means. He probably has not only hive backing but his own as well. His eccentricities might lead you to direct the conversation accordingly. Kohl is sourced where?"

Sophronia did not know; cosmetics was not her strong point.

Preshea spoke up. "Oh, me, me!"

"Yes, Miss Buss?"

"Egypt, my lady."

"Very good, Miss Buss." Lady Linette turned back to Sophronia. "What might you gather from that?"

"He has business concerns overseas, is possibly a collector of antiquities, or thinks his eyes are so pretty they must be exaggerated, which, given the length of his eyelashes, seems a waste of kohl."

Lord Dingleproops let out a guffaw. "Got you there, Felix!"

Lady Linette finally realized Sophronia's antics had distracted the entire class. "Ladies and gentlemen, please return to your own encounters! Sophronia, proceed with your discourse, applying our new information."

Sophronia sighed and faced Felix. "My lord, are you interested in ancient Egypt?"

"I'm interested in the fact that you noticed the length of my eyelashes."

Sophronia gritted her teeth. "Does your hive have historic ties to exotic lands?"

Felix's intense focus on Sophronia was momentarily distracted by the mantelpiece behind her. "Speaking of exotic, your reticule seems to have moved of its own accord."

Felix was not the only one to have noticed. One of Lady Linette's cats was a full fluff ball of bristling offense, staring up at Bumbersnoot.

Sophronia hurried over. In the guise of retrieving her shawl, she gave Bumbersnoot an impressive whispered lecture on sitting still. The mechanimal crouched down with a small steam puff of slowing gears. The cat took further offense and hid under a sofa.

"What, for aether's sake, is wrong with Artemisia?" asked Lady Linette, distracted by her cat's behavior.

Felix followed Sophronia and leaned in to whisper, "Italian design, did you say? I must see about getting my mother one. Then again, if all the best households have one, she may already be blessed."

Luckily, shortly after that, they were required to switch partners. Then the class got thoroughly distracted by the spectacle of Dimity Plumleigh-Teignmott, normally a placid young lady, positively bristling at a surprised Lord Dingle-proops. Their vampire-meets-maiden conversation was full of hissed undercurrents. Sophronia observed that when Dimity flashed her letter at the young man, he shook his head violently, not understanding her ire. He was either a very good actor or had no involvement in the fiasco on the squeak deck. Sophronia was relieved that she had interfered and set the airdinghy falling. But if Lord Dingleproops wasn't embroiled, who was? The flywaymen? The Picklemen? How did they get hold of the stationery? And the question still remained, why Dimity?

Sophronia tried to approach her friend after class with her concerns. "Dimity, about that letter..."

Dimity, practically in tears, only brushed by and scuttled off as fast as she could, trailing a worried-looking Agatha and Sidheag in her wake.

*Felix*, thought Sophronia as she made ready for supper that evening, *is liable to be a problem.* Despite all due attention to deportment, she could not help thinking of him as Felix, even while addressing him as Lord Mersey. They shared several lessons—including tea and delusions with Mademoiselle Geraldine and portion allotment, puddings, and preemptive poisonings with Sister Mattie. He would keep flirting, despite more tempting prospects like Monique and Preshea, who practically hurled themselves in his direction. *I wonder if I should warn him about Preshea. She does so desperately want to murder her first husband.* Sophronia had no idea why Felix was so intent upon her. She had not yet received lessons in seduction, or she might have understood the appeal of sharp confidence, a topping figure, and green eyes. All Sophronia's intellect was directed at something *other* than attracting male companionship. These things combined to make her particularly appealing to gentlemen. Soap could have told her that.

The boys were permitted to take supper with the girls, distributed among the tables. Lord Mersey, Lord Dingleproops, and Mr. Plumleigh-Teignmott sat with Sophronia's group because they were the youngest of the gentlemen visitors. Pillover was the youngest of all, at thirteen, and was distressed at having been singled out for special treatment.

"I'm not that good a student," he confided in Sophronia. "This trip was supposed to be a reward for top evil geniuses. I've no idea why Professor Shrimpdittle chose me. It could be because I'm the only one with a sibling on board. What is going on with you and Dimity, by the by? My sister is a raging pain but not the type to snub a friend."

Sophronia winced. "Set up, I'm afraid. Some kind of test."

Pillover nodded. "Ah, well, she'll come around eventually."

"I certainly hope so. It's terribly boring without her constant gossip."

"Really? I don't miss it at all. You are an odd duck."

The supper was served—broiled salmon, hashed mutton, potatoes, parsnips, and baked apple pudding. The young men had passable table manners, but conversation was stilted at best, with the young ladies either flirting or nervously silent at the prospect of using the wrong fork.

Despite his best efforts, Felix was not sitting on Sophronia's left. She sat isolated at the end of the table next to Preshea, who turned to speak with Lord Dingleproops. Pillover was a godsend, sitting across the way, although he would shovel mutton into his maw as if sheep were soon to be obsolete.

"I must say," he commented between bites, "you eat better at this school than we do."

"And in greater style, I imagine."

Pillover looked at the tablecloth and flower centerpiece as though he had not noticed them before, which he probably hadn't. "Rather."

"We *are* training to handle such things for the rest of our lives. You are training to be evil geniuses. Table settings and the like are regarded, I am sure, as beneath you."

"You are disposed to see this as careless?" wondered Pillover.

"Some things are more important than they seem. Note, for example, that by having larger flowers in taller vases, you can prevent people from conversing across the table, thus confining them to their dinner partners. Wider arrangements with cascading ferns, and you might even pass notes or objects to a dining companion without anyone the wiser."

Pillover looked uninterested. Sophronia switched topics.

"I think someone is after Dimity."

"Well, despite what she claims about that silly letter, it isn't Lord Dingleproops. I can tell you that." Pillover appeared to be aware of the situation.

"Have you had any odd encounters?"

Pillover started. "Me? Who would be after me?"

"Well, who would be after your sister?"

"It must be some kind of lark. Or mistake. I wouldn't put it past the Pistons."

Sophronia detailed the events on the squeak deck.

Pillover shook his head. "Can't be Pistons, not that. Even they don't have access to an airdinghy. No, I think you're right that someone else wants my sister."

"But who?"

Pillover was remarkably unconcerned. "Isn't that your job?"

"Have you missed the part where she's not speaking to me?"

Pillover had once been made to wear Sophronia's petticoats in pursuit of information and safety. This gave him an inflated opinion of her abilities. "You'll manage."

"You'll give it some thought, please?" Sophronia pressed. "I'm a little worried."

"Well, she is my sister," Pillover reluctantly agreed.

The meal proceeded, and Sophronia and Pillover conversed civilly, in a manner quite in keeping with training, until the tables were cleared and the cards brought forth.

Given their new numbers, the girls were told that round games were to be played so the entire table might participate. Monique declared that they would play loo and dealt without waiting for a consensus. Since loo was best played with seven, Sophronia, without being asked, and Pillover, who cared not one jot, sat out.

They watched the others play for a while. Felix kept glancing up over his cards at Sophronia.

Finally, she asked Pillover, in a low voice, "What is it with Lord Mersey?"

Pillover's face darkened, and he shifted in his seat as though it were uncomfortable. "Golborne's a famously conservative family. Too much money, not enough new blood."

"Ah, anti-integration?" Sophronia prodded. Some of the aristocrats had fought hard against allowing the supernatural any part of government. That had happened centuries ago, but aristocrats and vampires had long memories.

"Worse. Picklemen."

Sophronia stared at Felix. "Really?"

Pillover, whose family was quite progressive, answered sarcastically, "Can't have monsters taking over the government, can we? We're *food* to them. You know the propaganda. Fear supernatural creatures! Forget the fact that they won us an empire."

Sophronia had come around to appreciating both the werewolf Captain Niall and the vampire Professor Braithwope as much as one *could* appreciate teachers. Even if Captain Niall had once accidentally tried to eat her. So she considered herself mostly progressive.

Her attention was diverted by a small, polite cough.

"Vieve?"

"Good evening," said the scamp, from near her elbow.

Pillover nodded at her. They'd met before, during the incident with the petticoats.

"Listen, Sophronia, Soap says there's something you might want to see tonight when we leave the moor. And I *know* I want to. I'll be by with the obstructor later, so you won't need to climb." She didn't wait for Sophronia's agreement and rabbited off.

"Did you understand any of that?" Pillover asked, in a tone of voice that said he didn't really care.

"You mean to say, you didn't?"

"Nor was I meant to. Are you going out this evening, then?"

"Possibly."

Pillover looked down the table to where Felix was once more staring in their direction. The viscount seemed distressed by the amount of attention Sophronia was bestowing upon Pillover. Since Pillover was customarily the victim of the Pistons' pranks, he was morosely pleased to be getting under the boy's skin.

"You want any company?"

"Oh, no, thank you."

"I wasn't thinking of myself."

Sophronia gave him a crafty smile. "Has no one officially warned you boys about Geraldine's alarms?"

Pillover looked as cagey as a round boy with an obvious stash of apple fritters could. "Nope. I know from Dimity, of course."

"In that case, you might mention to Lord Mersey that I'm planning a jaunt later tonight."

Pillover smiled for the first time in their acquaintance. "I might do that."

## FLIRTING WITH DECEIT

With the sun firmly down and card games satisfactorily completed, the students went to their next classes. The boys had lessons in mechanics and machinations with Professors Shrimpdittle and Lefoux. The girls, all forty-five of them, trooped down to a lower deck to disembark using the glass platform lift. They had their weekly lesson with Captain Niall. There was a palpable waft of excitement, not to mention perfume, as the werewolf was most every young lady's favorite teacher. He was also, by far, the handsomest.

Sophronia liked him, too, even though she knew the floppy, easygoing military man was a sham. In his werewolf guise, he'd tried to kill her and savaged her best horsehair petticoat instead. He'd been moon-mad at the time, but she'd never quite forgiven the lapse, nor the loss of the petticoat. Like a proper gentleman, the good captain never made mention of the undergarment murder.

The girls stood on the moor. The glass lift turned into a gaslight for evening fighting lessons. Captain Niall strode toward them—a dashing soldier with a beaver-skin top hat tied to his head and a leather greatcoat buttoned from collar to hem. He had a loose way of walking, as if he had temporary, and not very good, control over someone else's legs.

"Ladies, today we leave off knife fighting and move on to the most useful of all skills." The werewolf paused dramatically. The young ladies about him inhaled in anticipation.

"Running away," said Captain Niall with a flourish.

The faces about him were crestfallen; running away was hardly a romantic pursuit. Except when one was running to Gretna Green.

"Now, there are many ways and means to run. Today we will cover escape within a confined area—the fine art of dodging."

He divided them into groups, naming some rabbits and others wolves. The wolves were each given a short wooden spoon that had been dipped in red gooseberry jelly. They had to tap the bodice of a rabbit to eliminate her from the game. This added incentive for the rabbits to dodge, given that their dresses were about to be covered in jelly. Wolves could only chase assigned rabbits, and rabbits could not work together. Apart from that, they were free to be as creative as they liked.

Sophronia, Sidheag, and Preshea were the rabbits to Monique, Dimity, and Agatha's wolves. Sophronia was pleased with this arrangement. She was good at running away and saw nothing morally reprehensible in it. She promptly scampered off to a nearby copse and climbed a tree to watch the proceedings.

A game of chaotic tag commenced, with the werewolf

teacher moving so quickly among the students he was difficult to see. He yelled instructions and called out rabbits as dead. It soon became clear why Captain Niall had chosen this particular hill. It was littered with obstacles—shrubs, long grasses, the copse of trees, and an occasional boulder.

The game went on for some half an hour until all the rabbits had died and only Sophronia was left. When she was finally found, the wolves refused on principle to climb after her.

"Rabbits can't climb trees," objected Monique.

Captain Niall ignored this and gestured Sophronia down. "Ladies, what did Miss Temminnick do correctly?"

"There she goes again," sniffed Preshea.

Everyone was silent.

Sophronia jumped down. Monique instantly whacked her with her spoon. A great gob of gooseberry stained the front of Sophronia's dress, and her collarbone stung.

"Ouch," she objected.

Finally, one of the older girls answered Captain Niall. "She hid?"

"Exactly! If one is hidden, one does not need to run. However, Miss Temminnick, that was not part of the lesson. So, let's see you try again in a five-minute fray." He pointed to three older girls Sophronia knew only by sight. "You're the wolves. Begin!"

All three charged Sophronia, holding out their jelly-covered spoons. Sophronia dove to one side and broke sharply outside of spoon range. She hiked up her skirts, leapt over a shrub, and made for the high ground. One of the wolves got her dress caught in the shrub and tripped, falling to the side. The two others followed. Sophronia dashed to a boulder, scrabbling for the top.

The wolves did not coordinate or they would have had her easily. Instead, they each came after her alone. Sophronia kicked, which was considered quite shocking in a gentlewoman, but with her skirts hiked it gave her enough reach to stay out of spoon range. It was so unexpected the first wolf fell backward down the hill, her gooseberry jelly never even touching Sophronia's leg.

Sophronia managed to push the last wolf away as the older girl went for her bodice. The wolf almost managed, but Sophronia twisted at the last minute and then, with a tremendous heave, leapt forward over her fallen opponent to land down the hill on the opposite side. She skidded around and took refuge behind a very spiky bush.

Sophronia was panting from the exertion, but still alive. She had a brief moment of elation, and then a wolf came to flush her out. *Should have named this game fox and hound*, thought Sophronia, bending double to avoid the jelly-covered spoon and charging her enemy headfirst. Surprised by a frontal attack, the other girl fell backward into a prickly briar.

Captain Niall called time.

"Interesting, Miss Temminnick. Ladies, what do you think?" He turned to the row of watching students.

"She showed her legs by hiking her skirts."

"She kicked!"

"She charged with her head! Like a bull."

"It was all very embarrassing."

Sophronia stood at Captain Niall's side and crossed her

arms, panting. Certainly, she had conducted herself like neither a lady nor a rabbit, but Captain Niall hadn't given them any particular rules about conduct, except to survive. She had survived, hadn't she?

Captain Niall appeared to agree. "Miss Temminnick sought the high ground, a strategic choice if you know the number of opponents. Remember, however, that if there is a chance of reinforcements, the high ground exposes you to projectiles. Now, ladies, please jelly up your spoons and switch roles. Those who were rabbits are now wolves."

Sophronia saw Dimity lick her spoon surreptitiously before passing it on. Dimity was awfully fond of gooseberries.

So it went, switching back and forth, rearranging rabbits versus wolves, until all were exhausted. By the end, everyone, even Sophronia, had died several jelly deaths. Dimity enacted a dramatic Shakespearean soliloquy at the combined spooning of Agatha and Preshea to a round of polite applause.

After two strenuous hours, with the girls all sore in the calf and blistered in the toe, the captain called a halt. They lined up to be lifted, in groups of five, aboard the airship. Sophronia was pushed to the back because she was being given the cold shoulder by nearly everyone. Sidheag, however, was hanging back intentionally, edging toward Captain Niall.

Sophronia faded into the darkness, pretending to have dropped her reticule.

"Sir, may I ask a word of advice?" Sidheag curtsied, bending her head too far forward.

"About the game, Lady Kingair?" Captain Niall gestured for her to rise.

"No, sir, it is a matter of pack. Things are unsettled in Kingair. I think *he* may be losing control."

"He is one of the strongest Alphas in England." Captain Niall smiled as though alluding to a shared joke. "There are some who would say even the queen's own werewolf would lose three out of five challenges to your grandfather."

"It's not his strength I question; it's the behavior of the rest of the pack."

"They *are* Scottish."

"But never have they been this angry."

"Perhaps it's the Giffard dirigible run. If there is even the possibility he could open the aetherosphere up to vampires, even if it's only roves..." Captain Niall trailed off.

Sidheag filled in the rest. "Then werewolves have a right to be worried."

Sophronia puzzled over this. It must have something to do with tethers. Currently, one of the greatest checks on vampire power was the fact that it was limited to specific territories. The more powerful the vampire, the more confined the territory. Werewolves, on the other hand, had a greater range, since their tether was to other members of the pack, rather than an exact location. This was how England had won an empire abroad; packs could fight in armies. *Is there something about this dirigible flight that could change that dynamic? That's far more significant than Vieve's claims of shorter travel times. Vampires could be as mobile as werewolves if they tethered to aetherosphere-going dirigibles, possibly more so.*

"I've always wondered why Professor Braithwope was the only floating vampire," said Sidheag.

"He's a bit of an experiment."

Considering the vampire teacher's silly mustache, Sophronia thought, *Not only in that way. Are the vampires hoping to experiment further with Giffard's new technology? Is someone trying to stop them?* Vampires, to Sophronia, were mainly a concept rather than a practice—she hadn't much experience with them. But she found the concept more palatable when she knew there were limits to their supernatural abilities. The werewolves, she must assume from this conversation, felt the same.

Sidheag said, "Do we consider the professor a successful experiment?"

Captain Niall touched the tall girl affectionately on one shoulder. "You know I can't tell you that."

"Of course." Sidheag pressed one long finger to her mouth. Then, glancing around, she said, "Oh, dear, it looks like I'm the last." The glass platform waited for her, so low Sidheag need only step up onto it.

"Not entirely. Miss Temminnick?" Captain Niall turned into the darkness to where Sophronia skulked.

She moved forward, not at all ashamed. This was, after all, what they were trained for. "Did you smell me or hear me?"

"Both. Even you cannot quiet your own heartbeat. And, as you have been told before, perfume will always work against you with the supernatural, unless you have scattered it everywhere."

Sidheag, at least, seemed gratifyingly surprised to see her.

"What did you hear?" she hissed as Sophronia stepped up onto the platform next to her.

"Enough."

"That's personal pack business!"

"And I won't mention any of it if you tell me everything you know about this possible vampire plot."

"I can't be *seen* talking to you." The platform rose slowly toward the underbelly of the airship. At the same time, the massive craft lifted higher into the sky.

"Then you had better do it fast."

"Has anyone ever told you you're awful contrary, Sophronia?"

"Frequently. Now explain."

"It seems the werewolves think the vampires are trying to master aetherosphere travel for themselves. There are rumors Giffard's been funded by vampire backers. Even though he's French."

Sophronia's mind whirled at the implications. "Is our school floating to town to support or fight this possibility?"

"I've no idea."

"How do our visiting boys figure into this?"

Sidheag shrugged. "Bunson's is pro Picklemen."

Sophronia nodded. "And the Picklemen will want to control any aetherosphere travel for themselves." She was thinking about the prototype kerfuffle at her sister's ball. Both the government and the Picklemen had been after the technology then. "No wonder we are floating to town."

"You think there's going to be some kind of contest for control?" Sidheag nibbled her lips. The werewolves, as a rule, were uninterested in advancements in science that did not pertain to munitions. Sidheag had not been raised to think in terms of patent control or manipulation of technological discoveries.

Sophronia said, "I'm not sure what I think yet, but that seems likely."

It was far easier to get around the ship with Vieve. Sophronia didn't have to climb the exterior to avoid patrolling mechanicals. Vieve had an invention of her own devising, the obstructor, which froze a mechanical in its tracks long enough for two girls to slide around it.

They sped through the central student section and then into the forbidden section. Dangling red tassels all around demarcated the highly restricted forward segment of the ship, which included the teachers' quarters, the record room, and... the boiler room. Everything was going smoothly, even the most dangerous part: passing the doors of slumbering teachers.

Then a loud whistle reverberated through the airship, picked up and repeated by every mechanical within range. They hadn't had to use the obstructor for two hallways, so it couldn't have been their fault. The alarm was triggered by some other miscreants out after hours.

The two girls squeezed behind a massive marble bust of Pan and a once-underdressed nymph in the corner. The nymph had been clothed in skirts and a lace hat, to make her more the thing. This meant there was plenty of room for concealment. Just in time, too, for doors to teachers' rooms popped open and heads stuck out.

"Is there no peace for the naked?" Sister Mattie wore a bed cap of sensible white lace.

"I think you mean peace for *the wicked*," corrected Lady Linette, wrapped in a voluminous silk robe of apple green trimmed in black velvet. Her hair was loose and flowing, her face free of paint. She looked lovely and fresh.

"Why would that apply?" asked Sister Mattie, before closing her door on both the problem and the noise.

"What's going on?" The headmistress voiced that query, her rinsed red hair crowned by a great pink floof of crochet.

"I shouldn't worry, Geraldine. It's probably our young gentlemen guests."

"I warned you no good would come of having boys on board!"

"Might have told that to me, mum, whot?" joked Professor Braithwope, shimmering out of his room fully clothed and dapper. His mustache was a fluffy caterpillar of curiosity, perched and ready to inquire, dragging the vampire along behind it on the investigation.

"Oh, Professor," simpered Mademoiselle Geraldine, "you don't count. You're a *gentleman*, not a boy, and *qualit-tay* to boot."

The vampire looked around the hallway, noting no mechanicals or culprits who might have set the alarm. He was the only one dressed, his boots mirror shiny and his trousers cut to perfection. Sophronia wondered how such a nobby little man could manage to fade to the background so often. It was a real skill.

"Where's the revolution?"

"Student quarters, I suspect. One of the boys. Our girls know better than to risk it at night. Or they know how to avoid setting off alarms." Sophronia could have sworn Lady Linette glanced in their direction.

The vampire nodded. "I'll see to it, being as I'm all gussied up and proper for public consumption. Plus, put a bit of fear into those monkeys, wrath of a vampire, whot?"

"A most excellent notion, Professor."

Sophronia, forgetting her own first encounter with the vampire, suppressed a giggle at the very idea of Professor Braithwope, with his quizzical mustache and undersized frame, putting the fear into anyone—except perhaps the fear of growing the wrong facial hair.

The alarm, painfully loud, continued. There was no maid nearby to receive shutdown protocols. Professor Braithwope hurried off, and the other teachers disappeared into their rooms, presumably to hide from the noise.

Sophronia and Vieve continued on their way, reassured that attention was directed elsewhere.

"What was that about?" Vieve wondered.

"Viscount Mersey might have taken something Pillover said after dinner as encouragement."

"Sophronia, you didn't plant ideas in that poor nobleman's head? You are a naughty girl."

"Where's your aunt? I didn't see her just now."

"Down in the laboratory with Shrimpdittle, I think. They're working on something together, despite bad blood over the prototype."

"Is that the real reason the boys are on board, as cover for this project?"

"Possibly."

"Vieve," said Sophronia slowly, "how would vampires handle floating through the aetherosphere?"

"I've no idea. Ah, here we are."

When entering the engineering chamber from the proper door, rather than the outside hatch, they came in from above onto a wide landing with the whole of the massive room spread out before them. Sophronia loved the view. It was so impressive, with multiple boilers flaming and smoking, engines and machines moving and sparking, sooties running between massive mounds of coal. Usually, two-thirds of the sooties slept during evening shift, but tonight everyone was awake. A full complement of supervisors stood guard—firemen, greasers, engineers, and coal runners. *Something is definitely afoot. Or should one say "a soot"?*

Sophronia and Vieve, unnoticed, made their way down the spiral staircase and through the crowds to the far corner of the room, ending up behind the coal pile that had long since become their regular meeting spot.

Soap was waiting, fairly vibrating with anticipation.

"What took you so long?"

"Someone set off the alarm."

"Not you two? Never you two." Soap's faith was endearing.

"Course not. Sophronia set up a patsy to take the fall."

Soap swung to look at her.

Sophronia smiled slyly. "What can I say? Boys need lessons sometimes."

Soap arched an eyebrow at her.

"Not you, Soap. You're not a *real* boy. But Felix is being difficult."

"Felix, is it?" Soap did not look pleased.

"Lord Mersey, I mean," Sophronia corrected herself.

Soap looked even less pleased.

Sophronia didn't quite understand where she'd gone wrong. Soap was usually such a good-natured chap. She changed the subject. "So, what's the surprise?"

Soap brightened. "We're going undercover for the next three days. Weather not being obliging."

"What do you mean? It's been lovely for March."

"Just so. We can't go sailing to London all visible. So they brought out the steam machine. We're going *to white*!"

"Well, that explains all the extra water that tube took on."

"You saw that?" Soap looked away from Sophronia. "What else did you see?"

Sophronia tried to look more mysterious than embarrassed.

Vieve was not interested in innuendo—a *new machine* was about to be cranked up! "I've heard about it but never seen it in action."

"I've only helped do it twice before," said Soap. "Come watch." He led them to sit atop a pile of coal. "Don't interfere!" He shook a finger at Vieve.

The sooties wheeled out a massive apparatus, one that usually huddled at the back of the room. They arranged it to sit straddling the distribution hatch—a massive opening used to bring in coal and shovel out ash.

The contraption was hooked up to boilers and attached to a complex series of metal tubes, springs, and gears, the range of which charmed Vieve.

"Oh my goodness, is that an electrosplit goopslimer port? I do believe it is. And is *that* a Thrushbotham pip-monger swizzle sprocket? Oh, *two* swizzle sprockets!" Vieve was practically squeaking in excitement.

The machine was cranked up and began to puff.

Never before had Sophronia seen such a massive amount of steam at once. The boiler room filled with hot white moisture. All her curls fell flat—Mademoiselle Geraldine would be so upset.

There was a great deal of yelling and some crashing, and then the sooties had the device corked up. All the steam, one must presume, was now flowing outside the ship.

Soap sauntered over, hands deep in his pockets. The soot on his face was clumped and spotty from the steam, and he looked inordinately pleased with himself.

"Wanna see?"

"Of course!" said Sophronia and Vieve in unison.

Soap helped Sophronia down, and she was shocked by how large and strong his hand was. He led the way over to the small hatch Sophronia used on her solo visits.

They stuck their heads out and saw...nothing. Only white.

"We are our own cloud! Ingenious." Sophronia was impressed. "And it will hold day or night, despite temperature shifts?"

"Of course!" Soap took this questioning as doubt of his own actions and integrity. "Designed by Professor Lefoux, this was!

She don't make mistakes, that one. Except bringing this bit of trouble on board." Soap pulled off Vieve's cap and ruffled her hair.

Vieve swatted him.

Sophronia nodded. "Thank you, Soap. This has been most entertaining. But we should be getting on." She was profoundly relieved. *At least for a while Dimity will be safe from attack. No one will be able to find her.*

Soap looked surprised; normally Sophronia lingered. "You should? Right, then." He led them back to the staircase. Vieve scampered up, but before Sophronia could follow, Soap touched her arm. "Who is this Felix chap?"

"Just an impossible boy. I shouldn't let him bother you."

"You need me to teach him any lessons? A little boxing 'round the ears?"

"That's very kind, Soap, but I can fight my own battles."

"I don't like you fraternizing with boys. Ain't normal."

Sophronia quirked her head in amusement. "No? And here I was thinking that's how society worked. Might as well learn the way of it."

"Oh, you believe so?" Soap leaned in. Even though she stood on the first step, the sootie towered over her. He smelled of wet coal and engine oil. It must be quite strong, as it seemed to be affecting her breathing. He leaned in, his normally cheerful face quite serious. "I could teach you a bit."

He was so close, Sophronia thought for one delusional moment that he intended to actually kiss her on the mouth! *Imagine that? Soap!* Instead he reached for her arm, the exposed piece between glove and sleeve where his filthy hand would not soil her dress. He raised it to his face and kissed her just there, his lips impossibly soft.

Sophronia froze. *But I don't think of Soap like that* was her first reaction, and then she felt a tiny bit of annoyance. *Why would he want to complicate our friendship?* And then caution. *It's up to me to ensure he doesn't.*

She recovered her powers of movement and extracted her arm gently. She decided to take his overture as a jest, a mockery of polite society, and laugh it off. "Oh, Soap, you *are* silly."

Jaunty Soap was instantly back. "See what I mean? I can teach you."

"Very gallant," Sophronia said, smiling and backing up, almost tripping over the next step up. *Look at me, made clumsy by a sootie!* "It's not exactly the lesson I need, however."

"I'm thinking it's the same kind of lesson this Felix is after."

Feeling she had entirely lost control of the conversation, Sophronia did as Captain Niall had so recently instructed; she ran away.


When Sophronia caught up to Vieve, the girl was trotting purposefully down the hall, obstructor at the ready. It was proving unnecessary, as the mechanicals had all been diverted elsewhere. Probably to monitor the boys.

"Can we swing by your aunt's classroom on our way back?"

"Need something?" Vieve's mind ever jumped to supplies.

"No. Didn't you say your aunt and the visiting professor were holed up there?"

"You want to see what they are up to?" Vieve changed course

and headed toward the teaching area outside the tassel zone, rather than across to the student residences. Soon, they found themselves at the classrooms. The dark hallway was lit only by a small beam of light emanating from the crack under Professor Lefoux's lab door.

Sophronia went for Sister Mattie's room.

Vieve, confused, followed.

Sister Mattie never locked her door. She maintained that if a student needed to pollute, cure, or improve nutritional health, she should do so with impunity. Or, as she put it, "One woman's petunia is another one's poison."

Sister Mattie's classroom abutted Professor Lefoux's. Sophronia made her way through it in the dark. This was not difficult, as she knew which plants were thorny and which were sticky. She ended up behind the rubber tree, where a small door let out onto a balcony covered in large pots of rhubarb and tomatoes, alongside foxgloves and rhododendrons. Sophronia brushed through, mindful that tomato leaves would deposit telltale yellow streaks on her dress. She climbed up and balanced precariously on the railing so she could lean over to the small round window of Professor Lefoux's lab.

She peeked inside. Under bright gas lighting, Professor Lefoux and Professor Shrimpdittle stood together over a large table spread with the parts of some disassembled apparatus. They were not working on the gadget. They were arguing. Sophronia fished in her reticule and brought forth her latest prized acquisition, an ear trumpet. It had taken a good many letters to persuade her mother that she was losing her hearing and in desperate need of the medical device. It was invaluable for eavesdropping, and she'd decorated it to look like a morning glory flower. She pressed the flared end to the glass and the nozzle to her ear.

"...needs to be done!" Professor Lefoux was saying. Her words were almost indecipherable, her French accent was so strong.

"That's ridiculous. Breathing is irrelevant!" Shrimpdittle objected. His voice was one of upper-crust education, all toffy-nosed and toothy.

A knock sounded at the door.

Professor Lefoux went to open it.

Monique de Pelouse came inside. *Holy smokes!* thought Sophronia. *What's she doing here?* She whispered to Vieve, "Monique's turned up. I thought she was in disgrace. Why on earth would they let her wander around after hours?" Sophronia felt unsettled, possibly even a little jealous. Monique knew more about what was going on than she did!

The professors were obviously expecting Monique. For a moment, Sophronia wondered if the dismembered gadget was meant for her.

"I'm to ask if it's ready," the blonde said. "Is it?"

"Not yet," Professor Lefoux answered.

With no further exchange, Monique pirouetted to leave.

"One moment, Miss Pelouse. Was that you who set off the alarm?"

Monique stuck her nose in the air. "Of course not. I have permission to be out. You know that; you gave it to me." She gestured rudely with her thumb at Professor Shrimpdittle. "A couple of his charges thought it'd be fun to sneak out."

Professor Shrimpdittle looked contrite. "Oh, dear. I do hope Lady Linette isn't upset."

Monique smiled evilly. "Not at all. She sent Professor Braithwope to handle the matter, knowing how little Bunson's cares for vampires." With that, she let herself back out of the room.

Professor Shrimpdittle whirled on Professor Lefoux. "If your bloodsucker has harmed one hair on any of my boys' heads!"

"Professor Braithwope is a perfectly respectable teacher. Your boys should not have been out! You were told. *They* were told!"

"I wager they only did it because your girls taunted them."

"Don't be ridiculous, Algonquin. It's what boys do!"

"Who's he feeding from? That's what I want to know."

"As if I should inquire into your personal life and diet!"

"Who is his drone?"

Sophronia perked up. This was a question that troubled her on a regular basis.

"None of your concern!"

"I think it is my concern, with my boys on board! What if he goes for one of them?"

"Professor Braithwope is a gentleman! Not to mention a vampire. He never goes anywhere without proper invitation. You should know that! His kind invented the concept!"

"Well! I like that." Professor Shrimpdittle's tone clearly said that he didn't.

"So you should! Would you rather our school were so deep in the Picklemen's keep we couldn't claw ourselves away . . . like you? Going to sell this invention to them to keep it out of vampire hands? Or are they still after the valve?"

Sophronia hissed back to Vieve, "I think that mini crystalline valve frequensor is involved."

Vieve's eyes shone. "I've been researching that. The one you gave me, I think—"

Sophronia held up a hand, back to eavesdropping.

Professor Shrimpdittle said, "This is getting us nowhere. Perhaps we should stop for the night?"

"I think that's a capital idea." Professor Lefoux was struggling to control her emotions.

Until that moment, Sophronia would have said the austere teacher didn't have emotions.

"You should examine your loyalties, Beatrice. Someday you will have to choose." Sophronia could hear the slamming of books as Shrimpdittle packed.

"Choose?"

"Between science and the supernatural."

"I wasn't aware they were on opposite sides."

Sophronia heard the door slam.

"Oh, that man!" Professor Lefoux exclaimed in French to the empty room. Then there was silence.

Sophronia peeked through the window. The teacher was cleaning up the apparatus on the table, systematically putting everything away.

Sophronia signaled Vieve.

"Take a look," she whispered, making room on the railing and assisting the smaller girl to look in. "What do you make of those parts?"

Vieve didn't answer, face pressed to the glass, until the gas in the room was turned off and the interior black.

She swung her weight back and slid down off the railing. Sophronia followed.

"I don't know. It looks almost like armor, but for what? Undersea exploration?"

"Perhaps it has to do with our trip? Perhaps we're going to London because of your aunt or Professor Shrimpdittle and this invention."

Vieve considered. "It's possible. It'd explain why they need the whole school—access to my aunt's laboratory."

"You were saying about the valve?"

"That one you gave me, I have to run further tests. But I don't see how it can affect mechanicals or the oddgob."

"Keep at it, will you?"

"Until I get caught or something more interesting comes along."

Sophronia patted her friend on the head in the manner of Soap, a thing she knew the girl found particularly annoying. "Good little inventor."

## THE 6TH TEST

# GARNERING INVITATIONS

The girls entered the breakfast room to find the postal steward calling names and passing out correspondences. Since they had gone to white, Captain Niall must have undertaken a run back to Swiffle-on-Exe to retrieve missives. The teachers were always saying that the captain was not an errand boy at the beck and call of young ladies' whims, but on occasion he did perform groundside services made convenient by his land-bound state and supernatural speed.

There was nothing for Sophronia, who sat bleary-eyed and exhausted at the end of the table while the other girls exclaimed. Her fellows exhibited new trinkets to their male dining companions and shared the latest gossip from home. It was an orgy of batted eyelashes, and Sophronia was finding herself unable to cope with fluttering on only a few hours' sleep.

Felix Mersey ostentatiously picked up his place setting and

moved it next to hers. "What's wrong, pretty Ria? You seem to have lost your customary aloofness."

"Oh, do go away. I'm not up to dalliance this morning."

He pouted at her. "Is that all I am to you? A plaything, a speck of dust on a sunbeam, a bit of dandelion fluff on the breeze?"

"Yes, that's it exactly." Sophronia hid a smile at such silliness. *No sense encouraging the blighter.*

"Hard-hearted, that's what you are."

"You're an imbecile, you do realize?"

Any further conversation was interrupted, as it was surely meant to be, by a squeal from Monique. It was emitted upon reading a gold-embossed letter and caught even Mademoiselle Geraldine's attention from the head table.

Felix moved hastily out of indiscreet proximity to Sophronia.

"Miss Pelouse, have you something of note to share with the assembly?" wondered the headmistress.

The blonde girl stood gracefully, glancing over the entire room with a beneficent smile. She looked like a queen addressing her subjects, holding her gold missive in one hand as though an award received from on high. Her dress that morning was of royal blue with butter-lemon stripes, a row of gold pom-poms down the front in increasing size. It was almost as though it were intended to match the letter.

"Nothing of any consequence, Headmistress," she said, blushing prettily. "It's only that my dear mama has informed me that she intends to hold my coming-out ball when we arrive in town!"

Pandemonium reigned. The announcement of a trip to

London had been one thing, and the presence of boys another, but this was the Thing to End All Things—a ball!

A breakfast selection of German sausage, broiled kidney, dried salmon, and muttonchops arrived, but few registered it. Some of the young ladies even ate the salmon without concern to vital humors—when everyone knew colored fish flesh could bring on an attack of hysteria.

Sophronia refused to be ruffled. She ate the same thing every morning: porridge.

Girls began to find excuses to call at Monique's table to compliment the horrid girl on the cut of her dress or the size of her pom-poms, angling for an invitation.

"What lovely earrings, Monique."

"Yes, aren't they pretty? My father purchased them in Spain. Such an expense for little me!"

"Did you do your hair differently this morning, Monique?"

"No, but it is looking quite shiny, isn't it?"

Pillover glanced up from his plate of sausage. "What a revolting spectacle."

Sophronia privately agreed and contemplated breaking from her normal dietary routine and eating a sausage in order to cope.

Monique, mistress of the British Empire at that moment, seemed willing to gratify all sycophants. Most of the older girls, cronies of hers, were told right off that of course she could not do without them in attendance. A few of the middle girls were told they might be allowed in, but the debuts—who shared her table and chambers—were left in suspense.

Preshea, at Monique's right hand, smirked, anticipating an

invite. "Can I pass you the butter, Monique? Would you care for a little more tea, Monique?"

Agatha looked terrified and Sidheag indifferent; they'd rather not be invited. Dimity kept glancing in Sophronia's direction as if she wished they were on speaking terms so they could discuss this new kink in the workings of life.

Lord Dingleproops, Monique's dining companion, paid her marked attention—to her evident enjoyment. Sophronia felt sorry for Dimity. Whatever false hopes he had once given her must now be crushed.

The ordeal of breakfast eventually ended. As they rose and made their way toward the exit, Sophronia snaked up behind her erstwhile best friend and whispered, "I shouldn't be too upset. Lady Dimity Dingleproops sounds quite ridiculous, anyway."

Dimity smothered a giggle and turned, eyes animated, prepared for a bit of a gossip—in that instant all ill feelings were forgotten. But Agatha, of all people, swooped in and linked arms with Dimity, practically dragging her away down the hall.


Through the course of that day, Monique became increasingly intolerable. She had Preshea and others running errands for her, bringing her little gifts. She would send one girl off and then make some snide comment about the poor thing's appearance and lack of funds. Then she was all sugar when the girl returned, bearing a posy of violets or glass of barley water.

By the time Professor Braithwope's etiquette class rolled around after sunset, everyone was beginning to show strain.

The boys escorted the girls to the vampire's door, but they had a lesson with Professor Shrimpdittle instead. Their presence made Monique worse. She latched herself onto Felix's arm when he tried to leave her.

"Abandoning me to monsters, my lord?"

Felix chuckled. "Now, now, Miss Monique, I'm not so bad as all that. I never said they were monsters, only predators."

"You're so wise," simpered Monique, still clutching.

Lady Linette paused in the hallway at the sight. "Miss Pelouse! How can you be so forward? Have you learned nothing? Lord Mersey, let go of her this instant!"

Felix lounged against the wall insolently, still attached to Monique. "I'm afraid, my lady, you must persuade *her* to let go of *me*."

"It's my ankle, Lady Linette. It's feeling poorly," professed Monique.

"Oh, does it? Should I send you to matron?"

"Oh, I shouldn't trouble yourself. It isn't that bad."

"I'm certain it isn't. Now, let go of the young viscount this moment and behave like a proper lady!"

Monique, pouting prettily, let go of Felix and marched into the vampire's classroom with no sign of a limp. Felix made good his escape with a wink at Sophronia. Sophronia, smiling at both the rebuke and the wink, followed Monique.

Monique sat down on a fainting couch next to Preshea, and before anyone else could take the opportunity, Sophronia sat down on her other side. She wasn't really planning anything; she only wanted to make the older girl uncomfortable.

Monique didn't register Sophronia at first, engaged in an

animated discussion with Preshea. The topic appeared to be Lord Dingleproops's chin and whether its absence was all that important to the state of the Empire. When she turned to her left to find Sophronia sitting there primly, Monique twitched and made as if to rise.

But Professor Braithwope started class, so the blonde contented herself with turning her back on Sophronia. Sophronia had Bumbersnoot the reticule with her and placed him on the carpet behind her feet, well concealed by copious skirts.

If asked afterward, she would have explained that there was no *technical* way to train a mechanical into any action outside its initial basic protocols. So it must have been without her knowledge that Bumbersnoot made his way from her skirts to Monique's. She could never have known he would belch steam up the older girl's drawers and deposit a pile of ash on her very expensive pink kid slippers. *Never have known.*

Monique got the most peculiar expression on her face and let out a muffled squawk.

She leapt to her feet and turned to glare at the obvious culprit. "Sophronia!"

Realizing that Bumbersnoot must have done something, Sophronia used her foot to shift him back to his starting position behind her own skirts and looked up innocently at the raging Monique.

Professor Braithwope whirled from where he was demonstrating entering and exiting a hive house with grace and concealed weaponry. He'd been using an arrangement of unstable top-hat boxes as steps and was not happy at being distracted.

The act of whirling caused him to go through the side of one of the hatboxes in a manner most clumsy for a vampire.

"Sit down this moment, Miss Pelouse!" he barked.

"But Sophronia squirted steam up my drawers!"

Dimity let out an uncontrolled giggle. The others in the class looked either surprised or amused, according to their nature.

"Whot, whot? I hardly see how she might have done that. She hasn't moved."

Monique sputtered. Then, knowing she could not defend herself to the teacher, she sat back down and hissed in Sophronia's ear. "You certainly won't be invited to my ball!"

Sophronia smiled. "My dear Monique, I never for one moment believed that I would."

"Unnatural girl!" Monique turned to glare across the room at Dimity, who had one gloved hand pressed to her mouth and dancing eyes.

"And you! Why would I let you come, either? Who are *your* parents? Nothing more than scientists who can't decide which side they're on. Not to mention the way you dress, like some market doxy!"

Dimity's eyes instantly filled with tears, and she let out a whimper, mouth still hidden under her hand.

Sophronia sprang to Dimity's defense. "As opposed to an eighteen-year-old girl who is only *now* having her coming-out ball, who failed to finish properly, and whose parents are quite probably in *trade*?"

All the girls in the room gasped. Even Professor Braithwope was rendered momentarily speechless by such cutting remarks.

The vampire recovered his power of speech. "Ladies! Manners, whot?"

Dimity mouthed "Thank you" at Sophronia, which earned her a harsh look from the vampire.

After that, class settled down, but something in the atmosphere had changed. As the class practiced walking up and down hatboxes, swinging skirts to conceal weapons in as elegant a manner as possible, Dimity came to stand firmly next to Sophronia.

Professor Braithwope noticed and was perturbed, but he continued the lesson. "Any vampire may be addressed properly as 'venerable one.' Alternatively, you may use his title, if an aristocrat. All queens have titles; they are given a baronetcy if not already holding, although that has not been necessary for centuries. Very few women survive being bitten, so rarely is there a new queen. This is why there are always fewer female drones than males."

Sidheag raised her hand at that and asked, "Why bother?"

"Whot? Oh, to be a female drone? Well, the reward is unparalleled. Aside from immortality, if a woman survives metamorphosis, she is automatically a queen. But there are other reasons, before the bite. Drones are protected, fed, and cared for by their vampire. After a period of menial service, they are given patronage to pursue their own desires. Vampires tend to be wealthy and powerful, so they make very good *friends*, whot. There are drawbacks, of course." The professor touched his own neck, hidden under the high collar.

After prancing up and down the stacked hatboxes several

more times, Sophronia decided she could risk one more inquiry. "Could you tell us a little something about tethers, Professor?"

Professor Braithwope considered both Sophronia and her question. "Tethers, whot? Very well, I will indulge in a digression, but only because you'll never understand vampire etiquette if you don't understand our limitations. Queens cannot leave their hive house, and hive-bound vampires cannot leave the vicinity of their queen. How far they can go depends mainly on age, but it's generally no more than a borough. Rove vampires usually have the range of an entire city, but they also remain tethered to their home. They will not stray into a hive's territory unless invited and never enter a hive house unless they have petitioned for one of their drones to be bitten by its queen."

Sophronia prodded further; she was wildly curious. "How does this work for you, Professor?"

"I am tethered to this ship, but I can leave it to walk around the moor."

She pressed. "Are there other vampires tethered to airships?"

"No, we are social creatures, and mine is now such a solitary life. None have followed my example. Although you ladies make it interesting, whot."

"What about your drones?"

"Ah, now, ladies. This brings us back to etiquette, and the purpose of this lesson. It is rude to ask after a vampire's drones, either in courtesy or curiosity. Drones are a bit of an embarrassment. After all, you would not ask a lady about the nature and quality of her pantry, would you?"

All the girls in the class shook their heads emphatically.

The vampire turned cold eyes on Sophronia, his mustache stiff with accusation. "Anything *else*, Miss Temminnick?"

"What happens when a vampire goes beyond the limit of his tether?" Sophronia knew she was pushing the bounds of propriety.

Professor Braithwope paled and stilled. If a vampire could be said to go pale. Sophronia hoped never again to see a teacher whom she respected look so frightened.

The room hushed. Normally the vampire was such an easygoing teacher. Even Monique looked up, her coming-out ball forgotten for one brief moment.

Eventually he said, "Nothing good, Miss Temminnick."

Class ended, and the girls gathered up their reticules, hats, parasols, and shawls in subdued silence. Dimity held back when the others left and waylaid Sophronia with a hand on her arm.

"Professor Braithwope, might I have a private word?" she asked their teacher once the room cleared. "Sophronia, please stay, this concerns you."

"Yes, Miss Plumleigh-Teignmott. How may I help?"

"It's this matter of our orders from Lady Linette. You're aware of them?"

The vampire looked back and forth between the two girls and then nodded.

"Well, I'm not going to do it anymore. Sophronia is my friend and it isn't fair."

"Intelligencers don't play fair, Miss Plumleigh-Teignmott," he replied.

"Well, then I'm no intelligencer of merit. You may send me

down, if you like. I always felt I was ill suited to this lifestyle, despite my parents. I'd rather be loyal than right."

Professor Braithwope smiled, showing fang. "Very interesting way of putting it, Miss Plumleigh-Teignmott, and commendable courage, whot. We had thought you were not capable of independent action. You have, thus far, been rather dragged along in Miss Temminnick's shadow."

Dimity brightened. "My speaking out is a good thing? You aren't going to report me to Lady Linette?"

"I didn't say *that*, Miss Plumleigh-Teignmott."

Dimity looked crestfallen. "Whatever you think is best, venerable one."

The vampire only tilted his head at Dimity's use of the recent lesson.

Sophronia put two and two together and looked at her friend. "You were *instructed* to ostracize me?"

Dimity nodded, clearly ashamed.

Sophronia narrowed her eyes at Professor Braithwope. *Are you testing all the other debuts in the same way, or were instructions different for each girl? Is the ostracism also a test for me?*

The vampire met her speculative gaze calmly. "Did you guess, Miss Temminnick?"

Sophronia knew better than to admit to anything. "I did think it interesting that they were all so eager to blame me for high marks and react in the same way. Even Dimity. And Sidheag, who doesn't care for the machinations of girls." A thought occurred to her. "Were my marks inflated in order to run this test?"

Professor Braithwope's mustache fluffed in amusement. "You

would think of that. No, they were not. But Professor Lefoux did emphasize your superiority in order to drive a wedge. Now, ladies, run along or you'll be late for your next lesson."

They exited into the hallway, and Dimity instantly linked arms with Sophronia. It felt good to have Dimity's bubbling presence back at her side. They trotted down a hall crowded with fellow students. Agatha and Sidheag were waiting for them.

"Tell me," instructed Sophronia, once they were all four gathered in one corner.

"It wasn't our fault," defended Dimity instantly.

Agatha nodded. She lowered her head, trying to hide her face under her bonnet. Sidheag was characteristically nonchalant. Sophronia could almost hear the taller girl's thoughts: *So we weren't talking to Sophronia and now we are? Ho hum.*

Dimity burbled, trying to explain. "You see, we were each taken aside individually, after our exams, and made to promise to ostracize whichever girl had the highest marks."

Agatha whispered, "We all thought it would be Monique."

Sidheag added, "She had taken the test before and had four more years' training."

"Exactly," jumped in Dimity. "That's what I thought, too. Lady Linette told each of us that this was the second half of our exam. That if we didn't do as instructed, our official records would be marked incomplete."

"She said they'd send me down if I didn't obey." Agatha looked tortured. "I tried to keep Dimity in line, too."

Dimity nodded. "Our continued presence at the school depended upon us not speaking to you."

"Now we'll probably all be dismissed," said Sidheag brightly.

"Better than being disloyal! Besides, you two didn't renege, I did." Dimity had all the conviction of one who has taken uncertain action and now must justify the consequences. She fiddled with the glittery ruby-and-gold broach at her throat—paste and gilt, of course.

Sophronia chewed her lip. "What if I admitted you were with me last year for the record room break-in? What if they knew how well you did then? Do you think that would count in your favor?"

Dimity was skeptical. "You would have to confess to something that we got away with. *And* pinned on Monique. They might count an admission against both of us."

"It's all so convoluted," said Sidheag, exasperated.

"It always is." Agatha was philosophically despondent.

"I hated to do it," admitted Dimity. "Well, right up until you scared off Dingleproops."

"It wasn't him, Dimity. Please believe me. I don't know who it was or why they set you up, but it wasn't him, I promise you that."

Dimity looked nonplussed. "He said as much, but I thought I'd been the butt of some cruel joke. Who was it, then?"

Preshea came bustling up. "If you ladies are quite finished? Sister Mattie wants to know why you aren't in class."

The girls glanced around. The hallway was empty except for them.

Preshea said to Dimity, "I see you broke your word to Lady Linette."

Dimity huffed. "It was going too far. *We* were going too far."

"Far is where they will throw you." Preshea turned away.

"I'll take *that* over being mean to a friend," said Dimity staunchly to the girl's retreating back. "Not that you would ever understand *that*, Preshea."

Sophronia let out a small breath of relief. She hadn't realized until that moment how unhappy she'd been without Dimity's friendship. She thought she'd been rattling along fine on her own, but now she noticed the knots in her stomach releasing and the undeniable sensation of wanting to cry from relief.

Sophronia's little band had reunited just in time. Monique's promises of ball invitations were causing social mayhem. Snide comments and sharp elbows abounded. It was all much easier to endure now that the four of them were together again. They heard nothing from the teachers as to the repercussions of Dimity's staunch decision, and they avoided speculating on that, at least. Everything else was fair game.

Sophronia brought them up to speed on some of her private investigations.

Sidheag put it together without frills, as her werewolf-trained mind was prone. "I've been wondering about this. Captain Niall said the vampires might be involved with Giffard's flight? Why?"

Sophronia said, "If Professor Braithwope can tether to an airship, so could other roves."

"Yes, but why now? Presumably old Prof has been doing it for simply ages."

"Perhaps this new ship of Giffard's is more vampire-safe. Or perhaps it has to do with the new technology Giffard is employing. If it works, it'd be much faster than other airships. Perhaps the vampires want access to that speed. I don't think they like to be limited."

Dimity looked at her friend. "I thought you were a progressive."

"Maybe, but I don't know if it's right. I mean to say, Professor Braithwope is nice, but vampires need to be kept in check, don't you think?"

Sidheag nodded vigorously. Dimity shrugged. Agatha looked at the floor.

Dimity said, "Mummy and Daddy have arguments like this. When Daddy says something like that, Mummy calls him a Pickleman."

Sophronia nodded. "Well, I haven't taken sides yet."

Agatha said, "Oh, dear, are there sides?"

"Very likely. Speaking of your parents, Dimity, they haven't upset anyone recently, have they? Anyone important or powerful? On either side, perhaps?"

Dimity frowned. "I don't think so, why? Oh, because of that odd thing with Lord Dingleproops's letter? You think someone might be trying to influence my parents through me?"

"It's one explanation."

"I don't know." Dimity brightened. "I shall write and ask them directly. Or better, I'll get Pillover to do it. They will be delighted he's finally taken an interest in something besides Latin verse. They might even tell him something truthful. I think they gave up on me when I announced my 'hankies for hackneys' good works plan."

"What?" Sophronia was distracted.

"London cabbies are so very often under the weather," said Dimity with a sniff. "One does what one can."

"Oh, well, yes. And getting Pillover to write, good idea." Sophronia was determined to be nice and not to take Dimity for granted ever again. Especially with the possibility that Dimity's time at Mademoiselle Geraldine's was soon to end. Even if Dimity had some harebrained scheme about hankies.

Sophronia remembered the previous evening, when she and Vieve had spied on Professors Lefoux and Shrimpdittle. "I think Monique is somehow in on it, too. I know she's been crowing about this ball of hers, but she's at least involved in Professor Lefoux's experiment as an errand girl. We should run an infiltration on her."

Dimity nodded. They'd taken instruction recently from Lady Linette in the planning of provocational action. Time to put that lesson to use.

"She'll not believe it, if it were me," said Dimity.

Sophronia agreed. "Nor Sidheag." The taller girl looked up at her name. "You would never change your personality so drastically as to be interested in a ball. You might betray us, but not for an invitation."

"I'll take that as a compliment," said Sidheag.

"It'll have to be Agatha," said Dimity.

Sophronia and Sidheag looked doubtful. Agatha was definitely their weakest link.

The redhead looked back and forth between them with

dread in her eyes. "Oh, dear, scheming. I was afraid this would happen if we got chummy again."

Sophronia hunkered down conspiratorially. "You're the only possible choice, Agatha. You need to infiltrate Monique's group."

"Wait! What? Me?"

"Yes, simply pretend you really want an invitation to her blasted ball. Start lurking on the fringes. Keep an eye on her," instructed Sophronia.

"Then report back to us with the details!" added Dimity triumphantly.

"Oh, I don't know about this." Agatha's eyes were huge in distress.

"You don't have to *do* anything, only watch." Sidheag tried to be reassuring.

"It'll be good for you, Agatha. Show the teachers you've got acumen." Dimity was optimistic.

Agatha brightened. "Oh, do you think it might?" Unlike Sidheag and Dimity, Agatha actually wanted to stay at Mademoiselle Geraldine's—to please her papa.

"And," added Dimity brightly, "it might net you an invitation to the ball."

That was not the right tactic. Agatha looked terrified at the possibility.

Sophronia said hurriedly, "Oh, I don't think Monique would, no matter what you did. I shouldn't worry about that, Agatha."

"Oh, good."

"So, are you game?" prodded Dimity, titillated at the prospect of gossip.

Agatha straightened and looked pugnacious. "I'll do my best!"

Sophronia didn't expect much to come of it, but Agatha did try. She began, with remarkable subtlety, to lurk among Monique's followers. She inched her way down to that end of the table at meals. She offered to lend Monique her jewelry. Agatha had a great deal of nice jewelry, the real stuff, unlike Dimity.

Unfortunately, her reports were unsatisfactory. "The ball is all she talks of," she kept saying, and, "When can I stop?"

Then a few evenings later, when Dimity and Sophronia were getting ready for sleep, a demure knock sounded at their door. Dimity, in her nightgown, squeaked and dove for her bed. Sophronia, still dressed, went to answer.

It was Agatha. "Sorry to disturb you so late, but . . . Monique's gone."

"What?"

"I did like you suggested and went to her room just now, pretending I wanted that necklace back. Preshea tried to hide the fact, but Monique's not there. She's definitely snuck off. I think it has something to do with a message she got earlier. One of the mechanicals delivered it and she went all red."

"Oh, goodness. Thank you, Agatha!"

Agatha shuffled away. Sophronia closed the door and headed for her wardrobe.

"You're going after her?" asked Dimity.

"Here I was, proud all this time that I was out regularly, climbing the hull, visiting sooties, and spying on teachers, not even thinking Monique might be doing the same! She had permission to be out the other night, but I never thought she was a sneak like me...."

"Be fair, she can hardly be visiting sooties."

"Good point. Oh, none of this will work!" Sophronia slammed her wardrobe door. "I'm going to visit Sidheag. It's time to follow Vieve's example."

"What...?"

Before Dimity could finish her question, Sophronia was away.

She knocked on Agatha and Sidheag's door, hoping to be let in before Preshea noticed. When Sidheag opened it, Sophronia pushed past and closed the door quickly behind her.

"Sidheag, I need to borrow clothes."

Sidheag blinked. "Now? It's one in the morning."

"So?"

"Nothing I have could possibly fit you. You're shorter and curvier."

"Not dresses, silly. I need boys' clothes. I thought you might have some."

"What?"

Agatha looked up from the vanity, where she was brushing her hair. "You're going after her, aren't you?"

"Yes. And if she's climbing, I have to climb faster. It's time to get rid of skirts. Now, Sidheag? Please hurry."

Sidheag grinned. "How sensible of you." She dove for her wardrobe, which was in an unholy state. The act of opening the door caused a straw bonnet, a parasol, and a patchwork goose to fall out on her head. The taller girl barely noticed, batting away hats, gloves, and a single red stocking like so many gnats. She rifled through the contents, hurling items behind her in a deliciously enthusiastic way.

Agatha gave a whimper of distress. Her side of the room was neat as a new penny.

"Aha!" Sidheag resurfaced, triumphant, with a pair of tweed jodhpurs, of the type country squires used for hunting, and a wrinkled man's shirt.

Agatha helped Sophronia out of her day gown and petticoats. Sophronia pulled on the trousers, buttoning the front and tucking her chemise in at the top. They were scandalously tight about the derriere. She put on the shirt, pushing up the sleeves. For the first time in her life, she was finding it easy to dress herself. *Vieve might have something in this garb.* But then, she supposed, that was because she was wearing a rather pedestrian outfit. *True gentlemen need a valet to help with the cravat.*

Sidheag gave her a funny look. "You're leaving on your stays?"

"Of course! I haven't lost *all* sense of propriety!"

Sidheag snorted. "Corsets constrict movement. I always take mine off when I wear that outfit."

Sophronia gasped. "Bare?"

"We've been over this before—raised by werewolves, remember? What do you think they do before they change shape?"

Agatha gasped, then whispered softly, "You've seen men with no clothing?"

Sophronia tried to stop herself from blushing, remembering her illicit observation of swimming sooties.

Sidheag did not look ashamed. "Of course, silly."

Agatha took a deep breath and then blurted, "What's it like...when they...you know...?"

"They shape-shift? Gruesome. All the bones break and then re-form into wolf shape. Most of them howl in pain. There's a reason it's called a curse."

Sidheag was going to make Agatha say it out loud. The red-head whispered, "No, what's a man like down there?"

"Oh." Sidheag wrinkled her nose. "Unimpressive. They have"—she gestured toward her own nether regions with one hand—"a sort of dangly sausage—lacks tailoring."

Sophronia blinked in surprise. That sounded worse than Sidheag's description of a werewolf shift. She hadn't seen any of the sooties that close up. "Really?"

"Yes, like it wasn't fitted into its casing properly. And hairy." Sidheag was enjoying shocking them.

Agatha thought Sidheag was pulling her leg. "I don't believe you."

Sophronia interrupted this fascinating subject. "Ladies, thank you very much for your help. But I really must be off." She managed a creditable bow, scuttling away before Sidheag could say anything more licentious.

## THE 7TH TEST

# WIELDING A BALLISTIC EXPLODING STEAM MISSILE FIRE PRONG

I t was much easier to climb about the airship in masculine garb; Sophronia regretted not trying it sooner. True, petticoats had saved her life once, but this! This was liberty. She resolved, once they reached London, to acquire gentlemen's dress, upper- and lower-class. Plus a fake mustache. *Where does one purchase a mustache in London? Fleet Street?* Not that she would ever wear such things in public, but for midnight jaunts to visit sooties, why be modest?

She skirted the outside of the residential areas, then the classrooms, and soon she was outside the tassel section. It was a bit challenging to climb surrounded by a cloud of dense white damp. Twice her foot slipped, and she thought fondly of gentlemen's riding boots and then wondered if that might be taking things too far. Footwear, after all, was a serious commitment.

She moved as quickly as she could; with all the white she wouldn't know she'd found Monique until she was right on top of her. Then, as Sophronia was jumping from one balcony to another, she caught a flicker of skirts above her doing the same.

The blonde was heading toward the upper front starboard section of teacher residences. Sophronia knew the area well, even which balconies belonged to which teachers. She usually avoided them assiduously.

She took out her grappling rope and swung it up onto a balcony above. It caught and hooked. She shimmied up—*so much easier in trousers!*—and retracted the hurlie, taking a moment to run her hand along the railing. There were little scrapes and nicks—some fresh, some ancient—indicating that other grappling hooks had been used. *Why should I be surprised? This is a school of espionage, after all.* She swung, hurlied, and climbed up another level so that she was above Monique and could follow her from there.

Monique was not the most graceful climber. She was wearing an evening dress and was hindered by the length and fullness of her skirts. Even at her most prudish, Sophronia wore her shortest dress with only one or two petticoats when climbing. Nevertheless, Monique moved as if she did it regularly and was following a pattern. She did not look around to see if she was being pursued. Eventually, she stopped at a balcony, climbed over the railing, and knocked on the door. All the other quarters nearby had attractive French doors with stained glass. Professor Lefoux's glass was all gears in grays and blues, Lady Linette's was roses in reds and pinks, and Sister Mattie's was vines and flowers in greens and yellows.

This door had no glass, and the porthole window to the room was blacked over—Professor Braithwope's rooms. Vampires did not like sunlight, and floating high above cloud cover, the sun beat down on Mademoiselle Geraldine's more than anywhere else in England.

The door swung open and Monique entered the vampire's nest.

Sophronia made her way over. It was a risk, but the only way to listen was via the cracks in *that* door. She'd have to be particularly quiet, given Professor Braithwope's supernatural hearing. Hopefully, Monique would be talking loudly about herself, as usual.

Sophronia hooked her grapple over the railing, then unstrapped and lowered the wristband end of the hurlie, careful to let the excess come to rest without slapping. Then she swung herself over and by slow degrees climbed down.

Her weekly visits to the sooties and other extracurricular excursions had given her arm muscles no young lady of quality ought to have. She'd had to let out the seams on most of her sleeves. Thus far, no one had noticed. She was certain to get a lecture on her diet if Sister Mattie did. Mademoiselle Geraldine's young ladies were not supposed to become portly.

Sophronia attained the balcony and padded to the door. Taking out her ear trumpet, she pressed it against the crack between the hinges.

"…there must be *something* you can do!" Monique's tone was wheedling.

"I'm afraid not. She is not my queen, even were I hive bound, whot. The words of a rove hold little weight. It's too bad you gave Lady Linette a reason to send you down. You pushed her too far with that prototype business, and then poor testing marks. They have a legitimate excuse that can be justified to the trustees, and your parents."

"But I've given you years of my blood!"

*Monique is Professor Braithwope's drone*, Sophronia realized. Somehow she wasn't surprised. He would be a perfect advocate. It was a little creepy that he fed on a student. But then again, the very idea of him sticking those fangs into anyone's neck was creepy.

"Nothing I can do about it, whot. You should have stayed in everyone's good graces until this Giffard nonsense passed, as I instructed. I will have a better standing with all hives after. Now, you must leave the ship as soon as you come out. Our contract together ends the moment we land in London."

*I wonder if Professor Braithwope is the reason we're called to town*, Sophronia thought. It would make perfect sense. *He is the only teacher who can't travel there on his own. The whole school has to go with him. He is, after all, tethered to the airship.*

Professor Braithwope's tone became almost kindly. "You are more connected to her than I at this point, whot. After all, I did not authorize the redistribution of the prototype; you undertook that at her request."

"You thwarted me and them in that matter," said Monique. "They aren't happy with either of us."

Sophronia rubbed at her forehead, trying to make her brain's inner cogs tumble smoothly. Last autumn, when Monique tried to steal the prototype, Sophronia had thought she was working for the government. This conversation indicated that Monique was working for a vampire hive instead. If they wanted the prototype valve then, did they still want it now? *Goodness, I wish*

*Vieve would tell me what that newer one from the oddgob was for. Is it still all about communication across distances? Or do the mini ones do something more sinister?*

"Hence the reason I do this test with Giffard," said Professor Braithwope.

*Well, that cinches it. Professor Braithwope needs to meet with Giffard and his new dirigible; that's why the school is going to London.*

The vampire continued. "What will you do to get back in their good graces?"

Monique said nothing. Sophronia wished she could see their faces. Eavesdropping was difficult without a window.

Finally Monique muttered, "I don't know."

*I'd wager she already has a plan,* thought Sophronia.

"I wager you already have a plan," said Professor Braithwope.

"And you're hungry enough to let me get away with not telling you about it."

Sophronia realized, for the first time, that Monique had always favored high-necked gowns. She also liked silk shawls and ribbon chokers. *How could I not have realized it was to disguise feeding bites? I'm going to have to pay better attention to that aspect of fashion in the future.*

"Oh, no, my dear, you forget, I no longer care," said the vampire, sharper than Sophronia had ever heard him speak to a student. "Now, come here."

Sophronia prepared to shimmy back up the rope.

After a long silence, Monique spoke, her voice weaker than before. "Since you are no longer looking after me, Professor, you must consider this our last meal together."

Professor Braithwope said, "Of course, wouldn't want to impose."

"You have . . . *alternative* options?" Monique sounded jealous.

Sophronia began to make a mental list, trying to think of all forty-five students and which ones might be hiding the mark of Professor Braithwope's favor.

The vampire did not answer Monique.

Sophronia considered offering herself. There would be quite an advantage to having a vampire's help. But it smacked of cheating. Also, the idea made her squeamish. It was a mark of how far she had come during her time at Mademoiselle Geraldine's that it didn't make her *more* than squeamish.

"Well, Professor, will you be able to attend my ball?"

"I'm afraid not. That's well within Lord Akeldama's territory. I'll stay with the ship around Hyde Park, neutral ground, whot."

"Shame," said Monique.

"I am certain you will catch London afire with your charm," said the vampire gallantly. Professor Braithwope never forgot his manners, which was why he taught lessons on them.

"I'd rather do it with my looks," snapped Monique.

Angry footsteps headed in Sophronia's direction. She scrabbled backward, sacrificing silence for speed. She grabbed her rope at the edge of the balcony and shimmied up, coiling it behind her.

The door below burst open, and both Professor Braithwope and Monique walked out.

"I heard something!" said the professor.

"No one is here." Monique glanced around but did not look up.

But Professor Braithwope did, just as Sophronia tumbled over the railing of the balcony above. Their eyes met for one startled instant.

The vampire winked at her. Actually winked, his mustache bristling conspiratorially. "Ah, perhaps you are right. Simply the wind, whot?"

There was no wind.

Monique had her own concerns and let the matter drop. It was one of the things that made her such a poor intelligencer. She was good at putting lessons to use, but only in the service of her own ends.

"I can't believe it," said Dimity over breakfast. Her objection was almost loud enough for Monique to hear at the other end of the table.

Monique, fortunately, was in deep counsel with Preshea, Lord Dingleproops, Lord Mersey, and several of the older girls on the subject of decorations. Who supplied the best fresh flowers in London? And did they want ribbons, rosettes, and streamers, or only two fluttering options?

"He's her advocate on staff. Or he *was*. I suppose it makes sense, but I never should have believed it of *him*. I was certain Prof B. had better taste. And"—Dimity's attention was caught by the end of the table—"why must Preshea flirt with him so outrageously?"

Sophronia was accustomed to her friend's lightning-fast change of topics. "Lord Dingleproops?"

"Of course, Lord Dingleproops! I could hardly mean Lord Mersey. He's obviously yours. And Pillover doesn't count. Pillover never counts. They are the only three assigned to our table."

"Not that Monique would ever flirt with me," added Pillover, staring glumly into his bowl of porridge. Sister Mattie had put him on a diet. He was, if possible, even more morbid as a result.

"Lord Mersey is *not* mine," Sophronia protested rather too vehemently.

Dimity got coy. "Does he know that?"

"Now, now, we were talking about Lord Dingleproops. I thought you had moved on. The lack of chin. The nasty joke missive."

"Well, I genuinely think he didn't know about that. I compared handwriting. It wasn't his on that letter requesting the assignation."

Sophronia nodded. "Still, I thought you were no longer tempted to partake."

"I wasn't, until Preshea came along and stole him away from me."

"Dimity!"

"Well, it's true. I'm a terribly, terribly shallow person."

Pillover nodded into his gruel.

Dimity turned on him. "Speaking of which, have you heard back from the Parental Evils yet?"

Pillover shook his head even more glumly, practically sinking face-first into the porridge, he was hunched so low.

Dimity went back to commenting on the other end of the table. "Oh, would you look at Preshea, flashing that diamond necklace around? One shouldn't wear diamonds to breakfast, so gauche. As if she came from real wealth!"

"Doesn't she *have* money?" Pillover looked up. "She acts like she has money."

"Which is the most certain indication that she does not. People with money never act like it. Take Agatha, for example."

"Which one is Agatha?" wondered Pillover, in a tone of voice that said all girls looked the same.

"The redhead."

Pillover glanced at Agatha, who was dutifully pretending to be part of Monique's inner circle. Her bonnet had slid back, her hair was coming undone, and she'd forgotten her lace tuck—again.

Pillover looked understandably doubtful as to the girl's substance.

Preshea's tinkling laugh rippled down the table. The pretty brunette pressed a hand to Lord Dingleproops's arm and looked up at him adoringly. Her diamonds sparkled almost as much as the avarice in her eyes.

Lord Dingleproops seemed stunned. His cravat was tied so nicely, one could almost, reflected Sophronia, forgive him the lack of chin.

Dimity said, "I wrote him poetry!"

Preshea let go of the young lord and continued with her conversation. Dingleproops brushed at the spot where her hand had been, straightening his jacket.

"Dimity," Sophronia said, horrified by such an admission, "you didn't *give* him the poetry, did you?"

"Certainly not."

Sidheag tilted back in her chair, grinning. "Well, let's hear it."

"Oh, no. I don't think that's a good idea at all," Sophronia said.

But Dimity was already dipping into her reticule and pulling out a scrap of paper. She gave it to Sidheag, who read it with a perfectly straight face, her tawny eyes dancing, and then passed it to Sophronia.

> My love is like a red red rose
> occasionally he has a red red nose
> he could keep me warm in the snows
> I wager he has very nice toes.

Sophronia could think of nothing to say except "Oh, Dimity."

Things might have continued in this vein except a violent jerk shook the entire airship, accompanied by a rumbling clunk and then a sinking sensation.

The girls looked at one another.

Dimity glared suspiciously at Sophronia. "What did you do now?"

Sophronia widened her eyes. "Not me this time, I promise."

"It's *always* you," accused Sidheag in an appreciative kind of way.

"Are we sinking? I do believe we are sinking," said Lord Dingleproops a tad loudly.

"Falling, my dear Dingleproops," corrected Lord Mersey. "We are not at sea."

"Landing, perhaps?" suggested Dingleproops, obviously uncomfortable with the concept of falling out of the sky.

The girls were also discombobulated, but they were not so gauche as to talk about it. They looked to the head table to see how the teachers were behaving. Aside from Professor Shrimp-dittle, none of them were reacting. Even Mademoiselle Geraldine was calmly consuming crumpets. Professor Braithwope, it being daylight, was still abed.

Sensing the shift in student mood, Lady Linette rose to address the masses.

"We are lowering for a refuel and groundside layover. Students will engage in various land-bound activities, including an al fresco luncheon during which time you will be expected to undertake consumption, courting, and conspiracy over calico cloth. After sunset, there will be a lesson with Captain Niall for the ladies, and badminton in the dark for the gentlemen. Be certain to gather all your necessities after breakfast; you will not be permitted back aboard until supper."

Mademoiselle Geraldine added, "Ladies, be certain to wear your wide-brimmed hats. You know how I feel about freckles."

This announcement was met with enthusiasm. Outside classes? All day and evening? How thrilling. Plus, picnics were widely considered a wheeze.

Everyone attempted to finish breakfast posthaste, the better to have extra time to change into walking dresses and outside bonnets.

Shortly thereafter, they found themselves trotting down the steam-powered drop-staircase onto a grassy hilltop pasture near a diminutive forest. Sophronia spared a moment to wonder what locals might think of a random low-floating cloud. However, it was romantic to imagine being seen descending out of it.

"As if we were cloud princesses," suggested Dimity. She'd chosen to branch out from her customary vibrant dresses for one of ruffled cream-and-dove-gray chiffon, looking very cloud-like herself.

As soon as all the students and most of the teachers were disgorged—Professor Braithwope and Mademoiselle Geraldine remaining on board—the airship cloud rose majestically back into the air and drifted out of sight behind the trees.

It was a beautiful day, not a cloud in the sky—which made a random airship cloud all the more peculiar. The girls looked a picture. It was still cold for spring, but out had come pretty flowered muslins and striped seersucker walking dresses. There were parasols galore, and embroidered fringed shawls, not to mention shepherdess hats and Italian straw bonnets. Admittedly, the stylish dresses had been modified by belts with dangling gadgets, wrist attachments, suspiciously heavy chatelaines, and, in Sophronia's case, a large reticule that looked like a metal sausage dog.

Lessons, it must be confessed, were not a resounding success. The students were distracted easily. Sophronia and the debuts joined with some of the middle-level girls and all of the visiting boys for a lesson with Lady Linette in how to stroll in Hyde Park. Much time was spent going over the different ways to cut an unwelcome suitor, how tightly a man's arm might be grasped, and the best way to engage in espionage under direct sunlight. They also discussed the distribution, use, and application of stealth spy rocks.

There was a picnic of broiled beef, roast duck, braised pork pie, cold poached chicken in cream sauce, pickles and relishes, crusty French bread, and stewed fruit, accompanied by punch, which was followed by tea with pear turnovers, cabinet pudding, and apricot macaroons. They learned how to sit on wet ground and still eat with delicacy. Conversation centered mainly on the various evil projects under the purview of their gentlemen visitors, with the young ladies inventing new uses and applications. It turned into a kind of game. Lord Dingleproops, for example, was working on mustache-curling and -waxing technologies, and the girls wondered if his wax might be used to convey secret messages, or even if the curl of a man's mustache might function in such a manner. The discussion evolved to the interesting question of whether a gentleman could tattoo a secret message upon his chin, then grow out his beard, thus transporting said message into enemy territory with no one the wiser. Would a man want a message permanently upon his chin? That was the quandary. And could one legitimately ascribe nefarious intent to any man with a full beard as a result?

"I've always thought beards suspicious," said Dimity with conviction.

Sophronia felt that Lord Dingleproops might be improved by a beard. After all, no one would know his chin appeared to have eloped with, quite probably, Monique's brain and Preshea's sense of humor.

After the picnic, the ladies and gentlemen were permitted to socialize further. Flirting was cautiously encouraged, with Lord Dingleproops and Lord Mersey being instantly subsumed by Preshea and Monique, respectively. Sophronia and Dimity linked arms and tootled around. Agatha trailed dutifully behind her mark, as ordered, along with a small gaggle of fellow syco-phants. Sidheag mooched off with a stick to beat a tree or something. The teachers settled into a group near the hilltop to keep an eye on the mingling young people.

Sophronia and Dimity wandered into the small forest, where they found an empty patch of ground and put Bumbersnoot down to have a snuffle in the fallen leaves. He was given strict instructions not to catch anything on fire, although it was damp enough that he would have had to put considerable effort into the attempt.

He squeaked about, his stubby mechanical legs getting caught on twigs, his ears flapping with toots of smoke, and his tail wagging back and forth eagerly. Sophronia did not bother to remove the lace bits wrapped about him, so that he trailed ribbons and straps in his wake like an entirely disreputable bride.

They talked of nothing consequential and watched the mechanimal's antics. Bumbersnoot was wrestling with a large stick, and Sophronia couldn't tell whether he wanted to swal-low it into his storage compartment or his boiler. Suddenly, the little creature sat back and whistled, pressing out steam force-fully in some kind of an alarm, like a teakettle.

Both girls were startled. They'd had no idea he could make any noise whatsoever, aside from the clang when he stumbled into furniture.

Moments later three slablike men materialized out of the trees. One of them grabbed Dimity, and another Sophronia. The third stood with arms akimbo, as if he intended to make a speech.

Sophronia found herself most indelicately confined. There was one beefy arm about her waist, trapping her arms against her side, and another over her mouth, preventing her from shouting for assistance.

"Where's the boy?" demanded the third ruffian, looking around. "We need him as well."

Sophronia tried to kick her captor, lashing out with one booted foot, but heavy skirts and copious petticoats prevented her from doing any damage.

Dimity was also struggling. Sophronia could see her friend's wide hazel eyes above the other ruffian's arm.

Bumbersnoot, ignored by their attackers, took temporary refuge behind a stump.

Sophronia really didn't want to, but she did the only thing she could. She opened her mouth and bit down hard on the man's sweaty arm.

The man howled in pain but didn't let her go, only jerked her head back and tightened his grip over her mouth in a most uncomfortable manner.

"The boy should be with them; they are siblings, after all."

*Pillover. They want Pillover, too.*

Bumbersnoot, not at all pleased with this treatment of his mistress, circled about and approached Sophronia's captor.

Sophronia couldn't give him any orders. Even if she were able to speak, he rarely obeyed verbal commands. She had no idea what he might do. She was terribly afraid he would get himself permanently damaged; one swift kick from the ruffian's anvil-sized boot and he was done for.

Her mind cataloged lessons. They'd had nothing on freeing

themselves from larger, stronger captors. Her elbows were tight to her waist, but she made an attempt to reach for her chatelaine—the Depraved Lens of Crispy Magnification hung there. It was a weapon, of sorts. She couldn't get hold of it, but she could reach her other wrist.

She still wore the hurlie. She rarely took it off except to bathe. She managed to use one hand to release the catch.

Bumbersnoot moved closer.

Sophronia couldn't point the grapple at her own captor, and she daren't risk hitting Dimity, but the man who had spoken was an easy target. She angled her wrist at him and fired. She got the grapple over the ruffian's shoulder, jerking back to bring the hook into the flesh of his upper back. The man screamed and turned, scrabbling with his hands.

"Get it off, get it out!" he yelled. There was blood leaking down his shirt—he was without a jacket. All three of them were. *So thuggish.*

In the same instant, Bumbersnoot snuck up against Sophronia's captor's leg and blasted hot steam on the man's bare ankle, scalding him badly. *That'll teach him not to wear hose,* thought Sophronia.

The man yelled in surprise and let her go. Sophronia dove down, scooped up Bumbersnoot, and rolled out of reach. Lady Linette had made them practice that maneuver in full skirts. The extra material actually helped, cushioning the somersault. Sophronia couldn't get very far, however, as her wrist was still attached to the other man via the hurlie.

At the sight of the blood, Dimity fainted, becoming a dead weight in her ruffian's arms. He swore and tried to keep hold, but Dimity's chiffon dress was slippery, and she hadn't Sophronia's propensity for covering herself with gadgets. Without handholds, the man lost his grip. Dimity collapsed to the forest floor.

The bleeding man managed to free himself from Sophronia's hurlie, which she retracted. Momentarily unencumbered, Sophronia pulled out her letter opener. She'd begun to carry it right after they started knife-fighting lessons, as soon as she realized it would work just as well and be more innocuous. After all, a lady might expect a missive at any moment. It wouldn't do to be without a letter opener. She made a mental note to start wearing and training with her hurlie in her left hand so she could use both as weapons in a fight.

With one ruffian trying to pick up a limp Dimity, another clutching his burned leg, and the third trying to grab his own bleeding back, it looked like Sophronia had the best of them. She was no fool, however. It was her and Bumbersnoot, whose ribbon strap she threw over her neck, against three fully grown men. She ought to run, but she wasn't about to leave Dimity in their clutches!

The men were wary of coming at her again. She was, after all, armed with a projectile. She wished for a gun. If this kind of thing were to become a regular occurrence, munitions lessons really shouldn't be left for older students. Then her training kicked in: *get them talking.*

"What do you want?" she asked, pleased with how steady her voice sounded.

"Oh, no, little miss, we know better than that," said one.

Another said to his companions, "We can't let her go. She'll alert the others."

"Good idea," said Sophronia, at which juncture she threw her head back and screamed at the top of her lungs.

Instantly, not so very far away, she heard someone crashing through the trees. She screamed again.

Apparently, deciding it was most important to hush her, two ruffians charged. Sophronia took aim and fired with her hurlie a second time. It hit the burned man in the chest and bounced harmlessly off. The hooks were made to catch on the draw back, not the firing. *I should get Vieve to mount a sharp point in the middle that pops out when I release the turtle.* Still the man howled in surprise; the spring-loaded release was strong, so it would at least bruise. Then the other man was upon her.

Sophronia fell into Captain Niall's best defensive stance for the smaller personage when faced with a large opponent, and raised her letter opener. The ruffian moved in, no doubt relying on the fact that she was female and could not possibly know anything about fighting. Captain Niall had only taught them a single attack, but he had made them practice it over and over and over. Sophronia slashed out, opening up a long gash on the man's arm.

He backed away warily.

The other ruffian stopped, grabbed at her grappling hook, and began tugging on it. Soon he would have Sophronia by a leash, and she had no time to undo the turtle from her wrist, focused as she was on fighting the first man. Sophronia prepared to kick. That was a dirty tactic, not taught by Captain

Niall, but Soap had shown her a few tricks and she was prepared to use them if necessary.

It was not necessary, for a rescuer appeared out of the forest.

"You screamed, madam?"

"Why, Lord Mersey, what are you doing here?"

"Following you, of course. Spot of bother?"

"Little bit of one, yes."

The young man looked with interest at Sophronia's opponents, one holding a collapsed Dimity, one bleeding from a gash to the arm, and the third bleeding from a wound to the back.

"My dear Ria, you hardly need my help."

"Hardly."

"Have I told you recently how much I admire a capable woman?" As he spoke, the young lord reached inside his coat and produced the most remarkable gadget. It wasn't very big and was rather flat, which explained how he could keep it in his coat without upsetting the lines, but it was extremely evil looking. It was long and sharp, with multiple attachments and a nozzle blackened from extruding some toxic substance. It looked highly flammable and quite deadly. Vieve would have been enthralled.

The ruffians were suitably impressed. They stopped.

"Put down the young lady," said Felix.

The man holding Dimity hesitated.

Felix was an aristocrat and accustomed to instant obedience. "This moment!" He swung the weapon to aim at the man and Dimity. "I assure you, I am a very good shot. I will most certainly hit you, not her."

"What is that thing?" quavered the ruffian.

"Oh, this?" Felix was casual. "*This* is a ballistic exploding steam missile fire prong. It's my latest invention, and it's very, very good at being deadly."

That did it. The ruffian holding Dimity dropped her once more, and she flopped becomingly, like a sleeping princess from a fairy story.

The man who had been hurlied said to the other two, "We ain't paid enough for this."

The others apparently agreed. "Leave it."

With little more to-do, the three ruffians dashed away into the forest.

Sophronia and Felix looked at each other.

"Nice prong," said Sophronia after a moment.

Felix grinned and waggled his eyebrows lasciviously. "Thank you for saying so."

Sophronia was instantly suspicious. "You mean that isn't a ballistic exploding steam missile fire prong?"

"No such thing, my dear Ria, but it certainly sounds wicked, doesn't it?"

"Then what is it?"

He handed the evil-looking object over. "Ah, a portable boot-blackening apparatus with pressure-controlled particulate emissions, and attached accoutrement to achieve the highest possible shine. For the stylish gentleman on the go." He presented his own well-turned-out leg, proving that his boots were as shiny as could be, despite exposure to the outside environment.

Sophronia looked down the barrel of the thing and,

accidentally, pulled the trigger. A fine mist of boot black hit her in the face, making her squeak, sputter, and drop the object.

She pulled out her handkerchief to repair the damage but left the apparatus where it lay in the leaves. "Automated shoe-shining kit?"

"Shoe-shining *prong*." Felix picked it up and moved closer to her. "You are unhurt?"

Sophronia nodded, still trying to clean her face.

After a moment, Felix took the handkerchief away from her and began to tenderly remove all trace of the black. Sophronia submitted to his ministrations in a momentary lapse of training. Her mind went blank, and she couldn't determine how to extricate herself from the intimacy. She was not prepared for tenderness.

A small cough and rustle of leaves interrupted the tête-à-tête.

Dimity was awake.

Sophronia grabbed her blackened handkerchief from Felix and ran to kneel next to her friend.

"What happened?" wondered Dimity.

"You fainted."

"Yes, I know that."

"And then Felix...uh...Lord Mersey came to our rescue with a shoe-shining kit."

"Sophronia, have I told you recently that your explanations often lack a certain *panache*?"

"Well, you will keep fainting during the best bits."

Felix ambled over. "How are you feeling, Miss Plumleigh-Teignmott?"

"Oh, perfectly topping, Lord Mersey. I'm always topping. And you?"

"Tolerably well. Shall we rejoin the rest of the party?"

"Jolly good idea," said Dimity, accepting his hand up and his offer of an arm.

He offered his other arm to Sophronia. "Ria?"

Sophronia took it, not wishing to be churlish.

"Now, ladies, do we say anything of this to anyone?" he asked, not being trained by Mademoiselle Geraldine's into the custom of never saying anything unless instructed otherwise.

"Of what, exactly?" wondered Sophronia.

"I fainted. I've no idea what you are on about," added Dimity.

"Ah," said Lord Mersey, "quite. I see," just as if he did quite see.

Dimity and Sophronia looked at each other. Dimity nodded. Now they both knew for certain that someone was after Dimity and Pillover. *I hope their parents can shed some light on this situation,* thought Sophronia. *Or Dimity and I are going to have to take some seriously restrictive precautions.* She was already planning ways to booby-trap their room of an evening.

# THE 8TH TEST

## THE SOOTIE CHALLENGE

S oap, where did you go after you let us off for the picnic?"
Feeling she ought to take every advantage of the general
befuddlement of a day spent groundside, Sophronia had
decided to visit the boiler room that very night.

Soap paused in an attempt to sound out a word in his reading primer. "We went to take on more water, fuel, and a certain
*delivery.*"

"Delivery of what?"

"Ah, miss, that I don't know. But it must be important
because we went *well* out of our way."

Sophronia nibbled her lower lip. "Did Vieve notice anything?"

"Did Vieve notice any what?" asked Vieve, wandering up.

"This delivery the school took on. Soap says...wait a
moment!"

"No, Soap didn't say that," said Soap.

Sophronia had noticed something unusual, or rather someone unusual, trailing Vieve. There was the expected crowd of nosy off-duty sooties, but there was also...

"Dimity! What are you doing in the boiler room?"

"Good evening, Sophronia. My, it's rather dingy down here, isn't it?" Dimity came forward out of the pack of sooties, looking embarrassed. The sooties were accustomed to Sophronia and Sidheag in their parochial garb, but Dimity wore a visiting gown and a bonnet with silk flowers. They had never seen the like in the boiler room.

"I had to bring her," said Vieve. "I dropped in to check on Bumbersnoot, but you had left. She insisted."

"*How* did she insist?" Sophronia found it difficult to persuade Vieve to do anything Vieve didn't want to.

Vieve blushed. "She simply *did.*"

Dimity was self-satisfied. "I blackmailed her with a hat!"

Sophronia cocked her head. "Dimity, why are you down here?"

Dimity proclaimed, "I brought pamphlets!" and produced a small stack of parchment, homemade and cut to resemble those of the temperance movement.

"What?" Sophronia took one.

"To help the poor dears improve themselves, of course. There's a whole section on cleanliness. See, here?" Dimity pointed to a drawing of a bar of soap. She began handing out the pamphlets to the sooties, none of whom were particularly impressed. A few checked to see if they might be rolled for smoking tobacco, and one used a corner to pick his teeth. Soap took his with alacrity and began to try sounding out the words.

137

Sophronia said, "Oh, Dimity, they can't read, remember?"

Dimity was crestfallen. "I forgot that bit."

"I'm learning, miss," piped up Soap, waving both primer and pamphlet.

"Very good, Mr. Soap, most improving," said Dimity, clearly under the impression that it was her charitable efforts that had encouraged his interest in education.

"You must excuse Dimity," said Sophronia to the sooties at large. "She believes that to be a lady she must practice acts of charitable benevolence. She has selected you lot as her victims." The sooties laughed. Dimity was not very prepossessing. She looked as though she couldn't victimize a beetle.

Dimity ignored this slur on her character. "I do hope you don't find my efforts condescending."

"Not at all, miss," said Soap. "This is my very first personal bit of paper. I've never owned a pamphlet afore. Thank you." He wasn't joking. Sophronia looked at her tall friend with new eyes. He always seemed to be so happy; did he actually suffer from deprivation?

One of the others asked, "Will your charitable actions come with more of them little cakes?"

"Oh," said someone else. "Is she *that* Dimity?"

Dimity had encouraged Sophronia to filch nibbles from tea and pass them out to the sooties. Sophronia attributed the largesse to her friend. Thus, while none of the sooties had actually met Dimity, they all knew of her. They had been thinking of her as a kind of angel of pudding mercy.

Dimity brightened as the sooties turned more affectionate

eyes upon her. "I shall do my best. I'm certain stealing for charity is a worthy application of my intelligencer skills."

"You and Robin Hood," said Sophronia.

"Oh." Dimity was confused. "Was he a spy, too?"

Soap had only really spent one evening in Dimity's company, and that was during an infiltration. He turned to Sophronia at this juncture and said, "Is she always like this?"

"Pretty much," answered Sophronia.

Soap returned to the pamphlet. "Prop-per, high-gine-y," he read out. "What's high-gine-y? Some kind of animal?"

"Nope." Sophronia giggled. "It simply means clean."

"I'm so stupid," muttered Soap.

"You're brilliant!" Sophronia defended him staunchly. "You simply haven't learned yet. I'm sorry, I didn't mean to laugh at you."

"S'all right, miss. You really think I'm brilliant?" he fished hopefully.

"Of course," said Sophronia without hesitation. "Book learning will only take you so far."

One of Soap's quick white smiles flashed.

Dimity finished passing out pamphlets and turned expectantly. "Right. What do we do now?"

"Usually, practice dirty fighting. This young man will help." Sophronia beckoned Furnival over.

Furnival Jones was a kindhearted, scruffy boy and one of Sidheag's favorite fighting partners. He had a perpetual expression of mild surprise on his face due to a near absence of eyebrows, the result of a close encounter with a boiler.

"Miss?"

"Be a dear, Furnival, and go at Miss Dimity here for a bit?"

Furnival looked Dimity up and down doubtfully.

"Oh, must I?" Dimity hated to fight.

"Certainly."

"Oh, very well." Dimity kilted up her lovely skirts and gamely grabbed a stoking pole, aiming it limply at poor Furnival.

The sootie backed away and looked helplessly at Soap.

Soap gave him the nod.

Sophronia said, "I know she doesn't look like it, but she's trained like Sidheag and me."

The boy swung his own pole tentatively at Dimity.

Dimity blocked.

Sophronia, Vieve, and Soap watched for a bit. Dimity wasn't very good, but Furnival treated her gently. Unless Sophronia missed her guess, the poor lad was already developing romantic feelings toward her friend. Many of the sooties probably were. Dimity was so pretty and chattery, she quite overpowered the average male. Many gentlemen were unable to cope with abundant chatter, which is why they so often married it.

Soap went to encourage the fighters. Dimity developed a bit of backbone under his tutelage and struck with more firmness. Furnival scrambled to block.

Sophronia turned to Vieve. "Anything new on that mini-prototype?"

Vieve's small face went serious under her oversized newsboy cap. She dipped into her waistcoat pocket and produced the faceted crystalline object. "It's giving me stick. Why put a communication device inside an oddgob?"

Sophronia took it from her, rolling it about in her hands. "Definitely for communication?"

"Yes, and I have a few theories as to application."

"Of course you do. Anything you wish to share?"

"Sophronia, my dear," said the ten-year-old, sounding not unlike one of the professors, "I must *test* the theories first."

"Of course. Silly of me to even ask."

"What are you two plotting?" asked Soap, leaving Dimity and Furnival to whack irresolutely at each other.

"Nothing," said Sophronia and Vieve in unison.

Soap was not convinced and took the mini-prototype from Sophronia, his soot-covered fingers brushing the back of her hand most unnecessarily as he did so. He held the valve gingerly, as though afraid to smudge it. "What's it for?"

"That," said Sophronia, "is the question."

A set of birdlike whistling noises floated into the air, the sootie version of a proximity alarm. The boys who were assembled to watch Dimity's duel shuffled about uncomfortably and looked over at Soap for direction. It was not unlike a group of pigeons disturbed by the presence of a partridge in their midst.

"Oh, ho, what's going on here?" said a cultured male voice.

Felix Mersey slouched up, as if he always wandered the boiler rooms of floating girls' seminaries. He was dusty with coal, having obviously climbed in from the outer hull through the hatch.

Sophronia's first thought was: *Oh, dear, he's figured out how to get around the ship.* Her second was: *Thank goodness I wore a dress this evening.* Her third was: *Life probably would have stayed easier had Felix and Soap never met.*

At an almost imperceptible hand signal from the taller boy, the young lord found himself surrounded by sooties, none of whom looked pleased to see him. Vieve melted into the shadows. Dimity came to stand with Sophronia.

Soap straightened, put down his primer, and walked over to the viscount. Felix Mersey might be the cream of the aristocracy, but in the boiler room Soap was undisputed king—grimy empire though it might be.

Felix was not impressed. "Who are you, darkie? And what are you doing with a guidance valve?"

Sophronia didn't like anyone disrespecting Soap. But even while battling anger, she filed Felix's comment away: the mini-prototype was called a *guidance valve*. She jerked forward to take back the guidance valve and show her allegiance to Soap.

Dimity held her back. Her friend was remarkably strong for such an innocent-looking creature. "My dear, we'd best let them deal with this in their own way."

"But—"

"This is not a matter for ladies." Dimity considered. "Or even intelligencers."

"Oh, but I—" protested Sophronia.

"No, dear, no."

Soap smiled his big, wide, welcoming grin at Felix. For once, it did not look friendly. "Ah, now, little lordling, you're in our world. I'm thinking a bit of politeness might be in order."

"To commoners? I think not."

"We can boost you right back out that hatch you came in."

"Hardly sporting. There's plenty more of you scrappers than there is me."

"Ah, yes, but if you're going about not treating us as gentlemen, we don't have to behave like 'em, do we?"

"As if you knew how."

Soap made a perfect bow, precisely the kind due to a viscount. "How do you do? The name is Phineas B. Crow."

Goodness, if Soap didn't *sound* exactly as if he were a gentleman. *He's been practicing the accent.* Sophronia wondered where he'd learned it in the first place.

Shocked into an instinctual reaction, Felix bowed back. "Felix Golborne, Viscount Mersey."

"Lord Mersey, I've heard of you." Soap looked over to where Sophronia skulked.

*And he knows how to shorten the name of an aristocrat as well?*

"Funny," said Felix, watching Soap's gaze rest on Sophronia, "but I hadn't heard of you."

"Some of us know how to keep secrets." With that, Soap ostentatiously returned the valve to Sophronia.

Felix colored. *So he wasn't supposed to tell anyone it's a guidance valve? Or is he embarrassed to catch Soap and me on terms of any intimacy?*

"Be careful," whispered Sophronia to Soap.

The sootie winked and turned back to Felix.

The boys squared off. Felix stood about half a head shorter than Soap, but then most people did. His clothes fit him perfectly, while Soap seemed to have been shoveled badly into his, with wrists and ankles sticking out.

"What can we possibly do for you, Lord Mersey?" asked Soap.

"I have no business with you."

"Good thing, too. We have enough bother keeping this ship afloat. We don't have time to pander to layabout toffs when there's real work to do."

Felix ignored this. "I wanted to look in on Miss Temminnick."

Soap said, "Well, she has had a number of unwelcome visitors this evening."

"Oh, has she indeed?"

Soap declined to elaborate. As Felix had voiced his interest outright, the taller boy could not delay him further.

"Miss Sophronia," he said, "you have a visitor," as if he were her butler. "This boy wants to see you." He said it as though Felix were years his junior.

Felix turned the full force of his charm on Sophronia, presenting the back of his impeccable frock coat to Soap. "It is an odd place for us to meet, Ria, my dove."

Soap tensed.

Sophronia supposed she must play the game. "Very well, my lord, why tarry here at all? Your waistcoat will be smudged and your cravat gone gray; how will you survive such travesties?"

"For the pleasure of your glorious company, I should suffer a thousand smudges."

"Do they always talk like this?" Soap asked Dimity, loudly.

"Pretty much."

"It's revolting."

"I shouldn't let it worry you, Mr. Crow. She's only practicing."

Sophronia looked away from Felix. "And he's only play-acting. Training to be a rake and toying with my poor, weak heart." But even as she said it, she was forced to face the fact that this could be a lie. *What a pickle. Maybe if I ignore his overtures, the messiness will go away?*

"Oh, now, Ria, you malign me. I'm as honest as a rose garden is beautiful."

"And as full of dung," replied Sophronia without missing a beat.

Dimity said appreciatively, "Such language."

Soap was looking equal parts impressed and disturbed by this banter. He added, "Aside which, don't you know, Lord Mersey, Miss Sophronia doesn't have a heart?"

Sophronia didn't show it, but the remark stung. She was very fond of Soap. She didn't want him to think her cold. She said to Felix, "My lord, how did you follow me?"

Felix didn't answer, which was reason enough to be wary. *He's only an evil genius in training. He shouldn't be able to track me, a prospective intelligencer.*

"I need to know, my lord. It could cost me my life someday."

Vieve stepped out of the shadows. "My fault again, I'm afraid," she said, looking cheeky. "I told him how to climb and where to go, then left the climbing and the going to him."

"Goodness, why?"

"He's going to put a word in with the headmaster of Bunson's for me."

"What?" Sophronia was confused.

"Young Master Lefoux and I have struck a bargain," said Felix. "I'd campaign for his admittance to Bunson's, and he'd tell me were you went each evening."

Sophronia digested the fact that Felix, evidently, didn't

know that Vieve was female. She contemplated revealing this to him out of spite, but Vieve must have had good reason for betraying Sophronia's whereabouts. It was best to keep information as ammunition for when it might become useful, and not squander it on revenge. And, in the end, there was no *real* harm done in Felix following her.

One question did remain. "How did you know I went *anywhere* of an evening?"

"I might have seen you leave your chambers late one night."

"You know where my chambers are?" Sophronia was shocked. A girl's boudoir was sacred!

Felix issued her a crooked smile. "I've never seen the engine room of a floating school before."

"I see. Well, thank you, Vieve."

Vieve tried to explain. "I can't lark about here forever. I've been thinking Bunson's is a better place for me."

Sophronia handed her traitorous friend back the mini-prototype. "Guidance valve," she mouthed.

Vieve nodded, indicating she'd heard the name.

"What about Professor Shrimpdittle?" Sophronia was alluding to the fact that, as an old acquaintance of Professor Lefoux's, Shrimpdittle knew Vieve's true gender.

"I haven't figured that out yet. May need your help to reassign him."

"Oh? And here you betrayed me this very evening to both Dimity and Lord Mersey."

Dimity took offense at being lumped together with a boy. "Wait a moment!"

Felix watched the exchange with amused eyes.

Vieve had the good grace to look embarrassed. "Yes, well, I thought we might come to an arrangement. If I leave for Bunson's, I won't need the obstructor anymore, will I?"

Vieve had found Sophronia's weakness. "Fine, you rat, I'll put some thought into a discrediting action." Sophronia's mind was already contemplating how one might get a professor dismissed from an evil genius training school.

Vieve spat on her hand and offered it to Sophronia. "Done!"

Sophronia sighed and shook it. Luckily she was wearing her black cotton spare gloves, the ones dedicated to visiting sooties.

"I think that's enough excitement for one evening. Shall we head out?"

Soap said, "So soon?"

Vieve was dubious. "As a party of four?"

"Oh, you may take Dimity with you. Lord Mersey and I will go the normal route. I'd like to see his technique."

Felix looked uncomfortable but schooled his expression to one of bland superiority and marched off to the hatch. Clearly, he was not as relaxed about climbing as he pretended.

Sophronia held back. "Don't you worry, Soap. I'll give him what for!"

Soap looked pleased. "You will? Oh, good. But, erm, what for?"

"Disrespecting you, of course. Ignoramus."

Soap's face fell. "Oh, now, miss. Please don't. I don't need you to defend me."

"But your honor is at stake!"

"Honor's for toffs. In that, at least, he's right. I'm nothing but a lowly sootie."

"But—"

"You wanna give him a lecture for some other reason, please do."

Sophronia was disconcerted. What *else* had Felix done?

"Looking at you as if he wanted to spread you on toast and nibble!" Soap's voice vibrated with disgust, or something more dangerous.

Sophronia didn't know what to say to that, so she only nodded dumbly and scampered after Felix out the hatch.


Sophronia was none too thrilled to be stuck climbing. Vieve's method of getting around was faster and less strenuous. But exercise was good for her, and part of her wanted to show off for Felix—not to mention show him up.

If Lord Mersey was impressed by the smooth way she shot her hurlie and swung from balcony to balcony, he gave no indication. After an aborted attempt to assist her, as any gentleman would a woman into a carriage, he found she was more efficient than he, even in skirts, and hung back in an attitude of "ladies first."

Sophronia outdistanced him and, although she knew it was rude, decided to leave him eating petticoat fluff. If Felix had entertained any ideas of an assignation, they were quite thoroughly shredded.


"You're flirting with that boy shamelessly," accused Dimity, who was already undressed and abed when Sophronia entered their room.

"That's a lie! I'm not entirely certain I even *like* Lord Mersey. He's very involved in his own consequence."

"And why shouldn't he be? Son of a duke, long line of evil geniuses, even Picklemen in his pedigree. He is allowed to be arrogant. But I wasn't speaking of him. You flirt with him with aplomb and finesse. Lady Linette would be chuffed. In fact, I think your approach far outstrips that of Monique or Preshea. Insulting him and pretending you aren't interested; who'd have thought such a tactic might work?"

"Mademoiselle Geraldine," said Sophronia promptly. "She has advised the approach on a number of occasions." Sophronia puffed out her chest and assumed a mockery of their headmistress. "A lady of *qualit-tay* makes herself appear at all times *unwilling* and most of the time *unavailable*. Gentlemen adore the hunt." Sophronia frowned, considering her current circumstances. "Honestly, Dimity, I wasn't applying it intentionally, but I suppose Lord Mersey has had ladies after him most of his life. I must make for a nice change."

Dimity got out of bed to undo the buttons down the back of Sophronia's dress. "Regardless, it's Mr. Soap to whom I was referring. You'll break that poor boy's heart. He's leagues beneath you. Nothing can come of it."

"I won't!" Sophronia was stung. "I don't think of him at all in *that* way."

"You might be reduced to saying something quite blunt."

Sophronia blushed at the very idea.

"At least stop canoodling with him."

Sophronia was shocked by the accusation. "I'm not! There wasn't one single canoodle!"

"You are most assuredly flirting. I've suspected it before, but now that I've visited the boiler room, I'm convinced: *flirting.*"

Sophronia pulled on her nightgown. *Perhaps Dimity is right. Perhaps I am being unfair to Soap. But I do so enjoy his company. Soap's so much more fun and restful to be around than Felix. Or anyone else, really.*

"When did life get so complicated?" she wondered to Dimity.

"Boys," said Dimity succinctly. "Good night."

## INTERIOR DECORATION

A faint knock sounded at the parlor door just as Sophronia was drifting off to sleep, exhausted. She climbed out of bed, assuming anyone knocking at three in the morning could only be wanting her. A sinking sensation in her stomach suggested it might even be Felix.

Agatha met her in the parlor.

"For you, is it?" asked the dumpy girl.

"What are you doing awake?"

"You think you're the only one who sleeps light?"

"Were *you* expecting someone?" This seemed, given Agatha's character, highly unlikely.

Agatha gave her a look that said exactly that.

Sophronia opened the door a crack.

It was not Felix Mersey, thank goodness. Instead, she found herself looking down at Vieve's pert little face.

"You want to cash in on our gentlemen's agreement now? I haven't had any time to plan!" protested Sophronia.

The young girl shook her head. "No, these things take ages to sort, I know that."

"Have you found out something about the mini-prototype?"

"Not as such. I still need to run more tests. Although I do think it involves Picklemen, if that Felix Mersey knew it was called a guidance valve."

"Oh, dear. Picklemen and possibly vampires as well?"

Vieve shrugged as much as to say that the two were always involved in any technological advancement, so why fuss? "But I thought you might like to see what they went out of their way to bring on board."

Sophronia had nearly forgotten. "Of course! Soap said it was a special shipment." She began to follow Vieve out of the room.

Agatha, who had been listening with interest, said timidly, "You aren't going outside in your nightgown, Sophronia? What if someone catches you?"

"Loan me Sidheag's duds?" asked Sophronia. "I'll take the blame if she gets upset."

Agatha puffed out her cheeks but then nodded, disappeared, and reappeared with a familiar set of shirt and trousers. Sometimes even Agatha had gumption. Sophronia put them on and knotted her hair at the base of her neck. She was supposed to put her hair up in rags each night, but she rarely found the time. Plus, the only person any good with curling rags was Monique. Sophronia wasn't about to ask her for help, even at Lady Linette's insistence.

She followed Vieve down into the lower part of the rear of the airship, where storage chambers thrummed to the loud hum of the massive propeller.

It was via this warehouse that Sophronia had first entered Mademoiselle Geraldine's Academy for Young Ladies of Quality— an ignorant covert recruit. There was a massive hatch and a moving glass platform, used for loading students or goods. The cavernous storage chamber was lit only by a flickering orange glow coming through the slats from guidance engineering. There, specially trained sooties, greasers, and firemen manned the propeller's boilers and engines.

The noise of the propeller allowed the girls to be less cautious with their footsteps, but they still hugged the wall. At the far end, near the propeller room, was a small shed. Usually it housed cleaning supplies, but these were now stacked outside. Inside, someone had lit a gas lamp and was talking quietly.

Sophronia held Vieve back. The propeller was loud, but if it was Professor Braithwope inside that shed, he might still be able to smell them.

Eventually, Sophronia decided to risk it, inching forward slowly, her bare feet whisper-soft. Vieve took her cues from the older girl. They reached the side of the shed, and Sophronia pulled out her ear trumpet. She crouched low and pressed it against the small space at the bottom where wall met floorboards.

"...too bad these were delayed. We could have used this information months ago," Professor Braithwope was saying. "How could the intermediary let them all pile up like that?"

"She seized an opportunity to infiltrate flywaymen. The messages kept coming, but she was afloat, so no one was left to alert us. It wasn't until I realized we hadn't had a shipment that we thought to go after them ourselves." Of all the possible teachers with the vampire, it appeared to be Sister Mattie.

"Are they *all* from her?"

"No. She's our best, but even she is not that prolific."

"But all hers say the same thing, whot?"

"Indeed they do. The question is—how many are involved?"

The vampire's tone was resigned. "And why? They know we have to enter the results of the test into public record."

"Are we overlooking something, Aloysius? Are we certain this is only about the technology?"

"Isn't it always, whot?"

"I suppose we should head to bed, then. We aren't getting anything new."

Vieve and Sophronia dove to the back of the shed, squeezing in behind it.

The two teachers emerged, illuminated by a lantern Sister Mattie held high in one hand. She stood by while Professor Braithwope locked the door to the shed. Once finished with the task, the vampire tucked the key into his waistcoat pocket and turned to offer the lady his arm.

Then he stiffened, cocking his head to one side. "Who's there?"

Sophronia and Vieve barely dared breathe.

"You might as well come out."

The two girls exchanged terrified looks, and then Vieve got

a very set expression. "You stay," she mouthed at Sophronia. "I owe you."

Vieve unclipped the obstructor from about her wrist and passed it over. Then she carefully nicked one finger with the sharp edge of her shirt pin, drawing blood. *She's hiding my smell,* Sophronia realized. Vampires' senses could be befuddled by fresh blood. Then Vieve stuffed her hands into the pockets of her jodhpurs, pulled her cap over her eyes, and sauntered out.

"What ho, Professors," she said jovially. Just as though she strolled about the ship at all hours turning up where least wanted—which, Sophronia supposed, was exactly what she did do.

The vampire looked none too pleased to see her.

"Oh, it's only little Genevieve," said Sister Mattie, relief in her voice. *Really,* thought Sophronia, *she ought to be better at hiding her emotions.* Then again, acting was Lady Linette's speciality.

"You are a scamp, aren't you, whot?" said the vampire, not relaxing. "How much did you hear?"

"Not much."

Sister Mattie said wisely, "A little lovage is a dangerous thing."

"I think you mean knowledge," corrected Vieve.

"No, I do *not.*" Sister Mattie was very confident on the subject of herbs.

Quicker than the eye could follow, even had it been broad daylight, the vampire reached out and grabbed Vieve's ear.

"Ouch!"

"What did you hear?" he repeated, sounding much more vampirelike than Sophronia had thought he could. His mustache even managed to quiver with malice.

"Something about a technology, and whether they were interested or not, and how many."

"Anything else?"

Sister Mattie clucked. "Now, now, Professor, don't damage the girl."

Vieve began to struggle. The vampire lifted her by the ear. She struck and kicked out. "Stop it, sir! There's nothing more, I promise."

*That's odd behavior*, thought Sophronia. Not odd for a ten-year-old girl, but Vieve rarely acted like an actual ten-year-old.

Vieve began to whimper and scrabbled more, raking at the front of the vampire's chest. "Lemme go, that hurts!"

*It's quite a show*, thought Sophronia, *but it's definitely a show.* Vieve was no more an actress than Sister Mattie. *What is she up to?*

"You realize I will have to report this transgression to your aunt?" The vampire set Vieve down.

Vieve sullenly rubbed her abused ear. "I suppose so."

"Oh, you do, do you? You're too young to have transgressions. Now, here, wrap this handkerchief around that finger and come along."

With that, the two professors, trailing a protesting Vieve, walked the long stretch across the warehouse floor and left, shutting the door behind them.

The smell of blood, all that propeller noise, and Vieve's whining had effectively hidden Sophronia's presence. She wondered if the same trick would work on a werewolf. *I must really learn more about the limits of supernatural abilities.* She sent a thought of thanks after Vieve. *I guess that's a fair exchange for betraying my sootie visits to Dimity and Felix.*

She was mystified as to why the girl had thrown such a tantrum. She felt around the floor where the vampire had shaken Vieve. Sure enough, as she patted, she happened upon the key to the shed. Professor Braithwope had put it into his waistcoat pocket, and Vieve had thrown her fit in order to pinch it for Sophronia. *Blast it*, Sophronia thought, *now Vieve is one up on me and I owe her! I shall have to put some serious thought to getting rid of Shrimpdittle so she can go become an evil genius.*

Sophronia put the key in the shed door and turned it slowly. The bolt clicked over, but if the cargo was that important, there would be more than a lock guarding it. Inside Sophronia could just make out that the shed was set up like a lady's sitting room. There were multiple low couches, a very ornate chaise longue— all brass fittings and cream brocade—and fifty or more embroidered throw cushions. There was even a tea trolley near the door, complete with teapot and a plate of small cakes. She had no doubt those were from Mademoiselle Geraldine's collection. Sophronia was not fooled by all the detail; no one set up a shed like this except to try to hide something in plain sight. She checked the doorway for traps. She ran her hand cautiously along the jamb on each side and down the center for a trip wire. *Nothing. Most atypical.*

Cautiously, she moved into the room.

The ornate chaise across the way emitted a puff of steam from under its brocade ruffle and whirled to life. It had an affronted aspect, as though it were a mother goose and the decorative pillows strewn all about were its eggs.

The chaise charged Sophronia, who leapt to one side, bounced up onto a couch, and, in lieu of any other weapon, grabbed one of the cushions.

The chaise twirled on one of its legs, tassels flying. Its gilt decoration and upholstery disguised copious elaborate mechanisms. It faced Sophronia again, skittering from one side to the other, unable to jump up after her and unwilling to charge and break the other couch.

Sophronia waved the pillow at it.

The chaise puffed smoke out a back slat and waved two tassels with obvious menace.

Luckily, it didn't seem to be able to sound a whistle alarm like a maid mechanical, nor a trumpeting blast like a soldier mechanical, but it was not going to let her out of the shed, either.

*Its protocol probably dictates that it hold infiltrators here and not allow them to escape until someone checks. I could be at this all night.*

Sophronia glanced around. There was no way out except the door by which she'd entered, and the chaise had that defended. She couldn't see any weapons mounted on the angry furnishing. In fact, it seemed nothing more than a rather cushy—albeit autonomous—couch. Nevertheless, it looked as though it would crush her if she went for the door. It was certainly fast and heavy enough.

Sophronia considered firing her hurlie and swinging over the chaise and out like a circus acrobat, but there was no hook-ing point. Plus, she would not have gotten what she came for: the information Professor Braithwope and Sister Mattie had extracted from this room. There must be messages stashed somewhere in the arrangement of the shed.

They were at an impasse, Sophronia and the chaise longue.

She feinted left and the sofa followed. She feinted right. It mirrored her on the ground. She made as if to throw the pillow, and it huffed out smoke in indignation and reared on its two stubby back legs, fighting the air with its forelegs like an angry horse.

Sophronia frowned. They had been taught various forms of secret communication—quilting, knitting, crocheting, and lacework code. Perhaps the embroidery on the pillows conveyed information from active intelligencers trained at Mademoiselle Geraldine's. If it contained communiqués from London, this would make for important cargo indeed.

Ignoring the enraged chaise, which was holding position, Sophronia squinted at the cushion she held. It was too dark to make out any of the crewelwork. The code was probably contained in the colors and numbers of threads as well as the details of each image. It'd be impossible to interpret the meaning without a companion cypher book. Perhaps Sister Mattie had the cypher memorized and that's why she'd been along. Whatever the case, there was no point in Sophronia's stealing a pillow, tempting as it might be.

Sophronia suddenly remembered that Vieve had loaned her the obstructor. She wasn't certain it would work on a mechanical without a track, but it was worth a try. She aimed at the perturbed furniture and let loose a silent blast. The sofa froze.

It suffered this indignity with an aura of perturbation. Sophronia dropped the pillow, jumped down, and then leapt onto another couch before the chaise came back to life.

It whirred into animation, let out a puff of affronted smoke, and turned to charge Sophronia at her new location.

Sophronia blasted it again and repeated the process until she was perched precariously atop the tea trolley, which sat closest to the door.

She hit the chaise with one last obstructor blast before swinging herself around the jamb, crashing open the door with both feet, and landing on one knee in the warehouse beyond.

The sofa clattered back into motion and came after her but was confined to the shed. It stopped in the doorway, glaring at her and shaking threatening tassels—if an object without eyes can be said to glare. Sophronia felt sorry for the chaise longue, but she wasn't going to risk being caught in order to mollify a gaudy piece of furniture.

The next morning Mademoiselle Geraldine's left its Dartmoor home and began to float out over more populated areas. The students were reminded curtly at breakfast by Sister Mattie that "people who live in dirigibles should not throw chamber pots." The remark was met with censure by Mademoiselle Geraldine but appeared to have been predicated on action taken by the visiting boys, who snickered knowingly.

The propeller could no longer be activated during the day, for it blew too much of their cover away. They lost speed and bobbed up and down most of the time, trying to catch breezes heading toward London. Suddenly, Sophronia understood the excitement over Giffard's accomplishment. Riding those impossibly high-up aether currents would enable them to move with both speed and stealth. At present, only on cloudy days and at night could they could fire up the propeller and move with any kind of purpose.

That first day they had a lesson with Sister Mattie on the middle squeak deck on how to throw poison with accuracy. They were practicing with water in little perfume bottles. Sophronia asked if isinglass might be mixed with some of the poisons to turn them to jelly, allowing for less dispersal when hurled.

Sister Mattie went into a long diatribe about how different toxins changed when gelatinous, which had them all standing around dumbly staring at her for a quarter of an hour.

Then they heard "Clear the deck!" yelled in an excited voice, tinged with the hint of a French accent.

In accordance with their training, the young ladies scattered, running to the side or rolling away or, in Sophronia's case, leaping over the railing to hang suspended on the outside of the ship. She did it with the ease of a girl overly familiar with balconies. Her leap and twist placed her staring back in at the deck, so she was in a perfect position to observe Vieve when she charged across it.

The young girl had what looked like ice skates strapped to her feet, only these had multiple wheels on them and some kind of tiny propeller. They were manipulated by a large ball Vieve clutched in one hand. She would tilt the ball to one side or the other to steer, somehow communicating with the skates wirelessly. The skates were clearly firing at a much faster speed than anticipated. Vieve went bucketing all over the deck, weaving from one side to the other, eventually crashing into the well-padded form of Sister Mattie.

Vieve tumbled backward onto her bony bottom. Unprotected by skirts and petticoats, she fell hard, her skate-covered feet sticking up in the air, the wheels still going furiously.

Sister Mattie also went backward, making an "oof" noise.

Sophronia was the first one at her side.

The nun was nonplussed at having been attacked by a small French cannonball. "Dear me, dear me, dear me. My goodness gracious! Who? What?"

Vieve remained lying on her back with feet in the air, apparently unable to turn off her contraptions. She said cheerfully, "What ho, Sister Mattie. Apologies. Only testing a new invention."

Sophronia solicitously helped Sister Mattie to stand and brushed her off. "Are you all right, Sister?"

"Thank you very much, Miss Temminnick. Only surprised, not injured."

"May I get you a glass of water or smelling salts?" Sophronia was fond of Sister Mattie.

"No, thank you, dear, very thoughtful." The roly-poly teacher turned to glare at Vieve.

The other girls wandered back over. They surrounded the collapsed Vieve and stared down at her.

"You are a positive menace," pronounced Monique.

"I don't know why Lady Linette permits you on board," added Preshea.

"Professor Lefoux is an able enough instructor, but that can hardly be worth your presence," continued Monique.

"Useless creature," said Preshea.

Vieve only looked up at them, lips pursed. Her green eyes were wide and shocked by this attack. She was accustomed to being ignored by the students.

Sophronia was having none of it. "Enough. Things go wrong with science. It's the way of it. You're hardly upset that class has been disturbed, so there's no point in pretending you are."

Preshea sputtered at this unexpected defense.

Monique was rarely at a loss for words. "Oh, ho! Sophronia appears to have herself a little pet."

"Ladies!" Sister Mattie recovered her aplomb. "Enough." She turned to Vieve. "Miss Lefoux, do get control of your shoes and take yourself elsewhere. You realize I will have to speak to your aunt about this incident?"

Sophronia wondered if that weren't Vieve's intent. Was she trying to make herself as inconvenient as possible? Perhaps to convince her aunt to let her infiltrate the boys' school? After all, there were two other squeak decks, both vacant. She didn't have to test her foot thingamabobs here.

"My sputter-skates," corrected Vieve.

"What?"

"Sputter-skates, not *shoes*."

Sophronia, delicately testing the waters, said, "They look like the kind of thing boys might appreciate."

Vieve twinkled up at her. "Exactly." She sat up, carefully balanced on her backside so the sputter-skates didn't touch the deck. Then she reached down and pulled a small lever. The skates, true to their name, sputtered and died. The wheels stopped moving at last.

"I think," said Vieve to no one in particular, "I ought to install a safety shutoff."

"Do you indeed?" Dimity was droll.

Sophronia offered Vieve a hand up.

Vieve balanced precariously on her now quiet sputter-skates.

"Sister Mattie, could Sophronia help me over to those stairs, please?"

Sister Mattie, eager to be rid of the child and get back to lessons, waved her off. "By all means. Miss Temminnick, attend Miss Lefoux, if you would be so kind."

Sophronia grabbed her friend's bony shoulders and wheeled her across the deck.

When they were outside of listening distance, Vieve shoved the ball she'd been using to steer into Sophronia's hand. "Look at that."

It was leather and metal with a catch on one side. Sophronia opened it to find the mini-prototype—more properly, the crystalline guidance valve—nested inside.

"It transmits protocols via aetheric particles!" crowed Vieve. "Or at least I think so. The original prototype was designed for long-distance point-to-point communication, like a wireless telegraph. But this little beauty can be used for point-to-machine commands. The theory is, it uses ambient aether in normal atmosphere, but it would probably work better, faster, and over larger distances within the aetherosphere."

Sophronia was awed. "You think that's how Giffard is negotiating the aether?" She paused. "He would have to have very quick response times from all over his ship to float those crazy currents."

Vieve nodded, eyes shining. "These guidance valves are designed to work better up there. That's why he had to wait. We needed to develop and distribute this technology to him. Airships have been ready for ages. It's the navigation they couldn't master."

"Professor Lefoux was testing it with the oddgob machine, and when I removed it, she couldn't get the machine to shut down properly."

"Exactly. And I think she had it configured wrong. She was trying to send the signal to it. I'm using it the other way around. Plus, this school floats high enough up that aether particles are prevalent. Don't you see? The applications are endless. You could have multiple valves in a controller hub going to machines all over the ship. In theory you could even use it to remotely control mechanicals. I'm so stupid—last fall I thought it was going to be used for human-to-human communication. I was wrong. These things are meant to transmit protocols!" She looked down at her skates. "Of course, it's only on and off. And in my case, the off didn't work. But the very idea!"

"Fifty percent effective?" Sophronia wondered who was controlling this technology. Mademoiselle Geraldine's had an unknown patron; was he or she in on this? What about the British government? Bunson's had Picklemen ties—they had wanted the original prototype. And then there was the pillow shipment, not to mention Professor Braithwope and Monique's talk of vampires.

They had reached the staircase and could not delay matters

to discuss further, as Sister Mattie was watching. Hastily, Sophronia handed Vieve back the guidance valve and said, "Thank you for last night, by the way. It was most helpful. Come by my quarters during luncheon? I feel a terrible headache coming on that may require me to rest this afternoon."

"I'll filch some sandwiches," said Vieve.

"Excellent."

## THE 10TH TEST

### Finding Fortune

How will you infiltrate Bunson's without being found out as you get older?" Sophronia asked Vieve, gesticulating elegantly at the front part of her own corset.

"I come from a long line of bony women, so I shouldn't think that will be a problem. And I managed to fool even you, until you were told."

"True, but I was more thinking about the fact that some of them must already know you as *you* at Bunson's."

"Only Shrimpdittle, and if you can deal with him, I should be in form. So long as my aunt keeps mum, I don't see as there should be any real difficulty."

"If you say so."

"I know so. And I have a wonderful fake mustache I shall begin sporting in a few years' time. That will fool most anyone. Mustaches are like that."

"You'd make a terrible intelligencer," said Sophronia at that outrageous statement.

"I know. Hence the reason I want to infiltrate Bunson's, which is far more amenable to my personality."

"And contact between the schools? How will you handle that?"

"It is more amicable now than it has been before. But…" She trailed off, her small face thoughtful.

"You don't think good relations will last?"

"You serve different masters."

Sophronia sat up. "Do you know who is the patron of Mademoiselle Geraldine's?"

Vieve shook her head. "No, but I know it isn't the Picklemen, and they're the backbone of Bunson's. Those who aren't Picklemen don't get along with them, so…" She shrugged her conclusion.

Sophronia didn't think much of the Picklemen herself. "In that case, are you certain you want to go *there*? There must be other evil genius schools."

"None as good as Bunson's. It's a feeder to École des Arts et Métiers, the *best* university. Besides, I don't mind a Pickleman or two. They have the funds and an interest in technology. Do you think it's them Professor Braithwope was referencing the other night in the shed as wanting the technology?"

"Must be. Sister Mattie said the intermediary had gone to infiltrate flywaymen, we know the Picklemen are mixed up with them, and…wait a moment, what will I do about Bumbersnoot with you gone? Who will look after him?"

Vieve shrugged. "It's time you learned mechanimal maintenance, if you will insist on carrying him everywhere like he's a toy."

Sophronia grinned at her pet, who was lounging on the end of the couch, wearing lace and ruffles. "Oh, he doesn't mind, do you, Bumbersnoot?"

*Tick-tock, tick-tock* went Bumbersnoot's tail in apparent agreement.

"Come here, you charmer," said Vieve, scooping up the mechanimal and removing his reticule attire. "I'll show you how to clean and oil him and leave a few tools. You should try it before I relocate, in case you have questions."

Sophronia prepared to be instructed. If Vieve was set on leaving, Sophronia had better learn to fend for herself in the matter of technology. *Funny,* she thought, *I used to love to take things apart.*

"Oh, ho ho, look who's all chummy." Monique came into the room and cast herself in an unladylike manner into an armchair.

"I thought you had a terrible headache, Sophronia. You don't look like you're ill," accused Preshea, following Monique.

Sidheag, Agatha, and Dimity trailed into the parlor after them.

"Oh, Preshea, what do you care? You had Lord Mersey all to yourself at luncheon," said Dimity.

Vieve looked at the fashionable young ladies surrounding her. She issued an ironic little bow, packed up her things, and made good her escape.

"I don't know why you associate with that brat," said Monique. "Older girls shouldn't patronize younger ones."

No one replied, but there was a collective arching of eyebrows. After all, Monique was forced to spend most of her time associating with them, and even Sophronia—the eldest of the bunch—was three years her junior.

Monique wrinkled her nose, as if smelling the absurdity in her own words. She quickly moved the subject on. "Preshea, darling, is it only I who have noticed, or has this whole trip to London become excessively dull?"

"Don't fret, dear Monique. You still have your party to plan." Preshea was all optimism.

Monique brightened. "Oh, yes, the party. How droll of me to forget. Should we consider refreshments?"

Preshea and Monique then spent a quarter of an hour discussing the delights of the upcoming ball. They listed all the diversions and delicacies in a manner that emphasized the fact that no one else in the room would get to sample any.

Agatha played her role painfully well, pretending interest. *Really*, thought Sophronia, *she is a better intelligencer than the school gives her credit.*

Sophronia and her friends remained unaffected by the barbs. She and Sidheag played tiddlywinks while Dimity knitted. Dimity was fond of knitting and was currently attempting to craft small yellow booties for Bumbersnoot. She claimed this was practice for her future as a charitable lady of means. Sophronia secretly worried that the mechanimal would slide all over the floor—not to mention, why did a metal dog need warm feet?—but the act was kindly meant.

Then, in a twist of topic, Preshea and Monique began to discuss boys. "Lord Mersey, of course, is the cream on the cake. Getting him to attend can only be to the betterment of all concerned."

Monique was confident. "I'm assured he will come. As will Lord Dingleproops. Of course, we can't have young Vullrink, not after last night's supper. Imagine using a knife for fish? And Mr. Plumleigh-Teignmott is right out."

Preshea nodded sagely. "Too young?"

"Too ill connected." Monique looked pointedly at Dimity.

Dimity glanced up from her needles. "He'll only thank you for it. Pillover hates parties."

"Oh, wonderful. It's always so nice to know the unwelcome are also uncaring of their social standing," sneered Monique. She probably would have gone on with her commentary until their next lesson, but the perimeter alarm trumpeted.

Dimity put down her knitting.

The girls stayed in their parlor, as they had been instructed. Even Sophronia, who was inclined to take to the hull to investigate, remained seated. With all the manufactured fog, it would be impossible to see who approached, a fact that was worrying in and of itself. If someone had managed to spot and attack the school despite their cloud disguise, that someone had superior technology.

They waited with bated breath for the ship to shake with cannon fire, for the fateful lean and sway of a balloon collapsing. Nothing happened. They listened for the sound of timber splitting. Still nothing. In short order, the trumpeting stopped with no apparent reaction from ship, mechanicals, or staff.

"Must have been a false alarm," said Dimity into the ensuing silence.

The girls, with nothing better to do, prepared for their next lesson. Even Monique was sobered by the strange experience.

They had foreign languages and lip-reading with Lady Linette next. None of the boys were present. Apparently, gentlemen didn't require foreign tongues. They moved from there on to tea and subterfuge with Mademoiselle Geraldine. Since the headmistress had no idea of the true nature of her own school, the exact kind of subterfuge was always assigned by one of the other teachers. Today, however, Lady Linette informed them that this time they should know what to do when they arrived.

Excited by the mystery, the girls hurried through the hallways to be met in the tassel section by Professor Shrimpdittle, trailing a sullen-looking Lord Dingleproops, Lord Mersey, and Pillover Plumleigh-Teignmott. The ten of them entered Mademoiselle Geraldine's quarters together.

As ever, the walls were lined with shelves of fake pastries, and the headmistress rose to welcome them from behind a large table set with a full tea service. She had known to expect a larger-than-normal gathering, for there were twelve place settings. Her décolletage heaved with appreciation. Mademoiselle Geraldine loved company.

Sitting next to her, in the place of honor, was an elderly female. She wore eccentric dress for a woman in the later part of life. Her wild gray hair was loose and her forehead bound over with a colorful scarf, like a sky pirate. Her jewelry was bronze and gold and more prevalent than Dimity's at her most sparkly. The stranger's complexion was tan in a manner that young ladies of quality were cautioned against. Her eyes were lined thickly with kohl. Her attire seemed to be composed utterly of brightly colored scarves tied in layers.

Dimity gasped in appreciation. "A fortune-teller!"

"How very esoteric, Mademoiselle G.!" crowed Lord Dingleproops, striding up to the headmistress to clap her on the shoulder, rather as a man would approach a fellow at his club. Mademoiselle Geraldine looked at him as though he were a collapsed soufflé, and he backed away hastily.

The girls tittered in elation. Even Pillover looked pleased, and he was rarely pleased by anything.

*We didn't go down low to retrieve her,* thought Sophronia. *How did she get on board?*

"Very good, Miss Plumleigh-Teignmott. We have indeed been graced with the presence of a fortune-teller."

Sophronia wondered, "Did you set off the alarm?"

The fortune-teller's eyes sharpened on her.

Sophronia realized she had revealed more of her personality with that one question than was healthy. She was, after all, the only one who'd jumped straight to logistics rather than the exciting possibility of having her palm read.

"Ladies and gentlemen, please be seated. Madame Spetuna has been retained for the evening to tell your fortunes." Mademoiselle Geraldine was wearing a lightweight muslin gown of chartreuse with cream stripes. It was a dress that better suited one of her students. Each stripe was patterned with pink roses. There was fringe all up the length of the sleeves and about the low square neckline that displayed the headmistress's assets to great effect. Said assets heaved as she inhaled, and Professor Shrimpdittle looked as though he might faint.

She continued, "Given that there are ten of you, we must keep the readings brief. So tuck in quickly to the nibbly bits while we do so, and don't stand on ceremony. If Miss Pelouse would pour the tea? Miss Buss, why don't you sit first?"

Preshea took the seat closest to the fortune-teller with alacrity.

Madame Spetuna looked her over. "Ze cards, I think, for you, dark child."

Preshea was made to pick five cards from a deck and lay them out carefully on the damask tablecloth. Madame Spetuna rearranged them a few times before settling on a pattern she liked.

*This must be today's subterfuge challenge. We are to ensure that the fortune-teller doesn't reveal anything to Mademoiselle Geraldine about our real training.* Sophronia, nibbling a biscuit, sat back to watch. She wondered about the fortune-teller. *Does she know what we do here? Or does she, like Mademoiselle Geraldine, think it is a normal, albeit floating, finishing school?*

"Ah," breathed Madame Spetuna, "this is most interesting. Most interesting indeed. You, my child, will marry well. More than once. A charmed life, so long as you weave a tight net, little spider." The lady retrieved the cards and shuffled them back together into one stack in an attitude of dismissal.

Taking this as a sign her fortune was complete, Preshea stood. Looking particularly pleased with life, she passed over a few coins and gave Madame Spetuna a nice curtsy.

Mademoiselle Geraldine was fanning herself. "Oh, dear, oh, dear, Miss Buss. Let us hope it is widowhood and not"—she whispered the next word—"*divorce* that leads to your multiple marriages."

Preshea sat and sipped from a china cup. "I shouldn't worry, Headmistress. I am tolerably certain it will be widowhood."

Mademoiselle Geraldine was reassured by this. Preshea's future husbands probably wouldn't have been. Even Lord Dingle-proops, ordinarily unconcerned by those around him, looked apprehensively at the beautiful dark-haired girl. She gave him a wicked smile and a coy lowering of the lashes.

*Reel it in, Preshea.* Sophronia glanced nervously at the headmistress. But Mademoiselle Geraldine was waving the next victim forward.

Dimity took the danger seat. "I admire your fashion sense," she told the fortune-teller with absolute sincerity.

Madame Spetuna tucked a lock of hair behind her ear—in which there were *three* earrings!

Dimity's eyes sparkled.

"For you, the palm," said Madame Spetuna.

Wide-eyed, Dimity presented the fortune-teller with both hands. Madame Spetuna bent over them, the many rings on her fingers flashing as she traced the lines.

Sophronia heard Monique whisper to Preshea, "I wouldn't allow such a dirty common creature to touch me!"

Madame Spetuna gave no indication of having heard. "You wish for a simple life, magpie. You will not get it. You will choose, many times, between loyalty and peace. A terrible choice." She looked up at Dimity, her dark eyes sad. "I am sorry."

Dimity nodded, her round face somber. "That's all right, Madame Spetuna. I always suspected it might be so."

Since she had forgotten her reticule, Dimity slid off one of her own many bracelets and gave it to the fortune-teller. They exchanged the smiles of kindred spirits.

Mademoiselle Geraldine called Monique. The older girl hid her excitement with a haughty expression. She sat and took up the cards without Madame Spetuna suggesting she do so.

"You are attracted to the cards, moonbeam? Good. It is always better when one is summoned."

Once the icy blonde had selected five cards, the fortune-teller bent over them for a time. "You will never be as important as you think you are. That is all."

"What do you know, old woman?" Monique stood with a sneer and left without offering a gratuity.

When she went to sit, Mademoiselle Geraldine rapped the girl's knuckles hard with a fan. "Manners!"

Monique, without further comment, curtsied to the fortune-teller and returned to her tea and Preshea's questionable counsel.

Then it was Agatha's turn. The redhead asked, in a hesitant

voice, if her fortune might be told privately. Sophronia thought to warn her that this might not be permitted by Lady Linette under the subterfuge clause, but there wasn't time. Madame Spetuna agreed.

Agatha was also given the cards. After her selection was laid on the table, Madame Spetuna whispered in her ear. Whatever Agatha's fortune, it cheered the chubby girl. She was almost animated and passed over a ridiculously large sum to Madame Spetuna in thanks.

Sophronia wished she were a fortune-teller. It would be an admirable way to inspire discomfort. Professor Shrimpdittle, for example, might be shaken into distrusting Bunson's. *Then again . . . I wonder how much it costs to buy a fortune?* Sophronia assessed her own meager funds. Then while Agatha bumbled back to her seat, Sophronia pulled out a scrap of paper and a bit of graphite from her reticule. *Three shillings,* she wrote, *to imply that Bunson's headmaster no longer trusts Prof S.* There was no time to code the note; she simply had to hope the fortune-teller was capable.

Sidheag assumed the seat with a certain bravado. She held out her hands without being asked.

"You have done this before, wolf child?" Madame Spetuna's eyes were sharp on Sidheag's face.

Sidheag nodded.

"Then what I tell you will be no different. You know your fate and you cannot escape it. Why do you dally here pretending to be tame?"

Sidheag nodded and stood to resume her seat. Her curtsy was

perfunctory, but the fortune-teller did not take offense. It was almost as if she knew Sidheag's curtsies were always perfunctory.

Finally Madame Spetuna gestured to Sophronia.

Sophronia went eagerly. *Suspicious nonsense, of course, but terribly fun suspicious nonsense. I wish Soap could have his fortune told. He'd love it.*

Madame Spetuna looked her up and down. She said, "The palm, I think, for you."

Sophronia offered both hands.

The fortune-teller seized them by the wrists. Her touch was soft and dry, and she smelled of exotic spices Sophronia could not place. *I must train my nose*, she thought. *Such information could be important, particularly if a given smell is associated with an enemy or an informant.*

"Even now, you think only in terms of the game. You are well chosen, little bird. Or are you a stoat?" Madame Spetuna bent forward, looking even harder at Sophronia's palms. She was close enough for Sophronia to feel the woman's breath on her skin. "Give your heart wisely." She paused a long time over one particular wrinkle. "Oh, child, you will end the world as we know it." Madame Spetuna swallowed and then turned Sophronia's hands over and placed them, palm down, on the table. She leaned forward, pressing them into the tablecloth as though she might rub out what she had seen.

It was an admirable performance. Sophronia thought she ought to applaud. Everyone was silent in awe. Sophronia looked over at Felix. He was making a face.

Then Monique giggled. "Stoat, of course Sophronia's a stoat."

Mademoiselle Geraldine recovered her composure. "What a

very odd fortune, Miss Temminnick. What game could she possibly be referring to?"

"Oh, Headmistress, we have been playing loo these last few nights. Perhaps it is that?" Sophronia lied easily.

Mademoiselle Geraldine looked relieved. "Oh, yes, indeed. Now, which of the gentlemen would like to go next?"

Sophronia reached into her reticule and passed the fortune-teller a shilling and the note. Since handling and exchanging money was always an embarrassment, everyone made a point of not really watching the gratuity.

Sophronia pretended to get her skirt caught in the chair as she rose. In a flurry of long sleeves, she bent and almost tipped Madame Spetuna's teacup over. Under cover of this, the fortune-teller opened and read the note.

By the time Sophronia had sorted herself, and the chair, out—Mademoiselle Geraldine reprimanding her for such unladylike clumsiness—the note had vanished, and Madame Spetuna was giving Sophronia a funny look.

Sophronia arched one eyebrow. She'd been practicing that expression for days; it was a very intelligencer sort of skill, and she felt she ought to know how to do it. Her eyebrow twitched slightly and didn't arch gracefully, but it got her point across.

The fortune-teller nodded, almost imperceptibly.

Pillover assumed the seat. "It's all nonsense, of course."

Madame Spetuna used the cards on him. "You are greater than the sum of your parts," she said.

Pillover looked doubtfully down at his tubby form. Sophronia wondered at a woman dressed in scarves quoting Aristotle.

Madame Spetuna continued. "And you will never make your father happy. Stop trying."

Pillover drooped.

Lord Dingleproops was next. "What a lark!"

"Wager to win, my lord, not to lose."

"That's all you have to say to me?"

"Wager any more and you could earn nothing at all."

"You speak in riddles. Come on, Felix, saddle up."

Felix assumed the seat, lounging back as was his insolent manner. His posture always gave the impression of not caring. About anything.

"You will not repeat your father's mistakes. You will make new ones, all your own."

"Very meaningful, Madame Spetuna. Of course, you might suspect any young man of being somewhat at odds with his father." Felix's eyes were narrowed.

Madame Spetuna only looked at him and adjusted the red-and-gold shawl around her shoulders.

The young viscount slouched over to take a seat opposite Sophronia and next to Monique. He ought to have talked to Monique, but instead he said to Sophronia, "Occult nonsense."

Sophronia blinked at him, her green eyes very direct. "Well, are you, my lord?"

"Am I what?"

"At odds with your father?"

"Is that interest I see at last, Ria, my dove?" Felix smiled and turned to talk with Monique.

Sophronia was left in possession of the field but also feeling as though she had lost something. *I must get better at extract-*

*ing information.* She considered. *Perhaps he requires feminine sympathy?*

Mademoiselle Geraldine, meanwhile, was urging Professor Shrimpdittle to have his fortune told. The good professor looked as if he would rather not, but the headmistress's assets were clearly irresistible. He took the seat.

The fortune-teller grabbed his hand and said, "You have troubles at school? Your headmaster, he does not value your contribution? This trip, it is to get you away, to keep you from becoming important."

Professor Shrimpdittle was agitated. "How do you know?"

"The spirits do not lie."

"There are no spirits, not that science has proven. Ghosts, of course, but not spirits."

"And yet, you fear I speak truth."

Professor Shrimpdittle, attuned to the interest of his own students, fell silent. But the seed of suspicion had been planted.

Sophronia palmed three shillings, ready to complete her end of the bargain.

Madame Spetuna was about to say more when a knock on the door interrupted her.

"Who could that possibly be?" wondered Mademoiselle Geraldine. "Everyone knows I am in an important session."

*As if this tea were a meeting of Parliament.*

"Come in," yelled the headmistress.

Vieve poked her head in. "Sorry to disturb, Mademoiselle Geraldine, but I heard...oh, yes! Bully! A fortune-teller! May I have mine done, please?"

"Oh, I don't think we have the time—"

Professor Shrimpdittle delicately interrupted the headmistress by rising to his feet. "By all means, let the child take my place."

"If you don't mind, Professor?"

Vieve trotted over and sat, little legs dangling.

The fortune-teller looked the scamp over and then looked at her palms briefly. "You are too young, as yet, to be fully formed. I can tell you only one thing. You are doomed to be lucky in matters of the head and unlucky in matters of the heart."

Vieve grinned. "That's good enough for me. I'd rather the first over the second."

The fortune-teller shook her head sadly. "Which only proves how very young you are. And now I am fatigued. Mademoiselle Geraldine, if I might beg to rest before the next session?"

"Of course, my boudoir is just there. Please, avail yourself of the amenities."

Madame Spetuna left the room with barely a nod at her former customers. She brushed past Sophronia and scooped up the three coins, which Sophronia held casually behind her seat back. It was as if Madame Spetuna had been conducting covert operations her whole life. *Very professional.*

Sophronia turned to watch the fortune-teller retreat. The lady was quite short and she moved slowly. *I must remember that kind of garb as a good disguise. I should invest in colored scarves. My list of necessities gets ever longer. Perhaps I should also take the time to learn the basics of fortune-telling to go alongside.* It seemed a matter of making statements vague enough to be possibly true or predictions far enough in the future to be irrelevant.

*    *    *

The girls discussed their precognitive tea later that evening. After much analysis of their own fortunes, and everyone else's, Sophronia brought the subject around to the fortune-teller herself.

"Of course, she can't possibly be a *real* fortune-teller."

"Why ever not?" wondered Agatha, who wanted to believe in what she had been told. Whatever that had been. She was keeping her own counsel on the matter, despite Sophronia's wheedling.

"Don't you think she's one of ours?" Sophronia was casual in her assertions. "Returned to report in person on some dangerous matter?"

"Oh." Dimity was impressed. "You think she is an agent in disguise?"

Sophronia nodded.

"How do you know?" Sidheag demanded. "She realized that I'd had my fortune told before. She seemed genuine."

Sophronia did not want to tell them about the bribe and Professor Shrimpdittle. Discrediting a man's reputation was shabby work. They'd been taught a little of it, but it was considered dirty, even by Lady Linette. Character sabotage was morally hazardous to both parties. Sophronia was outside her depth with this operation, and her friends would take her to task for it. Especially as she was campaigning against an adult. Monique was one thing, but a teacher?

But there was something about the fortune-teller. A broach hidden among her scarves in the shape of an onion. The fact

that she had come aboard in secret and while they were floating. Combined with something Sister Mattie had said about
the intermediary, the one who missed the shipment of pillows.
*She had to take the opportunity to infiltrate the flywaymen.* Flywaymen were supposed to be very superstitious, so a fortune-
teller would make a great cover for a spy.

## HOW TO GRACIOUSLY RECEIVE A GIFT

T he next morning at breakfast, there was a postal delivery
waiting. Captain Niall was still gathering the mail
diverted to inns along the way. The offerings consisted
of flowery letters from beaux and the occasional familial
missive. Sophronia watched Pillover carefully, pleased to see
him receive a letter addressed in aggressive black script.

Their six-month review marks must have gone out, for the
girls in Sophronia's year all had correspondences from parents.
Agatha was in tears over hers. Sidheag snorted at her missive
and lit it on fire with a nearby candle.

Dimity nibbled her lip over a boldly scripted note. "Oh, dear,
Mummy is disappointed."

Her brother looked up from his own letter. "What did
you do?"

"It's more what I didn't do."

Pillover stared gloomily into his giblet pie. "I suggest you become accustomed to the sensation. I showed interest in their work and they're still critical."

Dimity peeked over his shoulder. "Anything *significant?*"

Sophronia squinted at both of them. They were attracting attention with their sibling fussing. "Later!"

If Monique's parents cared that she'd been sent down, she showed no sign. Instead, she said in a loud voice to Preshea, "See? Daddy has written to the trustees, questioning Lady Linette's leadership. That should yield interesting results. Oh, look, and Mama has rented Walsingham House Hotel's Tea Room for my coming-out ball! It is not quite so grand as I had hoped, but..."

"Oh, but it is very pretty and centrally located."

"True, true, dear Preshea. Mayfair is the *height* of fashion."

Sophronia saw Monique stash away two other letters. Letters that had already been opened, their wax seals cracked. Monique's hands trembled as she stuffed them into her reticule.

Sophronia had expected a message of congratulations from her own family, assuming that they had been told of her achievements in the matter of oddgob tests. But there was nothing.

They returned to their parlor after breakfast to find two large dress packages waiting.

Monique pounced with a squeal of pleasure. "My new ball gown, already! How exciting. Oh, no. They are addressed to *Sophronia.* Who would have guessed you ever got new clothes? I certainly should not."

*Nor,* thought Sophronia, *should I.*

She pulled the ribbon and opened the top box. There was a note in her mother's tidy handwriting. "Your father and I are thrilled with your results, and with your sudden interest in fashionable attire. We hope the measurements are still sound."

Inside was a day dress of royal-blue-and-black brocade. Its pagoda sleeves boasted modest black fringe, but otherwise the gown was unadorned. The fabric was lovely, and the simple cut allowed it to shine. It had a high neckline, giving it a mature aura. Sophronia wondered if her mother had ordered the gown for herself and then been displeased with the vibrancy of the color. It was not a dress Mrs. Temminnick might ordinarily have approved for a daughter, which made Sophronia like it all the more.

She held it up for the others to see.

"Oooo," admired Dimity.

"It's not something she would usually send." Sophronia was careful to look skeptical.

"Oh, is it not customary for her to actually spend money on you?" Preshea wondered, drawn into admiring the dress despite herself.

Monique's nose wrinkled. "It's terribly adult."

Dimity said, "Perhaps we might get hold of some black velvet ribbon and create military details up the front—to make it a little less simple."

Sophronia liked the simplicity, but she didn't want to crush Dimity's decorative dreams. "Perhaps."

Dimity clapped her hands in excitement. "Let's see the other one!"

The other box was larger. Sophronia dipped in to produce not one, not two, but three bodices and two large, fluffy skirts. This gown was of soft and filmy sage-green muslin. The over-skirt dipped and swooped like curtains. The underskirt was a darker shade of the green, with a scalloped edge. There was a good deal of detail work put in at the hem, stripes as well as embroidery. It had a wide sash and, unless Sophronia was very mistaken, could be worn without the overskirt for a plainer look. Of the three bodices, one was a heavily fringed, low-cut evening style, with a cinched belt sporting a pretty center clasp; the second was for visiting and had narrow sleeves and a but-ton front; and the third was a crossover fichu that could be arranged like a shawl over the evening top or as a cross-front variation on the visiting version on colder days.

"Three dresses in one," said Sidheag. Even she was moved to comment on the peculiarity. "How very practical."

"How very thrifty" was Monique's comment.

Sophronia loved it, but she knew better than to say so in Preshea's hearing, or raspberry cordial would be spilled all down the skirts the first time she wore it out. So she said, "I'm not sure about the color."

Dimity was not so reticent. "It will bring out your eyes beau-tifully. I've heard of this, you know. It's called a *robe à transfor-mation*, and it's the very latest *thing* in Paris." She said this for Monique's benefit.

"So optimistic of your mother to include a ball gown option," said Monique, smiling sweetly.

"Monique is right." Sophronia turned to Dimity. "I doubt I'll get to wear that bodice, but it was very kind of Mumsy to think of me. She must have spent her own personal dress allowance on it."

The other girls gasped.

"Sophronia, don't talk of such menial things!" reprimanded Agatha softly. Agatha found money terribly embarrassing, as she had so very much of it.

*Perhaps Agatha would consider being my sponsor in the intelligencer game,* thought Sophronia. *If she decides against taking it up herself, of course.*

She was rather gleeful later, putting her new gowns away reverently in her wardrobe.

"You like them, don't you?" accused Dimity.

"I shall like them better when I have a chance to sew in hidden pockets and holsters, and determine a way to hang my chatelaine from those cloth belts."

"Yes, you like them." Dimity bounced onto her bed, grinning. She possessed a generous and happy spirit that allowed her to enjoy a friend's good fortune.

"I wonder what was in Monique's letters. The ones she hid in her reticule at breakfast."

Dimity smiled. "You mean the ones that had been opened and looked at before she got them?"

"You saw them, too? Do you think she's begging to become someone else's drone? After all, she and Professor Braithwope have broken off."

"Does it work like that? I heard vampires come after you," said Dimity, playing with her bangles.

"Could be negative replies to her ball, I suppose. Did you get a look at Pillover's letter?" Sophronia closed the wardrobe door on her new dresses and went to the looking glass to prepare for evening lessons. They had Professor Braithwope next, and he was very particular about appearances.

"Yes. Mummy's still working on aetheric communication, and Daddy's on mechanical protocols. It's all rather dull. They've been stuck on those subjects for absolutely ever, since before I started school here. Is it relevant?"

Sophronia sat down on her bed in shock. "Relevant? Relevant!" She remembered that it was after visiting Dimity's house that Monique had first taken possession of the prototype valve. It must have come from Dimity's parents! They were the ones building them.

"Oh, good, it is? How nice!"

"Dimity, Vieve thinks your parents' activities are part of Giffard's upcoming dirigible test. They've invented new mechanical protocols to help negotiate the aetherosphere currents. Do you remember the prototype that caused all the fuss at my sister's ball?"

"Of course I remember. Monique hurled a cheese pie at you."

"Well, that's your parents' device. Someone is using a smaller version of that device to help Giffard float."

Dimity blinked. "And someone else is trying to get at me to stop them?"

Sophronia nodded. "Pillover, too, don't forget."

"Poor Pill. He's such a little guy, and he's had no training at all." Dimity sounded almost as if she actually liked her brother.

"Did the letter say whom your parents are working for?"

"No, they'd never tell Pillover that. Too adult for a child to understand and whatnot."

"Would either of them work for the vampires?"

"Mummy might," said Dimity. "Daddy wouldn't."

"How about the Picklemen?"

"The reverse."

"And the government?"

Dimity nodded, blushing. "It's embarrassing, and I'm only saying this because we are alone, you understand? But it would depend on the remuneration." She lowered her voice. "We aren't *made*, you know? We're earned."

Sophronia steered the conversation delicately. "Your parents are divided in their political leanings?"

"It's why unions between Bunson's boys and Geraldine's girls are not encouraged. We are allowed to flirt, but that's only to practice. We aren't meant to *marry*. Mummy and Daddy are aberrant. Kind of like Romeo and Juliet. Only with less poison. Well, less poisoning of each other." Dimity was proud of this fact. "The rumor is, Daddy gave up becoming a high-ranked Pickleman for love of Mummy. Very romantic, don't you feel? He might even have achieved Gherkin status."

Sophronia was enthralled. "Are you two the *only* siblings with a boy at one school and a girl at the other?"

Dimity nodded.

"Sadly, this doesn't help us determine which camp is trying to push your parents' hand."

"They could be working for any of the usual suspects, thus alienating any of the others. Hundreds of depraved people could want to kidnap us." Dimity sounded almost philosophical.

"What a mess," said Sophronia. "Why did your parents have to be evil geniuses? Good geniuses are much easier to keep track of."

"All the best geniuses are evil," replied Dimity confidently. "Oh, goodness, we're late for lessons. Should we tell a teacher any of this, do you think?"

Sophronia shook her head. "With no proof and no certainty as to who is after you? I'm afraid you simply must be careful, Dimity. And keep an eye on Pillover."

Dimity sighed. "And here I was so excited to be away at finishing school so I *didn't* have to spend time with my brother." She stood and checked in the looking glass to ensure her hair was in place, all her buttons secured, and her lace tuck lying flat.

Sophronia stood as well, wrestling a stray lock of hair back under her cap. "What subject do we have tonight?"

"Oh, Sophronia, didn't you do Professor Braithwope's reading assignment?"

"I was out late."

"Hive and pack dynamics as part of the modern aristocratic system." Dimity waved a copy of the *Evening Chirrup* at her. "We were to read six articles written over the last twenty years from the gossip column. We're to present on the treatment of supernaturals as teased out from society papers. It was actually kind of interesting."

Sophronia took the parchment from her friend. "Did we all have the same six pamphlets to read?"

"Of course."

"Who knew to collect and keep multiple copies of the same newspapers at various points over two decades?"

"You think these are fake?"

Sophronia raised one eyebrow; she was getting better at the maneuver. "Or Professor Braithwope has hidden quirks."

"Sometimes I hate the way your mind works."

They made their way to the lesson. Dimity guided Sophronia by the arm so she could read while they walked. It wasn't entirely successful, as Sophronia bumped into a wall, a statue of a nymph, and lastly Felix Mersey. She wasn't entirely certain Dimity hadn't guided her into the young lordling on purpose. Dimity thought rather too highly of Felix for Sophronia's good.

"Why, Lord Mersey. How nice to see you this evening." Dimity pinched Sophronia to make her pay attention.

"Miss Plumleigh-Teignmott. Miss Temminnick, are you all right?"

Sophronia, caught by a particular line in one of the older columns, looked up at him. "Oh, no need to apologize, my lord. My fault entirely."

"I didn't."

"Mmm? Ah, well, I'm that clumsy when I read and walk." She gave him a winning, if absentminded, smile.

"Fascinating transcript?" ventured Felix, slightly alarmed by her pleasant demeanor.

Sophronia thought he looked disturbingly adorable when confused. "Indeed it is. Ever heard of the Westminster vampire hive?"

"Of course, hasn't everyone? Not exactly my social circle, Miss Temminnick." The boy's lip curled slightly.

"Are there many hives in London, do you know, Lord Mersey?"

"My dear Ria, one would be too many."

"Well, perhaps Professor Braithwope will enlighten me. I take it you won't be attending our lesson with him?"

"Wouldn't be permitted, Miss Temminnick."

"Pity, he's a very entertaining teacher. If you would excuse us?" Sophronia and Dimity curtsied and made their way into the vampire's classroom.

"Now what are you about, Sophronia?" hissed Dimity, as soon as they were out of earshot.

"Me?" They took their seats, Sophronia back to reading.

Professor Braithwope entered wearing a velvet smoking jacket, an expertly tied Indian print cravat, and a pathologically unsteady mustache. "Welcome, little bites, welcome. Today we are on to an extremely interesting topic, whot. But first, your thoughts on the reading? Miss Pelouse?" The mustache arrowed in Monique's direction.

Monique made some offhand comment. Preshea was up next, equally vague.

The mustache drooped. "Ladies, this is vital high-society survival information. Even should your paths take you into a duplicitous union with a conservative family, you must know who sits where in government. Not to mention, who came out of which families into which hives and packs. Did *anyone* read the articles? Miss Temminnick?" He turned the mustache on Sophronia.

Sophronia looked up at the mercurial little man from the wingback love seat she shared with Dimity. "I think the articles are meant to demonstrate the gradual acceptance of vampires into London society via their image as presented in the popular press. The earlier articles emphasize vampires' monstrous nature, feeding habits, and visiting hours. *Shockingly late*, says one line. And *regrettable slurping*, says another. This article was all about so-and-so being bitten after only three dances. The later columns focus instead on vampire influence on complexion and dress, particularly driven by one Countess Nadasdy of the Westminster Hive. A recluse who never leaves her secret home yet has a significant effect on fashion."

Professor Braithwope stood silent under this assessment. "Excellent, Miss Temminnick." His mustache vibrated in approval.

"Do you think you might tell us a little more about the Westminster Hive?" asked Dimity, all innocent and pure. It was the perfect setup, for while she turned wide, honey-brown eyes on the teacher, Sophronia watched Monique. The older girl went still, her expression impassive, which was a giveaway.

*Now that the professor has dropped her as drone, I bet Monique wants to trade up to a hive. And she'd want Westminster. It's clearly the most stylish.* Sophronia would lay good money on it.

Monique fished about in her reticule, retrieving a golf ball–sized white powdery object, which she popped covertly into her mouth. She swallowed with the look of a cat forced to eat a carrot.

Professor Braithwope, in animated response to Dimity's interest, said, "The queen of the Westminster Hive, Countess Nadasdy, is old, mean, and wise. However, her success in making new vampires is no better than any other queen's. And therein, of course, is the immortal curse. Drones tend to die in the attempt, and *she* has to kill them. This makes most vampire queens a little funny about the head—all that murder." He looked pointedly at Preshea and then went on to detail the male members of the Westminster Hive—age, holdings, undocumented trade, technological interests, and rank, if any.

This lesson left the six girls with the distinct impression that it was better to play nice with the Westminster Hive. Or avoid crossing them altogether.

They moved on to discussing the reach of the potentate, a rove vampire but a powerful one, who sat on Queen Victoria's Shadow Council and advised Her Majesty on the running of the Empire.

The girls were beginning to look glassy-eyed. It was a great deal of information to absorb.

"There is one other rove of interest in London, no matter how frivolous he may appear at first. Lord Akeldama is a unique personage of considerable standing with a propensity to dandification—Miss Pelouse? Miss Pelouse, are you unwell?"

Monique had turned, throughout the course of the lecture, a chartreuse color not unlike that of Agatha's dress.

"You are sweating, Miss Pelouse, whot. Young ladies of quality are not supposed to sweat!"

"Oh, Professor, I believe I'm unwell." The blonde got shakily to her feet and then, in a dramatic show, fell forward in a dead faint.

Since they had been instructed many times *always to faint backward*, this was shocking. A forward faint was, to the best of their assessment, a *real* faint! Practically unheard of. Preshea bent over her friend, spreading her own lavender-and-blue skirts out prettily.

Professor Braithwope reeled, discombobulated by such frail mortal activity, and then minced out the door. "Matron! Where's the matron, whot?" Sophronia and Dimity followed him.

At his yell several of the other teachers opened their doors. Sister Mattie's round, friendly face was concerned. "Professor, may I be of assistance?"

"Miss Pelouse is unwell."

Sister Mattie bustled across the hall and into the room.

Professor Shrimpdittle emerged at the far end of the passageway, followed by his boys. "What's happening?"

Sophronia sent Dimity off. "Tell him something is terribly wrong with one of the girls in Professor Braithwope's class. Use a tone that implies the vampire is to blame."

Dimity gave her an odd look but did as requested. She wafted down the hall, smiled sweetly up at the Bunson's teacher, and then whispered to him. She might not be the best at acquiring information, but she was deliciously excellent at disseminating it.

Professor Shrimpdittle's boyishly handsome face became suffused with red, and he glared at the vampire teacher. Professor Braithwope, flustered by actually having to deal with an illness, remained unaware of the man's ire.

The matron arrived. She and Sister Mattie made a litter out of some parasols and carried the insensate Monique from the room.

By now, word had spread, and most of the lessons were on hiatus. The doors were crowded with curious students, a consequence of their education. A few milled about in the hallway, causing Dimity some distress in returning. Vieve popped up, watching with interest as the fainted girl was carried past. She exchanged a few words with Pillover, who was lurking near Professor Shrimpdittle.

"What did that vampire do to her?" the visiting professor blustered loudly.

"Don't be silly, Algonquin," Professor Lefoux sneered. "The girl fainted. Could hardly be Aloysius's fault!"

"No good can come of having vampires supervising a bevy of nubile young girls," insisted Shrimpdittle.

Pillover said something to Vieve that made her laugh. The girl then trotted back the way she had come. Sophronia realized Pillover must be included in the plot to get Vieve into Bunson's, as he knew her real identity. *How to persuade him?*

The girls returned to class, somber after the sudden illness in their midst.

"Imagine, fainting *forward!*" Preshea whispered, white with shock.

*What did Monique eat? Useful to know,* thought Sophronia. *I must ask Sister Mattie. Dover's powder, perhaps? And why did Monique want to get out of class so badly she poisoned herself?*

Over supper, Pillover agreed to Vieve's planned infiltration, because it was evil to hide a girl from his professors, and he'd yet to do anything truly evil. "If I'm found out, I'll probably be awarded top marks. So I'm game." His expression remained morosely impassive. Poor Pillover; everything was a struggle. Here he was, forced to be bad, when at heart he was really a rather agreeable fellow. No wonder he behaved like a pustule, as his sister put it.

Felix watched Sophronia's whispered interchange with the younger boy with an odd expression on his face. She made certain he could not overhear the actual conversation.

Monique looked none the worse for her faint. She must have used the illness as an excuse to read those other secret letters, because she promptly engaged in an odd role reversal.

She took a seat between Dimity and Agatha, not Preshea and one of the boys.

"Dimity, you're looking quite pretty this evening," she said awkwardly.

"Um, thank you, Monique?" Dimity was tentative as she frantically searched for the barb within the compliment.

Sophronia and Pillover stopped talking in order to watch this fascinating proceeding.

"Such a nice bracelet you have." Monique smiled. It looked like it pained her. The bracelet was one of gilt filigree with paste amethyst stones.

Dimity sniffed. "Thank you again. Can I help you with something, Monique?"

"As a matter of fact, yes. It seems that we must make up the numbers. I was hoping you and your lovely brother might honor us with your attendance at my coming-out ball."

Pillover choked on his mulligatawny soup, snorting a small bit out his nose. Dimity looked at Sophronia, eyes desperate.

Sophronia gave a slight nod and then pointed at herself.

Dimity nodded back. "We will, of course, consider your kind

offer, but you know I couldn't possibly attend without Sophronia. We do *everything* together."

Monique winced.

"And Sidheag. And Agatha." The other two girls looked up. Agatha pretended to be pleased. Sidheag attempted not to look disgusted. Sophronia successfully hid a smile.

Monique gritted her teeth. "In that case, you are all invited. I hope you have outfits suitable to the occasion." Poor Monique; she couldn't resist saying something nasty.

"I do now," said Sophronia, but she did not push. This was far too fascinating of a character change. Something in those letters had forced Monique to issue invitations to Dimity and Pillover, which was sinister considering the kidnapping attempts.

Felix turned to Sophronia. "I demand the first dance and the dinner dance, fair Ria."

Sophronia came over all coy. "Don't be greedy. You can have the third. I'll consider the dinner."

"You're a hard-hearted woman."

"I know."

Dimity mouthed, "Flirting," at Sophronia, which made her stop self-consciously.

"Oh, look." Sidheag was the only one not at all interested in this alteration to their London activities. Thus she had not been distracted by the conversation and was pointing at the head table, where the teachers sat.

Professor Shrimpdittle, at one end, had spent the entire meal glaring at Professor Braithwope. The visiting teacher's sandy hair was mussed, as if he'd been running his hands through it repeatedly. His blue eyes were watery from lack of sleep. His attitude and appearance were unsettling. The students sensed the tension and were embarrassed. Really, he should *try* to hide his animosity. It wasn't done to allow emotions to impact anyone else's enjoyment of a meal!

The lady teachers were holding their own, despite a grumpy guest, except Professor Lefoux, who was stoically shoving soup into her mouth in the annoyed manner of any woman when a man is misbehaving.

Sidheag's attention had been caught by the arrival of Madame Spetuna. The fortune-teller was making her way to the dining table. A place was laid for her, so she had been anticipated, although she had missed the soup course. She was permitted to sit, with only a dirty look from Mademoiselle Geraldine, who thought punctuality more important than anything else, including bathing, brains, and breathing.

Sophronia wished for an opportunity to talk to the fortune-teller alone, to test out her suspicions that Madame Spetuna was an agent. She considered breaking into the record room to see if there were any files on the lady.

Madame Spetuna sat next to Professor Braithwope. The vampire took no food, only sipping a little port. The two engaged in animated conversation, much to the continued annoyance of Shrimpdittle.

Sophronia said, "Professor Shrimpdittle seems quite emotional over the presence of a vampire. I wonder if he is entirely stable. One doesn't have to like them, but they are here to stay. One must at least be polite."

This caused all three of the young men at their table to look at her with varying expressions of confusion.

"He's all right, is Shrimpdittle," said Pillover. Sophronia remembered, at that moment, that he was the youngest of the boys on board and had said he was confused as to why he had been permitted on this trip—which was meant to be a reward for boys of high standing. Had Shrimpdittle insisted Pillover be brought along, intending to put the boy at risk? He could be working for the Picklemen. Did that mean the Picklemen were trying to kidnap Dimity and Pillover?

Sophronia nibbled her bottom lip, staring pensively at the head table. She was bent on getting Vieve's agenda enacted regardless of the man's motives. "He seems unhinged. Is he fond of the drink, perhaps? Don't you feel as if his objections against the supernatural are excessive?"

"What are you implying?" demanded Felix.

"Me, *implying*? Nothing at all. Although, it could be that he is trying to hide favor or income."

Monique, of all people, jumped on this idea. "Pretending to hate them, when he really is progressive? Are males of his scientific ilk any good at acting?"

It was a stylish trap, and Sophronia was almost grateful to Monique for staging it, so she didn't have to. Now the boys at their table had to either defend their teacher as faithful to the conservative cause but possibly insane, or allow the ladies to imply that Shrimpdittle was not honest to the moral foundation of their school.

The boys did neither, being trained only in the ways of infernal devices and not inferring derisively. All of them, even Felix, looked confused. Sophronia hoped that the rumor was out there now—was Professor Shrimpdittle to be trusted? Whose politics did he *really* back? Was he going mad?

Sidheag jumped in to help. "You know, the other day when we were grounded and Professor Niall was around, I saw them engaged in conversation."

The three boys only looked more confused.

"Professor Niall," explained Sophronia, "is a *werewolf.*"

"Never!" objected Lord Dingleproops. "Not Shrimpdittle!"

Agatha tried as well. "And I saw him being nice to a kitten, once."

Everyone looked at her, puzzled.

Agatha blushed beet red. "Well," she practically whispered, "that's hardly very *evil* genius of him, now is it?"

Dinner conversation evolved away from the topic at that point, but Sophronia was tolerably certain the school would be buzzing by bedtime with questions about Professor Shrimp-dittle's motives.

Her own mind buzzed. She was holding on to too many threads at once and attempting to solve too many puzzles. It wasn't only Shrimpdittle; there was the information on the throw cushions to consider. Why had that shipment been so important? Was Madame Spetuna involved? Who were the pillows warning about: Picklemen, vampires, or some other element? And how was the Dimity kidnapping attempt connected to this? Did it all come down to the new dirigible technology? And was the guidance valve at the center of the enigma?

The others chattered, leaving Dimity, Sophronia, and Pillover to themselves at the end of the table.

Sophronia looked at Pillover a long moment. "What do you think of this kidnapping attempt?"

Pillover's dour face brightened. "Spiffing. I could do with a vacation."

Dimity put it together. "Monique's sudden change of heart and ball invitation? You think it has something to do with that?"

"Of course I do."

"Could we turn it down, then?" begged Pillover plaintively.

Dimity whirled on him. "Absolutely not! We should take this as an opportunity to flush out our enemies! Right, Sophronia?"

Sophronia massaged her temples. "This is making my brain hurt."

"I thought you liked it," said Pillover.

"In moderation and not while I am also running a character-assassination campaign."

"Yes, what is this thing with Professor Shrimpdittle? Did he do something particularly awful to you?" Dimity asked.

"Now, Dimity, you know I'm not the kind to seek revenge."

"Not entirely."

"What are you girls up to?" demanded Pillover. "I wouldn't say I *like* old Shrimps, but he's not the worst of our teachers, that's the truth."

Sophronia puffed out her cheeks. "It isn't personal. He knows too much, and I have an arrangement that requires I remove him from his current position."

Pillover put it together. "Vieve! She wants to attend Bunson's, but he knows she's a *she*."

Dimity was shocked. "Oh, Sophronia, no. She can't be allowed. What if she's found out? The humiliation! Her aunt can't possibly entertain such a madcap scheme."

"If Vieve manages to arrange it so that no one knows, then Professor Lefoux has given her permission. I think her aunt is annoyed they don't allow ladies to be official evil geniuses. You should know how aggravating that is, with your mother."

Dimity looked like she didn't want to believe it. "But I thought Professor Lefoux was so proper."

"She *is* French," said Pillover, as if that could be used to explain all possible impropriety.

"How'd Vieve get you involved?" Dimity demanded.

Sophronia smiled slyly. "I get her gadgets when she leaves."

Dimity sighed. "I should tell Lord Felix Mersey that the way to your heart is paved with infiltration apparatus."

Sophronia pretended horror. "Don't you dare! I like watching him struggle. He's so handsome when he's flustered."

Pillover was disgusted. "Girls!"

# A WELL-EXECUTED CHARACTER ASSASSINATION

Sophronia felt it would take only one more delicate push to topple Shrimpdittle. Sister Mattie had instructed them in the fine art of skin dyeing for subterfuge only a month earlier. Sophronia concocted a plan based on this information. It would involve breaking into a gentleman's bedchamber, but if the professor was a solid sleeper, it shouldn't be difficult.

Of course, Sophronia had no way of knowing *how* Professor Shrimpdittle slept. Ordinary character assassinations required considerable research on the victim prior to enactment. Sophronia hadn't the time. She could only hope that given his fondness for wine, the man would slumber deeply.

Once she had possession of the obstructor, it was a simple matter to make her way to the teachers' section. Vieve yielded up the device easily, knowing Sophronia was using it for the Cause. Sophronia paused at one juncture, after blasting a maid mechanical, reflecting that she had become quite relaxed about running about after hours. She ought to remember to stay on her guard, for it was when an illegal activity became easy that one was most at risk of exposure.

Professor Shrimpdittle's guest rooms were in the forbidden red-tassel section. Sophronia thought she had chosen an hour late enough for everyone to be asleep. Except Professor Braithwope, of course. She rounded the corner to be confronted by a soldier mechanical, which she shot into stillness. Then, as she went to creep around it, she found the hallway occupied!

Someone in a long dressing gown and bed cap of matching emerald brocade walked down the hall and entered Professor Braithwope's room. Without knocking, mind you! Impossible to tell whether the wearer was female or male, but it was most certainly not the vampire—too tall. *A pox upon nondescript clothing*, cursed Sophronia—in knickerbockers, corset, and men's shirt. *Is Monique still feeding him? It could be her, I suppose.*

Sophronia was preparing to proceed when, of all people, Sister Mattie emerged from Mademoiselle Geraldine's quarters and hurried down the hallway. Sophronia had to blast the soldier mechanical again, as she caught the telltale whirr of the machine ramping back into action.

She was thinking of aborting—the chances of discovery were too great—but the gaslight from under the various doors went out, except Professor Braithwope's. The quiet murmur of voices from his room indicated he and his guest were settled into conversation. So, with silent footsteps, grateful for the plush hallway carpet, Sophronia crept to the very last room.

Sophronia opened Professor Shrimpdittle's door with her

lock pick, automatically checking the jamb for cords, bells, sticky substances, or traps. *Nothing. He really is an innocent.* Closing it behind her, Sophronia's eyes adjusted to the weak light of a white-misted moon. Professor Shrimpdittle snored loudly, in a gratifyingly deep sleep.

Sophronia crept over and removed a little perfume bottle from her cleavage. Inside was a mixture of concentrated walnut dye and beet juice. It didn't last long, but it would hold to the skin for a day or so even under strenuous washing, especially if it were left to sit several hours—while a man was asleep, for example.

Carefully, she touched the small end of the stopper to the teacher's neck, light as could be. Twice. She examined her handiwork. It looked exactly as if it might be the mark left by vampire fangs. She fervently hoped that the man wouldn't move and smear it while it dried. She hurried to the door and let herself out, mission accomplished.

"Well, well, what are *you* doing?"

Sophronia only just managed not to let out a shriek that would have awakened the entire front section of the airship. She whirled to find Madame Spetuna standing in the hallway, arms crossed. She'd lost several of her scarves and much of her accent. *She looks younger, too.*

At a loss, Sophronia curtsied. "Madame Spetuna, how do you do?"

The purported fortune-teller looked at the door Sophronia had shut. "Professor Shrimpdittle's quarters, is it? What could you possibly have to do there?"

Sophronia didn't answer.

"And you had me sew that button in his ear earlier as well. What are you up to, little covert recruit?"

*She knows that, does she?* "I might just as well ask what you are up to, Madame Spetuna."

"Touché."

They stood in the shadows, at an impasse.

"I have learned you are in possession of a mechanimal," the fortune-teller said at last.

"How?" Knowing she was a covert recruit was one thing, but Sophronia had hoped the teachers knew nothing of Bumbersnoot.

The diminutive lady cocked her head to one side and raised an eyebrow.

*Of course, if she was trained here, and she's as good as I think she is, she would have sources of information beyond the teachers.* "What's it to you?"

"Let us make a bargain. You give me the mechanimal, and I will not reveal your infiltration of the tassel section." Madame Spetuna gestured with one hand at the dark hallway.

"Why do you need him?"

"Let us say, I could use the status conferred upon owners of mechanimals."

Sophronia speculated, "It would be a help if one wanted to gain the confidence of, say, flywaymen and Picklemen. They do have a penchant for mechanimals, don't they?"

Another silence met that.

"You cannot have my mechanimal."

The fortune-teller's eyes narrowed. She cocked her head threateningly, like an angry rooster. A red fringed scarf about her neck contributed to the effect, looking like a wattle.

Sophronia added, "But you may *borrow* him for a time. Arrange to return him to me in, say, one week, and we have a deal."

Madame Spetuna pursed her lips. "One month."

"Two weeks."

"Three."

"Done. And I want to know why you came on board to report in. What was so important you had to leave your post and abandon all those embroidered pillows?"

"My, my, you are a devious little thing, aren't you?" Madame Spetuna made a decision. "I came to report that the flyway-men are assembling a float gather. This has not occurred in some fifty years. Also, they are allying formally with the Picklemen."

"Which is why you need Bumbersnoot. This is an opportunity for you to trade up to a more significant position in sky ranking."

"Bumbersnoot?"

"My mechanimal."

Madame Spetuna inclined her head.

"Why are they gathering?"

"Giffard's dirigible. If he can travel the aetherosphere, so could they."

Sophronia wrinkled her nose. "They aren't trying to kidnap my friend Dimity, are they?"

Madame Spetuna looked genuinely confused.

Sophronia nodded to herself. Either Madame Spetuna wasn't high up enough to know, or the Picklemen weren't revealing this plan to their flywaymen allies, or it wasn't the Picklemen. *Vampires, then?*

"When can I get the mechanimal?" demanded Madame Spetuna.

"Tomorrow evening, in the boiler room," said Sophronia.

"Done."

"How do I know you won't steal him forever?"

"You don't."

They parted, and Sophronia was left feeling both forlorn and triumphant, although her prevailing emotion was one of relief. She was wrung out, like wilted spinach. *I'm losing my touch*, she thought. *I got caught!* Her stomach sloshed. Confidence shaken, she took a long time to make her way back to her quarters.

By the next morning, however, Sophronia was more controlled. During the brief free time before breakfast, she went hunting for Vieve.

The thing about Vieve was that the scamp turned up when she pleased, and no one was entirely certain where she spent the bulk of her time. So when one was looking for Vieve, it could prove difficult to actually find her. Sophronia pestered the hall steward, one of the human staff members, into getting the word out that Vieve was wanted. And after searching for a bit, she gave up.

The younger girl appeared, dimpling excitedly, to escort her to breakfast an hour later. They hung back, despite Monique's teasing, for a quick exchange. Sophronia shook her head quite firmly at Felix when the boy looked as if he would come over and take her arm. She indicated that she already had an escort, and even Lord Mersey was well mannered enough not to interfere. He did, however, look offended.

"Quickly," said Sophronia. "Your Bunson's plan is getting me into heaps of trouble. I've had to promise the loan of Bumbersnoot to a *fortune-teller*."

Vieve gave her best effort at a guilty look.

Sophronia was not fooled—Vieve rarely felt guilty about anything. "Can you kit him out to emit a timed explosive? Set the timer for three weeks in the future, give her incentive to get him back to me quickly?"

"I won't ask for the details."

"Nor should you. Well, can you?"

Vieve scrunched up her nose. "Explosives aren't my strongest suit. It's ridiculously difficult to acquire them when one is only ten. Then again, I could link something under pressure to his own functionality, get the viscosity of the oil down enough to begin a gradual buildup." Her forehead wrinkled. "You'd have to shut him down and clean him out if you got him back early."

"Show me how?"

"Of course."

"The boiler room, this evening?"

Vieve nodded and then skittered off.

At breakfast Professor Shrimpdittle was red-eyed and panicky, with a very high cravat tied about his neck.

*    *    *

Soap was thrilled to see Sophronia that night. "My goodness, miss, I thought you'd forgotten all about us." His grin practically lit up the boiler room.

Sophronia thought he was looking remarkably fit. Had he got himself new clothing? Well, *newer* clothing. "Never, Soap. Things have simply been busy with this trip, that's all."

"And with all them fine visiting gentlemen?" Soap's tone was overly casual.

"Now, Soap. You know you'll always be my favorite."

Soap tugged his own ear self-consciously. "Aw, miss."

Sophronia unstrung Bumbersnoot from his reticule disguise and put him down on the floor. His tail *tick-tock*ed happily as he nibbled chips of coal and snuffled in the black dust.

"So, miss, what's the doggerel?"

Sophronia relayed to Soap some of what she was currently scheming—the bits she was tolerably certain wouldn't offend. She told him of Vieve's plan to relocate, her own plotting against Shrimpdittle, the fortune-teller spy, and the possible attempted kidnapping of Dimity and Pillover. And how it all might be tied to Giffard's fancy new dirigible technology and the guidance valve that was once a prototype.

It was like telling an adventure story to a child. Sophronia made the most of it, exaggerating her own actions rather more than was truthful, and detailing the Chaise Longue Attack as if it were some epic battle.

Soap and the small crowd of sooties who joined him were entranced. They gasped in all the right places. When Vieve arrived and scooped up Bumbersnoot, they barely noticed. The younger girl settled herself to tinker with the mechanimal, making a host of adjustments and configurations. Inside his storage compartment, she placed a round spidery thing that looked uncomfortably deadly, and hooked it into the dog's tiny steam engine with various cables.

By the time Sophronia had finished her tale, Vieve was done with Bumbersnoot. Sensing that story time was over, the sooties dispersed.

Vieve showed Sophronia the adjustments she'd made.

"You detach it here, like so." She tapped the side of the spider in a pattern of pressed buttons and twisted nobs.

Sophronia memorized it.

"That's the only shutdown sequence that will incapacitate the explosive. Otherwise, it's timed to be heat dependent. If you try to remove it early, it will explode. What I've done is connected it to Bumbersnoot's boiler. This will cause a slow buildup. He already has a safety thermometer in his storage stomach to prevent overheating; this will cause him to regurgitate the explosive in exactly twenty-four days, if my calculations are correct. Once the device is disconnected, it will explode in minutes. All this timing is rather delicate and requires that Bumbersnoot run standard practices. If he is walked at high speed too frequently, he'll emit the explosive sooner."

"Will there be any kind of warning?" Sophronia asked, patting Bumbersnoot's head.

"His tail will begin to wag faster and faster. When it's going as fast as a hummingbird's wings, he's about to regurgitate."

"How do we ensure that he himself gets out of the blast

range?" Sophronia was worried for her beloved pet's safety. "And how do I get him back?"

Vieve shrugged unhelpfully.

"Ah, is that the mechanimal?" Madame Spetuna appeared as if out of nowhere.

Everyone started, including the sooties, who were usually excellent at spotting an intruder in their domain.

"Who are you?" Soap demanded.

"Ah, Soap, this is Madame Spetuna. She is that fortune-teller I told you about."

"How do you do?" said Soap, intrigued.

Madame Spetuna nodded at him curtly. Clearly, she had no time for sooties.

After exchanging glances with Vieve, Sophronia said, "This is Bumbersnoot. Bumbersnoot, this is Madame Spetuna. You'll be visiting with her for the next few weeks."

Bumbersnoot's ears dropped. He whistled a bit of steam out his undercarriage in query.

"It's not that you've done anything wrong, Bumbersnoot. It's a covert mission for you."

Bumbersnoot did not look convinced.

"Come now, you want to be an intelligencer like me, don't you?" Sophronia patted the metal dog on his head and then handed him to Madame Spetuna. The fortune-teller began stroking the mechanimal covetously.

Sophronia said, "Vieve here has installed an exploding spider, and only the two of us know how to shut it down. If you try to take it out and keep him, it will explode in your hands. If you don't get him back to me in under three weeks, he will emit it and explode." Sophronia did not explain that said explosion would be slightly delayed. She wanted the woman to think that attempting to steal Bumbersnoot would be very hazardous. To provide further incentive, she added, "If you opt to merely drop him overboard, I will arrange for the flywaymen to learn who you really work for. I have broken into the record room before, you know."

"That was you?" Madame Spetuna looked impressed. "Very nice touch, missy. And, of course, you could be lying to me about any of this, and I've no way of knowing."

Vieve said pertly, "I assure you, she is not lying."

Soap followed this interchange with a look of skepticism. He was fond of Bumbersnoot. "Are you certain about this, miss?" he asked as Madame Spetuna trotted away, clutching Bumbersnoot under one arm.

Nibbling her lip unhappily, Sophronia watched the intelligencer disappear. "No, I'm not. We have to hope that Madame Spetuna and the flywaymen stick close. If they are after the Giffard test, then they'll be heading to London, like us."

Vieve was confident. "It will all work out in the end. Only think, Sophronia, how nice it will be to own all my gadgets."

Soap pursed his lips. "Is *that* your bargain?"

"The things I do for gadgets," said Sophronia.

Soap, fond of Vieve's inventions himself, nodded sagely. "Now, miss, you let me know if you need any help getting that critter back, you hear?"

"Soap, what could you possibly . . . ?"

"Why, miss, you think the flywaymen don't have sooties on

their big ships, too?" He gave her an almost evil smile. "My people are everywhere."

"Soap, have I told you recently how much I adore you?" Sophronia's heart lightened, her worries about Bumbersnoot allayed slightly.

Soap looked down at his feet and shuffled them in the coal dust. "Aw, miss, not again."

Sophronia stood on tiptoe and kissed his dusty cheek. "Thank you. You're a chum."


Madame Spetuna departed the ship before breakfast the next morning, Bumbersnoot with her. Sophronia felt his lack keenly. She hadn't realized how prevalent the mechanimal was in her life—puttering about her feet as she washed in the morning, blundering into the furniture while the girls gossiped, eating discarded gloves while they dressed of an evening. Her shoulder, without the weight of the lace strap from his reticule-disguised form, felt naked. She had only a few days to miss him, however, because they finally arrived in the great city of London.


Around midnight on a fine clear Thursday in mid-March, a lone cloud wafted over west London toward Hyde Park. There it stopped and hovered in a most un-cloud-like manner. It hesitated and then headed purposefully toward the grounds of the Crystal Palace, where the Great Exhibition halls were being torn down. It sank low enough to touch the top of the center post, where once massive buildings had housed engines of industry.

No one observed this odd behavior except two gin-soaked gentlemen. They watched the cloud slowly part, revealing itself to be, in actuality, a massive dirigible.

"Did we visit one of the opium dens this evening?" inquired one gentleman of the other, trying to explain away this hallucination.

"Dens? Hens?" said the second, tripping over a mulberry bush.

The two gentlemen swayed where they stood, leaning against each other, transfixed while the dirigible undertook a series of transformations. Dark figures swarmed up to the squeak decks and then climbed over the casings of the huge balloons, scrambling about with the aid of rope ladders, but looking, to the befuddled watchers, like so many four-legged ants.

Eventually, the ants unrolled a canvas banner that stretched the full length of the central balloon and read BLENHEIM'S BUILDERS & SAFETY INSPECTORS. FOR QUEEN AND COUNTRY. The ants then proceeded to rig scaffolding from the ship's decks down to the ground. After these adjustments the airship looked quite convincingly as if it were part of the Crystal Palace deconstruction operation.

In Hyde Park the only way to hide something as huge as a floating school was to pretend it was a tradesman's concern, a business that functioned through the use of day laborers. Anyone of note tempted to look must instantly look away in humiliation. After all, persons of consequence did not pay attention to buildings going up or down—they were too *exposed*. Anything to do with construction was highly embarrassing.

When Sophronia awoke the next day and trotted out on deck to investigate, she couldn't read the legend spread above them, but at breakfast they were told what it said.

There were a few cries of outrage from the young ladies. After all, they didn't want to be associated with builders any more than the aristocrats strolling through Hyde Park.

Monique was particularly upset. "We can't be *seen* to be here, on a ship emblazoned with an *advertisement*! It's simply too shocking! What if someone observes us disembarking?"

"Well, you'll have to be careful no one does, won't you? After all, young ladies shouldn't be around building sites regardless of signage. You are, as of this moment, restricted indoors. Is that understood?" Mademoiselle Geraldine was firm on this matter.

They all nodded.

Sophronia entertained herself by imagining what kind of disguise might best facilitate escape. She couldn't, after all, look like a builder. She hadn't the physicality for it.

"I guess if I want to wander around, I'll have to pretend to be a sootie," she muttered. After all, most industries required the use of small wiry boys in some capacity.

Dimity was shocked. "Sophronia, first men's garb and now *lower-class men's garb*? The very idea!"

Sophronia admitted, "It *is* daring. Luckily, I have no reason to leave the ship. Yet."

"You will not be allowed off school grounds regardless, ladies," continued Mademoiselle Geraldine. "It's too dangerous to parade around London without an escort. Those of you who have families in town will make special arrangements. For the rest, this is an educational jaunt, not a pleasure cruise."

Preshea was upset. "But the shopping! I have been given an extra allowance in anticipation of this trip!" She emphasized the final *p* so sharply it almost popped the eardrum.

"It will wait, Miss Buss."

"But Monique's party!"

"That's enough, Miss Buss."

Preshea looked sulky.

Monique was smug. Her parents were in town preparing for the ball. She would be allowed to shop as much as she pleased.

So they lodged in Hyde Park, and their classes continued despite the tempting activities outside the windows. The view included the aristocracy taking the air, hackney cabs rolling by, and the certain knowledge that just out of reach were all the luxuries and privileges afforded by town.

It was maddening, for everyone except Sidheag. Even Agatha, normally reticent, yearned to take in a theatrical performance. "Or perhaps an opera. I do adore the opera."

Sophronia ruminated over whether the ban was intended to drive them into transgression, or if there was some serious threat to the students that warranted keeping them holed up. The teachers were not revealing any secrets, and with only a few attempted escapes by some of the older girls, the day passed smoothly.

The only odd occurrence was later that night, when instead of having Professor Braithwope for evening lessons, they were put in with the older girls under Professor Lefoux. This was their first experience with Vieve's aunt as an instructor.

Professor Lefoux was patently brilliant and moved through the topic—industrial sabotage, tea, and supply trains—with such rapidity it left most of the class, regardless of age, utterly confused. Then she began to fire off questions in such a way as to make them all feel stupid. It was a traumatic experience and left them fervently wishing for the nice, easygoing, friendly vampire of their ordinary schedule.

Professor Braithwope was a dedicated teacher, and he didn't like to change his routine. A monster of habit, the vampire. What, then, could possibly draw him away?

His place was empty at the head table at supper, as was a guest spot set next to it.

"He has a visitor," said Sophronia, nibbling at some fried haddock.

"Oh, you think so?" Dimity was much less interested in the goings-on of teachers than Sophronia.

"I do. An important visitor."

Halfway through the meal, when the main course was to be brought out, Professor Braithwope arrived with a gentleman in tow.

The gentleman was tallish, not overly thin or overly fat. He wore proper dress to the height of style but nothing more elaborate. He had a long face with lines about the eyes that suggested exhaustion, not humor, and the general pallor of an invalid or an accounting clerk. The most remarkable things about him were his hands, which were long and elegant, mothlike in the candlelight. Mademoiselle Geraldine insisted on candlesticks for supper. Gas, she said, was too harsh for food.

The stranger sat next to Professor Braithwope as though it pained him to do so, and took no food, only a little port.

Sidheag, following Sophronia's gaze, said idly, "So that's why Captain Niall was so anxious."

"Captain Niall was anxious?"

"About coming to London. I thought it only that werewolves don't like town, except the West End. Now I suspect that it has to do with *him*."

Sophronia examined their visitor, trying to determine what it was about this man that the school's werewolf would find objectionable. "Why him in particular?"

"Don't you recognize our dear fanged member of the Shadow Council?"

"Goodness, no, why should I?"

Sidheag had been raised in Scotland but nevertheless enmeshed in supernatural politics. "True, he likes to stay out of the public eye, but that's him, all right."

"Him who?"

Sidheag nodded firmly. "Funny, me having information before you."

Now Sidheag was simply being obstreperous.

"Are you telling me that is the *potentate*?" Sophronia hissed her revelation. Things began to click into place in her brain. Not unlike the workings of the oddgob machine. Could this be the school's mysterious patron? Not just a vampire, not just the government, but *Queen Victoria's pet vampire*?

Sidheag chewed a bit of fricassee of rabbit and new potatoes. "Looks like."

The potentate glanced up and directly at them, as if sensing they were discussing him, although even with supernatural hearing there was no way he could possibly cut through the suppertime chatter all the way to the back of the room. *Or could he?*

Sophronia raised her water goblet in salute. Sidheag ignored him. As Lady Kingair, she was allied with werewolves. Wolves might shun polite society, but they equaled vampires in status.

Felix, observing this interchange, said from across the table, "Very unpleasantly august company you keep here, for a ladies' seminary. Now, where's the pudding course?"

"It doesn't look like your teacher is too thrilled," replied Sophronia.

Professor Shrimpdittle was looking bilious. He had a bright paisley scarf tied high about his neck. He was focused on his mutton and spinach with single-minded intent.

Felix said, "In no way are two vampires better than one."

*Especially not if you believe you've recently been bitten.* "Are you certain it's not the political power he wields?" Sophronia asked.

"Why, Ria, are you speaking in riddles? That's sweet. I might almost think you wished to lure me in." Felix batted long lashes at her.

The meal came to a close, the millet pudding and Norfolk dumplings consumed with gusto, especially by Pillover. Sophronia held back while most of the students crowded out through the door, eager for their brief spate of spare time before night classes began. The teachers let them go, lingering over their sherry or brandy, as nature dictated. In the case of Sister Mattie, nature dictated barley water.

Alone, Sophronia inched her way toward the front of the

room. She pretended interest in some leftover nibbles at one of the tables. She watched the teachers out of the corner of her eye.

Professor Braithwope stood to take his leave, and the potentate clapped him on the shoulder in a fair imitation of jocularity. There was no real friendliness to the touch. *I suppose they are nervous; one is inside the other's territory. This ship, after all, belongs to Professor Braithwope by vampire law. So the potentate is imposing, whether invited or not.*

She heard the potentate say, "For blood, queen, and country, Aloysius. You take a grave risk, my boy, a grave risk. You are to be commended."

Professor Braithwope replied, mustache under control for once, "Thank you, sir. I shall do my best." This was said in the tone of a son to his military father on the eve of battle.

Feeling that she was pushing her luck, Sophronia drifted toward the exit, only to find herself accompanied by Professor Braithwope.

"Sir," she said, politely.

"I don't like how obsequious they all get when he is around," said the vampire, as though answering a question she hadn't asked.

"He is a very important person."

"More than you will ever know, I hope. Don't try any of your tricks on him, Miss Temminnick. He won't put up with them the way I do."

Sophronia's mind was whirring. *If the school works for the potentate, does that mean graduates are agents of the Shadow Council?* "For blood, queen, and country, sir?" she said softly.

"So he says, Miss Temminnick. So he says."

Sophronia had always enjoyed the idea of intelligencer work but been worried about whom she might be an agent for. Queen Victoria and her supernatural advisers seemed safer than the Picklemen or the vampire hives, but were they really any better? *If I want to, will I be permitted to make my own arrangements? Can I choose a patron, or do we automatically go to the highest bidder? And if the latter is the case, how is that a fate better than an arranged marriage?*

Sophronia wasn't certain what instinct drove her to drop by the classrooms that night—but she did.

She saw the light on in Professor Lefoux's lab and climbed outside to peek in, listening with her trumpet pressed to the porthole. There was only one person in the room, and he wasn't talking. Professor Shrimpdittle was bent over the large metal suitlike object that he and Professor Lefoux had tinkered with earlier that week. He was working in intense silence, and though Sophronia watched him for a quarter of an hour, she got no information. She returned to her room, puzzled but with a certain sense of anticipation. Soon, she felt, all her questions would be answered. They were, after all, in London.

Her bed was lonely and cold without Bumbersnoot's hot metal body to warm her feet.

## HIGH FLOATING ABOARD

When she first saw Mademoiselle Geraldine's Finishing Academy for Young Ladies of Quality, Sophronia had been impressed by the size of the airship. But no one would ever make the mistake of calling it pretty. It was a cumbersome thing that seemed to stay up by will rather than ability, like a potbellied pig. One got the impression it didn't really want to float but was doing so out of a sense of polite obligation.

The same could not be said of Giffard's aether-current floater, christened the *Puffy Nimbus Eighteen*. It was a thing of technological beauty. Its bottom half was still barge-shaped, but all sleek and elegant. Its blimp was sleek as well, an elongated almond with no patches from cannon fire and no extraneous ropes or ladders. The balloon was made of silk and oiled to a dark midnight purple. The ship glided in over a jubilant crowd and sank to land at the center of Hyde Park, some distance away from the embarrassingly emblazoned Mademoiselle Geraldine's.

The girls were permitted to visit the assembly area to watch the landing, along with hundreds of others. They were under strict orders to stick together, paired into two long lines. They dressed in their best walking frocks and bonnets, parasols raised against an overcast sky.

"Pretty as a pineapple," pronounced Mademoiselle Geraldine, waving them off with a lace handkerchief. Mademoiselle Geraldine never left the airship if she could avoid it. "An Englishwoman's dirigible is her castle" was one of her favorite sayings.

The girls joined in the cheers of welcome. It was a magical event, for Giffard had managed the journey in under an hour. He'd come all the way from Paris, mostly inside the aetherosphere, higher up than any manned float-craft had ever been before. "He must have used the crystalline prototype guidance valve," insisted Vieve. "He couldn't have managed those currents any other way." Then she vanished into the crowd.

Henri Giffard pranced down the gangplank of his wondrous machine with all the fanfare of a circus ringmaster. He was dressed in a suit of cream check with a turquoise cravat and boasted a mustache the likes of which Sophronia had never seen before. Had he been awake, Professor Braithwope and his sad excuse for a lip curtain would have trembled in humiliation. Henri Giffard's mustache curled up and out like a corkscrew, waxed to within an inch of its life. It was too theatrical. Sophronia instantly stopped looking at him and looked about the crowd. *He must be intentionally drawing attention away from someone?*

The gathering was what one might expect of a Hyde Park afternoon. There were toffs in fancy carriages and on horseback. Mademoiselle Geraldine's young ladies of quality were companioned by a number of other students from surrounding schools, all allowed to walk out for the momentous occasion. There were groups of boffins from the Royal Society, distinguished by slightly rumpled attire and a predilection for spectacles and oddball gadgetry. There were riffraff as well: some chimney sweeps, the occasional shopgirl, greasers, and other representatives of the rougher orders. Before she had met Soap, Sophronia would have glanced over them, but now she examined all with interest. Intelligencers could be anyone, after all.

She wasn't certain exactly what she was looking for—something out of the ordinary, she supposed. She noted a group of extraordinarily well-turned-out dandies to one side. They were a bit out of place. It was early in the day for that sort to be awake, and they were not the kind of men to be interested in dirigibles. She stared at them for a long moment, but then Giffard hailed the pinks with a whoop, and they whooped back. *Chums from the gambling circuit?* Giffard was rumored to be a bounder. Several of the academics looked like they might be too well dressed; perhaps they were in disguise? Then again, they could be French scholars, over to observe the landing.

The *Puffy Nimbus* was locked down. Giffard gave a speech in broken English and was welcomed with all due honors by the queen's daylight representatives. That was when Sophronia spotted *them*.

Off to the far side, lurking under a weeping willow, were three men, all dressed to the height of fashion, carrying canes and wearing top hats. Around those hats were bands of green. *Picklemen.* They, like Sophronia, acted aloof from the excitement—watchers. As she looked at them, one spotted her. He tipped his hat with his cane. Sophronia twirled her parasol at him and then turned pointedly to take Felix's arm, smiling up at the startled boy.

"Are you unwell, Ria, my dove?" Sophronia had never taken his arm before.

*Let them guess at our relationship,* she thought. *Let them wonder. Son of a Pickleman, is he? How much does he know?*

Sophronia said sweetly, "A little overstimulated, Lord Mersey, that is all. It's unseasonably warm, don't you feel?"

Felix patted her hand on his arm in a condescending way. "Well, little one, you hold on there. I'll ensure you get back to the ship safely."

Sophronia couldn't resist. "That's my big, strong man."

Felix's eyes flashed at her suspiciously.

Sophronia only continued to smile, using her lashes to good effect.

Felix couldn't help but smile back. She was, after all, on his arm. Why question such a sought-after eventuality?

They returned to the school. Surprisingly, no one had tried to escape during the outing. The teachers were delighted with such unexpectedly good behavior. Accordingly, the girls were given the afternoon off to primp and prepare for London, whether or not they would get out into it for Monique's ball.

The ship was abuzz with the excitement of those who were

invited and the disappointed tears of those who were not. Sophronia and her friends pretended titillation. In Dimity's case it was probably genuine. She fluttered about, suggesting a way Agatha might better do her hair ("Really, *darling*, it's such a pretty red"), reprimanding Sidheag for the plainness of her gown ("Add a *little* lace, please?"), and insisting Sophronia wear more jewelry ("No, the obstructor does not count").

"It doesn't look at all like a bangle. Could we dress it up with jewels or something else sparkly?"

"Not without Vieve's permission. It isn't mine *yet*. Dimity, leave it alone! I'm far more concerned with being adequately kitted than fashionable."

"Oh, Sophronia, don't say such a horrible thing!" Dimity put her hand to her chest and gasped. One of Lady Linette's techniques. "As if anything untoward would happen at Monique's coming-out ball." Her eyes sparkled at the temerity of her own statement.

Sophronia felt guilty. After all, Dimity and Pillover were headed into certain danger. "Very well, you can sparkle up the hurlie if you must. But not the obstructor."

Dimity clapped her hands and dove for the device.

Over supper that evening, they were informed that night classes were canceled.

"We will all be leaving the school for several hours. I'm told the airship is required by the government for a very delicate test." Mademoiselle Geraldine looked as if she had swallowed a slug. "It is too dangerous to risk young lives. All students are to pack their most precious items into one hatbox  one, mind you!—and assemble amidships. You are to remain near the

Crystal Palace building site, where you will be permitted to observe the test. You will have a quarter of an hour after supper to pack and assemble for staircase deployment. There *will* be a counting."

A murmur of confusion went through the crowd at such odd instructions. Sophronia looked at Professor Braithwope for hints as to the nature of this *test*. It must have something to do with the vampires trying to conquer the aether. Professor Braithwope's expression was impassive. Even his mustache betrayed nothing.

Undaunted, the students did as ordered. Several of the girls found themselves very large hatboxes indeed, and all of them wore their best dresses under their winter cloaks, in case something *did* happen to the ship.

"Why tonight?" whined Monique. "Couldn't this have waited until *after* my ball?"

"No, dear, it couldn't," said Sister Mattie, coming up behind the fretful girl.

"Oh, but Sister Mattie, if something happens, my spare ball gown will be destroyed. Then what will I do?"

"My dear, if we lose the ship, it will be far worse than that."

Monique wailed in distress.

Sophronia was not impressed. She knew for a fact that Monique had insisted other girls carry her dresses in their hatboxes.

Sophronia inched her way over to the dumpy teacher. "Is there really a chance the ship may go down?"

"My dear girl, it is a *floating* school. There is *always* a chance." Sister Mattie could be rather fatalistic at times; it was why she was such a good poisoning instructor. Death, felt Sister Mattie, must come to everyone in the end. Sometimes it simply required a little help.

Sophronia glanced around. "Are the other professors not joining us?"

Sister Mattie pointed.

The forms of Professors Braithwope, Shrimpdittle, and Lefoux were making their way upward around the edge of the ship.

"What about the sooties?" wondered Sophronia. "If this test is really that dangerous, shouldn't they be allowed off as well?"

"Oh, they don't count," said Sister Mattie airily. "Besides, they are needed to run the boilers. Every engineer is on duty right now, too. It'll take all the muscle we have to get high enough."

At that, Sophronia understood exactly what was going on. Everything fell into place—needing a teacher, the school having to travel to London, the vampires' interest in aether technology. "Giffard is running another aether test tonight, and he needs our school to shadow him because Professor Braithwope is involved. His tether can't be stretched that high, right?"

"Now, dear, you shouldn't concern yourself." Sister Mattie dismissed her with forced casualness and moved away.

Vieve appeared at Sophronia's elbow, dark hair free of the chronic cap but dimples firmly in place. "Did you notice? They are taking the invention from the lab with them." Professor Shrimpdittle was carrying the metal suitlike contraption. "And you know what my aunt did? She installed one of the guidance valves inside it! Let's hope she is better than I am at getting it to turn off correctly." With that, she disappeared again.

Sophronia moved back to Dimity, Agatha, and Sidheag. "I do wish they would do the counting soon."

"Why?" Agatha was instantly suspicious.

"Because she wants to stay on board," explained Dimity.

Sidheag was having none of it. "What if they do another count when we are on the ground?"

"I have to chance it. I can't leave the sooties to go up alone. It isn't fair."

"Very noble, Sophronia," applauded Dimity. "I didn't know you had an altruistic bone in your body. Charity is so ladylike."

Sidheag snorted. "Nonsense. She wants to see what's really happening."

Sophronia grinned. "Can't it be both?" She looked with concern at Dimity and Pillover. "You two, please stick tight to Captain Niall? Just in case there are any further kidnapping attempts. The one contingent I can guarantee *isn't* after you is the werewolves. If you stay near the captain, he'll protect you as he would any student."

The Plumleigh-Teignmotts looked as if they would like to object.

"Please, Dimity. *Please?*" Sophronia was more earnest than Dimity had ever seen her.

Dimity nodded, her round face doll-like in its seriousness.

Sophronia turned to Sidheag. "Keep an eye on them, too?"

Sidheag nodded. "Kidnapping?"

"I'll explain later."

Sidheag nodded again. Sophronia blessed Lady Kingair's military upbringing. The girl knew how to follow orders.

"Oh, and Dimity, as you exit, could I have a little diversion?"

Dimity pursed her lips. "Of course. What kind—"

Mademoiselle Geraldine clapped her hands, and all the girls turned to face her expectantly. "Line up by year for the counting. Debuts this side, midranks there and there, oldest girls that side, boys at the back."

There was shuffling while they did as they were told. Felix took it as an opportunity to brush close to Sophronia.

"What's going on, do you think?" he asked.

"You mean you don't know?"

"No, why should I?"

"Your people are involved."

"What do you mean, my people?"

Sophronia gestured below, where a great number of benches were being put out on the green near the skeleton of the Crystal Palace. This was nothing like Giffard's landing earlier that day. This was a private nighttime affair, and the constabulary were present to ensure it stayed private. These were not any old crushers, either. They wore the silver and wooden weaponry of men who specialized in the supernatural. Not that there would be much activity in Hyde Park so early at night. After supper was a time used to dress. Things weren't actually supposed to *happen* at nine o'clock in the evening. It was a most unfashionable hour to run a test, even covertly. No wonder Mademoiselle Geraldine was disgruntled.

Under the moon's bright light, Felix could see what Sophronia meant by her slur. His *people* were indeed seated below. A goodly number of gentlemen wore top hats with green satin bands about the crown. There were others as well—a group of well-dressed dandies, some scruffy types who could only belong to a nearby werewolf pack, and two pale, debonair gentlemen who must be vampires. The potentate sat with them.

Sophronia noted that the sky was becoming overcast. Not with clouds but with airships. A small armada approached and hovered at a distance. There were little airdinghies with four small balloons and sails up high in the middle—flywaymen. There were larger, proper dirigibles, a matched set with dark-colored balloons—sky pirates or private-airs. *No doubt Madame Spetuna and Bumbersnoot are up there somewhere, watching.*

Mademoiselle Geraldine's Finishing Academy sank down as low as possible, proving that the scaffolding all around it was quite fake. A counting was conducted, and the staircase was cranked down. As they began shambling toward it, Sophronia drifted to one side, her eyes on the professors. Dimity gave a shriek and a wobble, veering toward the side banister of the stairway. She lurched, almost tumbling down several stories to the ground below. Agatha peeped in fear and pretended a faint backward. Sidheag made a lunge after Dimity and nearly went over the edge herself. They were doing beautifully.

Everyone burbled in perturbation. The crowd boiled upward as ladies rose on tiptoe to see what was happening. Teachers and other staff pressed forward to ascertain the cause of the commotion. Lady Linette, trained as she was, sensed the manufactured nature of the distraction and surveyed the crowd, but with over three dozen on the midship deck, it was easy for Sophronia to wait until her teacher's gaze passed her over.

The moment Lady Linette looked elsewhere, Sophronia crouched. The fashion for large hats, even at night, afforded her some protection from view. Removing her own bonnet, she made a break for the ladder that led to the upper decks. She'd be exposed if she actually took those stairs, but she could hide behind them until everyone had disembarked.

Sophronia waited patiently until blasts of steam and the sound of cranking indicated the staircase was being pulled back up. The ship lurched upward. It was safe to emerge.

Professor Braithwope was visible on the upper forward squeak deck far above. He was climbing into the contraption Professors Lefoux and Shrimpdittle had built. It fit him like those suits designed for undersea exploration. *What are they called? Diving suits.* Once it was fully in place, he looked a little like an oversized mechanical, only more liquid in his movements.

Sophronia made her way around to the far side of the ship, out of view from the watchers below. But not before she saw Sidheag sit next to Captain Niall, along with Dimity and Pillover.

Giffard's aether-current floater, the *Puffy Nimbus Eighteen*, swooped into sight, undulating in their direction. Sophronia had once manned an airdinghy, so she knew enough to admire Giffard's skill. Once the other airship was level with Mademoiselle Geraldine's, the school extended a long gangplank to it, and Professor Braithwope ran across with a tightrope walker's skill. The gangplank was drawn back and the two ships began to rise ponderously, keeping pace with each other. Sophronia had intended to check up on the sooties, but she was hypnotized by the action above her, so she stayed hanging where she was. Professor Braithwope and Mr. Giffard exchanged pleasantries, and then Mr. Giffard went back to work steering his small vessel. The two ships rose together, so high the people below became little specks. Then so did the trees of the park. Finally, London herself was nothing but a blob of twinkling lights. They were above the clouds at last, higher than Sophronia had ever floated. The air was glacial and the winds howled by; the propeller pushed hard against the breezes upon which the school normally drifted peaceably.

Sophronia wondered if there would be a defining shift when they hit the aetherosphere. She knew that it must be close, that invisible onion skin, the thing that protected them all from the void beyond. She couldn't believe they intended to take Mademoiselle Geraldine's up *that* high. Giffard's aether-current floater was built for the changeable humors of the upper sphere, but Geraldine's was not.

She turned her attention to Professor Braithwope. The vampire stood stiff and straight, leaning back against the railing of the *Puffy Nimbus*'s one squeak deck and looking up. Sophronia could hardly fathom that he intended to enter the aetherosphere. Very little was known about it, except that it was breathable but dense, not like normal air, and dangerous. Only humans had ever been inside it, and only very few of them. But no other vampire could float up even a short distance; Professor Braithwope was the exception, by virtue of his inhabiting their school. So the school had to go up with him as far as it could, keeping his tether as short as possible.

*They intended all along to send the vampire, suited in his protective gear, into the aetherosphere. He will be the first supernatural creature to enter aether. They want to know—vampires, werewolves, government, Picklemen. They all want to know: what happens to a supernatural creature in the aetherosphere? They built him*

*a suit as a nod to safety, but they really have no idea what will occur up there.*

Professor Braithwope was undergoing a very dangerous test indeed. *For queen and country*, the potentate had said. *For science*, Sophronia thought.

Mademoiselle Geraldine's stopped rising and held steady, the propeller fighting to keep the school in place. They had gone up as high as possible. *Directly above us*, thought Sophronia, *must be the aetherosphere.* It boggled her mind. She looked but couldn't see anything apart from very bright stars. The aetherosphere was invisible from below, and opaque from within, or so she'd heard.

Giffard gave some kind of signal and the *Puffy Nimbus* bobbed up, leaving Mademoiselle Geraldine's behind.

At first everything seemed fine. Then Professor Braithwope began to gyrate around in his mechanical suit, waving his hands about his face as if fending off a swarm of attacking wasps. *The mating dance of a mechanical* was Sophronia's hysterical thought.

Giffard seemed to be occupied doing battle with his navigation helm. Sophronia thought she heard Professor Braithwope scream. Then she saw him jerk wildly backward, come up against the railing, and flip right over it. At the time, and for years after, she was never certain if he fell accidentally or jumped in order to get relief from invisible tormentors.

Professor Braithwope, encased in his Lefoux-made suit, was tumbling down through the air. His body was limp and there was no sound coming from him anymore.

*He should be screaming,* thought Sophronia inanely. *I would be screaming.*

She watched, transfixed, as the vampire's body spiraled down into the clouds and out of sight.

Then she moved. He was supposed to have had a guidance valve in that suit of his. Presumably connected to their ship's boiler room, so they could follow him right away if anything happened. But he either hadn't used it or it hadn't worked, because Mademoiselle Geraldine's still held steady.

Sophronia had never moved so fast about the hull, hurling and jumping from balcony to balcony in a frenzy, working her way down until she could climb in the hatch to the boiler room.

Engineering was a swarm of activity, every sootie awake and at work. There were greasers, firemen, and engineers everywhere monitoring the flurry. It couldn't have been easy. All the boilers were burning, licks of flame coming from the fuel boxes. Steam that didn't make its way out through the pipes filled the room, clouding the upper portions of the cavernous space and making it seem more intimate. It was incredibly hot.

Sophronia's only thought was to find Soap. Fortunately, he found her.

"What ho, miss?"

Sophronia babbled, forgetting her manners and grabbing his arms in an excess of emotion. "Soap! The school has to go down with him! His tether will snap!" she yelled helplessly into the loud bustle of the boiler room. "Go down now! Take us down! Please!"

Soap put gentle hands on her clutching arms. "I don't know

what you're on about, miss, but orders have to come from the pilot's bubble."

Sophronia panicked. She remembered only Professor Braith-wope's face when she asked him about tether limits. How terrified he had been. They needed to follow him as quickly and as closely as possible.

"Soap, who is in charge of the boiler room?"

Soap looked at her, mouth open. "*What*, miss?"

"Take me to him, please? Now."

Soap led her through the craziness at a run. Sophronia dogged him in her full dress and hat, looking as if she were about to go for a stroll in Hyde Park. Her skirts were long enough to lift up the soot dust in her wake, like steam from a machine.

They ended up at the base of a tall platform that rose up to one side of the room, allowing the man standing on its top to overlook the entirety of the activity therein.

"You stay here, Soap. No sense in us both getting into trouble."

"Are you sure, miss?"

"Yes," said Sophronia. *No*, thought Sophronia.

Soap's face puckered in concern, but Sophronia turned her changeable green eyes on him and said, "Please."

So he let her climb up to the dais alone.

The man who stood on the top was dirty with coal dust and wore simple clothing—jodhpurs, boots, shirt, and vest. He had facial topiary sprouting off his chin and down his neck like a mountain goat. The beard was red, as was the man's cruel face.

"Who are you, missy?" he barked.

Sophronia quailed a moment—he was very fierce—and then she remembered Professor Braithwope's well-tended, if confused, facial hair and found her courage. *I must send a beard to rescue a mustache!* "Sir, it's Professor Braithwope. He fell. I saw him. We must track him down or he could be permanently damaged. Please, we have to follow quickly."

"That's not possible, little miss. The lever hasn't dropped. And this is no place for a young lady. Get along with you."

"Please, listen! We must go down. We must!" This was one of those times Sophronia wished she had blackmail material. Why oh why were those lessons only for older students?

"If we were to go down, that newfangled gadget would have told us." The man pointed to a small cradle, in which sat a guidance valve. It was partly encased in mechanisms that attached to a lever. Sophronia remembered what she'd learned about the first prototype—that it required two to communicate. This was the second, and Professor Braithwope's suit housed the first. She remembered Vieve and her troubles convincing the sputter-skates to turn off using her guidance valve. It hadn't worked properly because she'd needed a second valve. This, then, was supposed to have been the vampire's safety net. Professor Braithwope, or his suit, should have alerted engineering when something went wrong. That lever should have dropped. But it hadn't, and the professor was falling.

Sophronia might have argued with the man indefinitely, but there came a screeching, airy, puff noise, and a long metal tube, which ended above the platform, spat out a pelletlike object that nearly hit the man on the head.

He grabbed it out of the air and cracked it open on his knee; it split like an egg. Inside was a message, which he read, and then, giving Sophronia a suspicious look, he reached for a massive bullhorn. The brass horn was almost as tall as he, and all over covered in keys and levers. Raising it to his lips and adjusting the controls to his liking, the man yelled out over the chamber. "All hands, pull back, we're going down at speed. Propeller tilt to steady a rapid descent. Greasers Six and Fourteen, take your sooties up top. We're collapsing the midship balloon."

A collective gasp met that statement.

*So I managed to climb the ship and get him the message here before the pilot's bubble did. No wonder they want working guidance valves. No wonder everyone is so desperate to get their hands on these things. Everything about air travel could be faster—for everyone, not just those who float inside the aetherosphere.*

Into the resulting comparative silence—the machinery still clanged and the boilers still flamed despite the fact that all human movement had stilled—a small voice said, "Not *all the way?*" in a shocked tone.

The red-faced man said into the bullhorn, "Yes. *All the way.* The rest of you, perform your cool-down tasks and then brace for a rough descent. We aren't landing, mind you, but we are going down fast!"

The chamber sprang into action. It was as though everything were in reverse. Sooties who had been running one way began running the other. Stokers stopped stoking. A few even threw water on the burning fuel, the resulting steam adding to the congestion of the room.

The angry man looked at Sophronia. "You, get out of here! Find yourself a place to brace. This is no lark, you realize? And what's your name?"

"Monique de Pelouse," said Sophronia, without missing a beat.

"I wager it is. Now off with ya. Get!"

Sophronia got.

A truly harrowing few seconds followed. The ship sank so fast Sophronia could feel it in her belly. It was a wobbly sensation, especially when one was accustomed to not feeling anything at all on the floating school. She holed up in her favorite meeting spot behind a—now much diminished—pile of coal, near the floor hatch. Eventually, Soap joined her there. Together they watched the ground approach through the hatch.

"What did you do, miss?" asked Soap as London came into view.

"It wasn't me. I tried, but he only took instructions when some tube spat at him."

They could see Hyde Park at the city center and Regent's Park to the north.

"Pilot's orders. Must have agreed with you. But deflating a balloon? It's not done, not ever. The expense alone!"

They began to see streets and houses distinctly.

"Are we going to crash?" wondered Sophronia, her heart fluttering.

Soap inched one long arm about her waist with the excuse that she might need the support. Sophronia was somewhat reassured.

The bones of the Crystal Palace and the now empty benches came into view. Everyone was crowded around what could only be the fallen body of Professor Braithwope.

"Man the pull back, swell up inflation," came a yell over the bullhorn.

"Erp, that's me!" Soap dashed back to work.

Sophronia felt bereft.

Someone in the crowd below looked up, pointed, and screamed. It must be a truly terrifying thing to see, the massive school hurtling down toward them.

Then Sophronia felt a mighty jolt. They stopped falling and hovered, almost exactly as high above the ground as they had been before the whole thing started.

The sooties cheered.

Several of the young ladies in the crowd below fainted. Each faint was, properly, backward and caught by one of the many gentlemen in attendance.

Sophronia let down the rope ladder attached to one side of the hatch and climbed to the ground as quickly as she could.

## BALLS AND CHAINS

No one—at least no one who had anything to say about it at the time—noticed Sophronia climbing down. She made her way through the crowd, ending up between Dimity and Captain Niall. She noted with relief that Pillover was still there and nodded gratefully at Sidheag, who had forced them into continued proximity with the werewolf.

Sidheag smiled back. Genuine pleasure lit up her long, masculine face.

Professor Braithwope's body was bent in a most unusual way. Someone had removed the helmet of the aether-suit, and the vampire's face was gray-green in color. His mustache was deflated and floppy.

Monique de Pelouse was bent over the vampire, her face a study in tragedy. Sophronia wondered if it was a calculated expression, intentionally revealing her intimacy with the vampire to the other vampires present. Was she saying, in her best Monique way: I'm in the market for a new patron? She might as well have taken out a sign that stretched across Mademoiselle Geraldine's midship balloon.

Lady Linette was barking orders. "Get those stairs down. Quickly! We must get him onto school grounds immediately!" Sister Mattie was pulling and rearranging Professor Braithwope's limbs, attempting to get them back into alignment. Professor Lefoux's normal attitude of strict severity was in place, but her hands shook as she attempted to remove the aether-suit.

Then Professor Braithwope's eyes snapped open.

The crowd gasped in titillated horror.

The vampire's skin was drawn back flush against his skull as he opened his mouth in a silent scream, showing yellow gums and the full length of his fangs. They were a stark contrast to his fragility, all that wicked strength in such a small, sickly man.

"Oh my," whispered Dimity, "how monstrous!"

Sophronia inched closer to the vampire, trying to listen to the quiet conversation between his female attendants.

"Monique!" said Professor Lefoux. "You'll have to do your duty."

Monique, composed and regal, nodded and with a single lissome movement swirled off her cape. Without hesitation she pressed one of her wrists to the vampire's gaping mouth.

He bit down, hard. Blood splattered Monique's white skin.

The surrounding watchers inhaled as one.

Dimity, as was her custom, fainted.

Monique gave a delicate shudder but no other reaction.

*Well,* thought Sophronia, *that secret is definitely out. It's a good thing she's having her coming-out ball and leaving the school, or there would be questions from her parents after this.*

It could almost be thought romantic, if it hadn't been so gruesome. A tiny teardrop of blood leaked out the corner of the vampire's mouth; his eyes remained wide and staring. Behind him, the great staircase of the school cranked downward, white puffs of steam escaping into the night. The midship balloon was being inflated and the fake scaffolding put back into place.

"Pull her away," barked Professor Lefoux, without looking up from the suit. "That's enough blood for one girl to give."

Lady Linette yanked Monique's wrist off the vampire's fangs and pushed her back.

Monique swayed.

The crowd murmured in concern, but no one stepped forward to help. Monique's cronies and sycophants looked away guiltily. Even Preshea did not want to touch her.

Then, out of the crowd, came one of the other vampires. He was an impossibly handsome man, older than he looked, of course, but one to set any young lady's heart fluttering. Even knowing he was a vampire. For some, *especially* knowing he was a vampire. He took hold of Monique gently, his hands soft and supportive on her shoulders.

"There, there, pretty little nibble."

Monique looked up at him from dazed blue eyes. "Oh, thank you, kind sir."

Sophronia tried to memorize the man's face. He might be important.

"More blood," barked Sister Mattie. "He will succumb

otherwise. And he needs it now." She was looking at Professor Lefoux.

"Look at this." Vieve's aunt was distracted, gesturing to some section of the suit. "It's been tampered with! And the transmitter valve, it failed."

"Never mind that now, Beatrice. He needs you."

Professor Lefoux finally looked up. "What? Now?"

"Yes, now!"

"Oh, very well." Professor Lefoux rolled up one sleeve of her serviceable gown and placed her wrist to the vampire's still dripping fangs with an air of disregard.

The girls of Mademoiselle Geraldine's, the ones still sensate, sent up a gasp. The implication was unavoidable. Professor Lefoux was *also* a drone to Professor Braithwope!

*Everyone's secrets are coming to light tonight,* thought Sophronia, wondering how she had missed this little facet of inter-teacher dynamics. *I should have been a better observer. That must have been Professor Lefoux in the green robe the other night.*

Feeling self-conscious but knowing now was the right time to do it, Sophronia stepped forward and whispered in Professor Lefoux's ear.

"Professor, I hesitate to say such a thing, but I believe I saw Professor Shrimpdittle going into your lab alone last night. And he certainly hates vampires."

Professor Lefoux's sharp eyes turned toward her. "What are you about, Miss Temminnick?"

"Nothing out of the ordinary, Professor. Only letting you know, if there's sabotage..." She trailed off.

Professor Lefoux, as if she could not help herself, glanced

over the crowd, focusing on Professor Shrimpdittle. The boys' teacher stood at the very back, looking as though he might run. His milk-fed face was equal parts shock and horror.

Sophronia stepped back into the throng.

Sidheag, supporting the fainted Dimity under one arm, asked gruffly, "What's going on *now?*"

"Wait and watch."

Eventually, Professor Braithwope stopped feeding. He still looked awful, eyes unfocused, and remained silent. He was lifted up by a group of dandies and carried on board.

Mademoiselle Geraldine pressed a large handkerchief to her trembling lips and trailed after, whispering brokenly, "But a man of such *qualit-tay!*" A few of the young ladies, overcome with sentiment, followed.

Professor Lefoux, without bothering to pretend weakness, tied Sister Mattie's handkerchief about her own wrist, rolled down her sleeve, and bent once more to examine the aether-suit. Eventually, she looked up.

"It has been tampered with; the guidance valve is not set properly. Meticulous sabotage, of the kind only possible from someone who knew how the suit worked. There is only one other person who could have done such a thing."

"Well," said Vieve, appearing at Sophronia's elbow, "that's not entirely true."

"Vieve, you didn't!"

"No, I didn't, but I should like at least *you* to know that I *could.*"

Sophronia said, "Impossible child, better keep *that* to yourself."

Professor Lefoux continued, "I am saddened to have to do this publicly, but Lord Ambrose, if you might be so kind as to seize Professor Shrimpdittle?"

The handsome vampire who had been consoling Monique looked at Professor Lefoux and then, with a curt nod, flitted supernaturally fast to the edge of the crowd, scooping up Professor Shrimpdittle before the man could even start to run.

"I object!" yelled the teacher, his eyes wild.

Sophronia felt suddenly unwell. She didn't want to witness this, not after she had driven him to do it. *Because of me*, she thought, *the suit was sabotaged. Because of me, Professor Braithwope could be permanently damaged. And now, because of me, this man will be punished for it.* She wanted to be sick. She wanted to blame Vieve and her devilish bargain. Instead, she schooled her features, swallowed down the bile, and stood witness to her own actions.

"We protest," said one of the Picklemen in an autocratic tone. "Professor Shrimpdittle is a respected member of the Royal Society, not to mention a learned teacher."

"He is also a noted vampire hater," said Lord Ambrose, casually picking at his fang with a cravat pin while still holding Professor Shrimpdittle with his other hand.

The crowd separated. The vampires and their drones ranged against the Picklemen. The few ladies present, the remaining girls from the school, and Captain Niall held neutral territory between the two parties.

The potentate stepped forward, flanked on either side by two very large, scruffy men. Captain Niall did a strange thing at the sight. He bowed, tilting his head and baring the back of his neck in a gesture of profound submission. Sidheag did the same. The scruffy men both nodded, accepting this odd behavior as their due. Their top hats, while fine specimens to the height of fashion, were tied beneath their chins, the black velvet ribbon stark against the white of evening cravats.

"Who are they?" Sophronia asked.

"The one with the mustache on the left is the dewan, the queen's own werewolf and the potentate's counterpart. The other one is Lord Vulkasin Woolsey," explained Sidheag out of the corner of her mouth.

"Is there anything you don't know about werewolves?" Sophronia demanded.

"Nope. You try living with them for a few years running. They're not exactly subtle."

"Shush," said Captain Niall, coming out of his bow.

The dewan said, his voice gravelly, "You have an accusation to make, Professor Lefoux?"

Professor Lefoux looked up from the aether-suit. "I do."

Professor Shrimpdittle struggled. "He bit me!"

One of the Picklemen instructed, "Say no more, Algonquin!"

Shrimpdittle was wild-eyed in desperation. Lord Ambrose lifted him as if he weighed no more than a lady's muff, and carried him forward, depositing him into the even stronger embrace of Lord Woolsey. Vulkasin looked mean, even for a werewolf. His mouth was a hard line and there were no smile wrinkles at the corners of his eyes.

"I had to protect myself!" cried Professor Shrimpdittle, wiggling futilely in the werewolf's grip. "I had fang marks on my neck!"

"Poppycock," said the potentate. "Professor Braithwope would never bite without invitation."

"Shame on you," said Lord Ambrose, "to cast aspersions on a vampire who has recently risked so much for his country!"

"Hear, hear!" cried the vampires in the crowd.

"Lies!" screamed Shrimpdittle, spittle spraying from his mouth. "All lies!"

One of the other Picklemen shook his head. "Stop now, Shrimpdittle."

But the man was beyond reason. "I had to stop him! I had to."

Lord Woolsey had heard enough. His lip curled. "I arrest this man in the name of the queen, for sabotage and attempted murder. You will let me know, Captain Niall, how the fallen vampire fares. Whether I must change the charge to murder?" He clearly did not care either way. Vampires and werewolves might not like each other, but when it came to running the country and preserving the good name of supernaturals, they always found common ground.

Captain Niall saluted the other werewolf. "Sir!"

Sophronia closed her eyes involuntarily. Vulkasin was one of the nastiest-looking supernatural creatures she'd ever seen. *What have I done, delivering poor Shrimpdittle into his clutches?*

"Any challenge?" The dewan looked over at the crowd of Picklemen.

They murmured briefly among themselves.

"Bad form," Sophronia heard one of them say, "confessing like that. Very bad form."

Finally, the oldest of the lot tilted his hat politely at three of the most powerful supernaturals in England and said, "We will, of course, provide legal counsel, but we cannot forestall the arrest. It is justified. He will be immediately removed from all teaching responsibilities."

With that, Lord Woolsey and the dewan walked away. Lord Woolsey carried the frantic Professor Shrimpdittle under one arm like a rolled umbrella.

Sophronia glanced at Felix's face. The boy was shocked, but he did not look over at her, so he must not suspect her involvement.

Pillover, on the other hand, was glaring at her. "He really was one of the better teachers. It isn't fair! Take it back, Sophronia!" With that, he grabbed his sister, still in a deep faint, and stormed off to the airship—half carrying, half dragging Dimity.

Sophronia, still worried about their safety, gave Sidheag a lips-compressed head tilt of encouragement.

"What am I," grumbled the Lady of Kingair, "the nanny?" But she trotted after the Plumleigh-Teignmotts. She might be a grumpy old thing, but she liked Dimity and she trusted Sophronia's instincts.

Vieve, on the other hand, glanced up at Sophronia with shining eyes and said very softly, "All this for me? You're too kind."

"Oh, yes," replied Sophronia, riddled with guilt. "I ruined one man and by doing so nearly killed another, all so you could go to school. You had better earn the sacrifice."

"I shall be brilliant," said Vieve with confidence. "What happened up there?"

"The blasted guidance valve failed. Or the professor was too crazed to remember to trigger it. It was awful. It was as if he went mad. And when he fell, it took our ship forever to respond."

Vieve tried a smile. "Don't worry, both the professors will be fine." She had all the optimism of a child.

Captain Niall, supernatural hearing and all, stared down at Sophronia and Professor Lefoux's niece with a suspicious look. Apparently unable to fathom why or how Sophronia might have orchestrated the visiting teacher's mad act, he simply sighed deeply and said, "Why did I get involved with this kind of finishing school? Espionage is not for werewolves."

Vieve said pertly, "Boredom, sir?"

Captain Niall cuffed her ear gently and wandered off.

Lady Linette began marshaling the girls back on board. "Some of you," she reminded them, "have a ball to dress for!" That got them moving with much greater rapidity than anything else.

Sophronia, truth to tell, was having an internal crisis. She hadn't meant to drive Shrimpdittle to such lengths, but it was her fault. *She* had convinced the poor man that Professor Braithwope had bitten him. *She* had driven him to sabotage the guidance valve in the aether-suit. If Professor Braithwope died, she was to blame. *Are character assassinations always this awful?* she wondered. *Will I have to learn to live with such consequences all the time? Am I really cut out to be an intelligencer, if this is part of it?*

She responded like a mechanical to Lady Linette's instructions.

*    *    *

On board the ship, everything was forgotten in the excitement of a ball. Girls rushed between chambers, rendering gown judgments and borrowing accessories. Only Sophronia stayed worried about Professor Braithwope's condition.

Vieve showed up in their parlor, damning and approving the state of hair fobs and follies with great authority for a girl who only wore boys' clothing.

"No, Dimity, you should leave yours as loose as possible but still up in a ladylike manner. It's a real scorcher, your hair. Best display it to maximum efficiency. Agatha, try curls. No, bigger curls. Bigger!"

Monique and Preshea emerged from their room, and everyone stopped and gasped appreciatively. The two girls looked truly charming. Monique was all tall blonde elegance, with Preshea the velvet night to her moon. *Blast it*, thought Sophronia, *they look so good I'm coming over poetic. How humiliating.*

"Gold brocade?" said Vieve's little voice. "A bold choice for the first gown of the Season."

That broke the spell, because Monique turned sharply, squeaking due to the tight bodice of that gorgeous gold gown, and threw her fan at the young girl.

Vieve laughed, batting it away. "Oh, very ladylike. Aren't you all grown up?"

Sophronia was wearing her new sage dress with the evening bodice and the fancy overskirt. Her hair was up, though not very done, and her jewelry was minimal—paste pearls borrowed from Dimity. She looked lovely in her simplicity, or so Dimity insisted. "Like a fresh green sunflower sprout."

"I look like a sprout?" Sophronia pretended offense and tried to join in the excitement. But she felt distant and alone. She kept seeing Professor Braithwope's blank eyes and broken form.

Vieve came to stand next to her. "Aren't they a sight?"

"Who?" Sophronia was a tad short with her friend.

"All of them. You'd think this ball the most exciting thing to ever happen."

"When a few short moments ago a vampire fell from the sky?"

Vieve turned, tilted her cap back, and looked out from under it at Sophronia. "You may have arranged matters, but the actions of others are not your fault. You know that, yes?"

"How is he, Vieve?"

"We should talk in there." Vieve gestured casually to Sophronia and Dimity's room.

As soon as the door was closed, she said, "I overheard my aunt and Sister Mattie chatting with the potentate and Mr. Giffard. Despite Shrimpdittle's tampering, they don't think that was the cause of Prof B.'s condition. Giffard said the vampire went crazy the moment they entered the aetherosphere. One second he was standing there in his suit, the next he was gyrating around the deck as though on fire. It was as if he had an adverse reaction to the aether itself. Even if the guidance valve had been working, he was too insane to activate it. Professor Shrimpdittle's sabotage was irrelevant. And now Professor Braithwope is a babbling madman, and they aren't sure if it's the result of aetherosphere exposure, the fall, or a snapped tether."

"Are they confident that's exactly what happened?" Sophronia held on to her guilt.

"They should have made the suit impermeable to aether, if that's even possible, but they only thought to try to salvage his tether. If anyone should feel guilty, it's the people who sent him up there in the first place. It's been concluded that vampires can't go into the aetherosphere, ever. A major scientific breakthrough, so at least he didn't sacrifice himself for nothing." Vieve dimpled at her hopefully.

"But if the school could have followed his fall faster? If Shrimpdittle hadn't...if I hadn't tricked Shrimpdittle into..."

"Stop being so hard on yourself, Sophronia."

"Will he recover? Will he be mad forever? Will he die?"

"They don't know. Matron has never heard of such an extreme case of tether snap, even without the added aether exposure. There is no precedent. He'll be put under guard, but he may never regain his senses. Or he could expire within the hour."

Sophronia did not feel any better. She thought she might rush to Professor Braithwope's quarters and offer up her blood. She felt she should admit her guilt to Lady Linette. She wanted to do penance. Instead, numb with horror, she allowed herself to be shuffled along to a ball.

In no time whatsoever, those who had been invited to Monique's ball, a *select* group of almost half the school and all the visiting Bunson's boys, disembarked. A veritable herd of hansom cabs awaited them.

Sophronia, Sidheag, Agatha, Dimity, Pillover, and Lord

Mersey crammed into one together. Felix arranged it so he could sit between Sophronia and the door.

"How are you this evening, Miss Temminnick?" He was looking quite handsome. His evening dress was impeccable—crisp whites and silken blacks.

Sophronia could hardly believe such a man as this held her in genuine regard. "Well enough, Lord Mersey," she replied, uncomfortable with his proximity. She could feel the warmth of the length of his thigh against hers, even through all her skirts.

"Still upset, Ria, my sweet? Your gentle heart moved by this evening's calamity?"

Sophronia studied him from under her eyelashes. "Yes, I must admit, I was shaken. To see a man fall like that."

Felix patted her gloved hand. "Not a man, a vampire, and they are made of stern stuff. You must rise above it."

*Unfortunate choice of words*, thought Sophronia. "Oh, yes, thank you for such kind thoughts."

"To be sure, Ria, my dear. You lean on me if you are feeling unwell. Don't tax yourself this evening. And I demand the dinner set and the last dance, in order to better see to your health."

Dimity, on Sophronia's other side, stiffened at this audacity.

Sophronia pretended to blush. She couldn't blush on cue yet, but she *could* pretend. She lowered her eyelids and fanned herself with her free hand. "Lord Mersey. You already have the third. That would be *three* dances. I think not. As to the dinner, I said I would think about it."

"Well?"

"I'm still thinking."

Felix looked appropriately chastised.

*Such games we play*, thought Sophronia, rather tired of the whole thing. *As if I didn't have to hedge and speak in code most of the time, I must now do it as part of regular social interactions. No wonder Mademoiselle Geraldine's has such success training the female aristocracy to be intelligencers. It's most of our life already.* For some inexplicable reason, in a horse-drawn carriage on the way to a ball, sitting in close proximity to another boy, Sophronia found herself thinking of Soap. *He never plays any games with me.*

Felix was pressed against her, but she found herself thinking of Soap's long arm about her waist. She crushed the upwelling of warmth ruthlessly. *Soap is a friend. I don't want to destroy that. I don't want to change us.* Some small traitorous part of her whispered back, *Then what do you want?*

They arrived and Lord Mersey gallantly helped them all to descend from the carriage. Sophronia was first, so that by the time he had finished, she was already making her way into Walsingham House with Dimity. Felix was left to escort Agatha or drop the girl's trembling hand and run after Sophronia in a most unseemly manner.

Walsingham House Hotel was beyond lavish, and the Frond Court Tea Room was particularly grand. Monique's family must be very wealthy or very optimistic, for no expense was spared. The entire venue was decorated in a gold-and-cream tea theme. There were cream roses nested in large gold sugar bowls. The everyday chandelier had been replaced with one of lavish crystal in the shape of a massive teapot. No one but Monique had been permitted to wear gold, and she glided, in regal superiority, among the attendees in their muted pastels. A string quartet, sufficient but not boastfully large, sat in one corner near a raised dancing area. Long, lace-covered tables arrayed along one wall groaned under bowls of golden punch and cream-colored nibbles. The punch was served in teacups, the comestibles on saucers. All the food was made to look like tea cakes, whether sweet or savory. This got a mite confusing, but everything tasted delicious.

Sophronia did not want to be impressed, but she was. It made her sister Petunia's coming-out ball seem provincial by comparison.

Several guests had already arrived—enough young men to make up the numbers, some elderly ladies to act as chaperones, and a full service of flaxen-haired, arrogant fops who could only be Monique's relations. As the room began to fill, Sophronia noticed a bevy of dandies, slightly older and more refined than might be expected, take up position near the punch. The vampire Lord Ambrose lurked to one side. Captain Niall stood in the opposite corner. He saw Sophronia's group enter, his top hat tilted in Sidheag's direction like an arrow of inquisition. Sidheag nodded at him shyly.

Having played the appropriate ode to Her Majesty, the band struck up a waltz. Titters of shock permeated the room, excitement from young ladies and disapproval from chaperones. To have a small band was elegance; to commence a ball with a waltz was very daring *indeed*.

Nevertheless, Monique's first partner, Lord Dingleproops, led her gamely out onto the floor, and after a stanza or two, others followed. Lord Mersey accosted Sophronia, who gave him her hand willingly, despite her earlier reticence. He was the best-looking boy in the room and probably the highest ranking. With Dimity swinging happily around on some dandy's arm, a man almost as sparkly as she, and Pillover doing his duty by Agatha, Sophronia felt she might as well take to the floor. Besides, she was tolerably certain Felix wasn't getting the dinner dance, so she might as well take advantage of his interest. Even Sidheag was whirling about in the arms of a boy taller and gawkier than she.

Felix was an excellent dancer, his hand warm and firm at the small of her back. His frame was a little tight, drawing her in close enough for disapproval, but there was such a crush the chaperones did not notice. Sophronia looked up into his eyes for a long moment before lowering her gaze and allowing him time to recover. He did seem a little breathless for a waltz that was limited in aestheticism by the size of the venue and the number of dancers.

It was for him to open dialogue, which he did after they had learned each other's rhythm. "You're a wonderful dancer, Ria."

"Mademoiselle Geraldine's takes such things seriously."

"Ah. And how many ways do you know to kill me, while we dance?"

"Only two, but give me time."

"You have lovely eyes. Has anyone ever told you that?"

"What rot. They are a muddy green. What are you about, Lord Mersey?"

Felix sighed, looking genuinely perturbed. His air of ennui was shaken. "I am *trying* to court you. Truth be told, Miss Temminnick, you make it ruddy difficult!"

"Language, Lord Mersey." Sophronia felt her heart flutter strangely. *Am I ready to be courted?*

"See!"

"Bunson's and Geraldine's don't mix. We practice, but we don't finish, not with each other."

"It's happened before."

"You mean the Plumleigh-Teignmotts? Yes, but they both had to give it up."

"Give what up?"

"Their training."

"I'm not asking you to marry me, Ria. I'm asking you to let me court you."

"To what end, exactly, if not marriage?"

Felix winced.

"I'm not willing to stop learning. Are you?" Despite her guilt over Professor Braithwope's fall, as she said it Sophronia knew this was true. "As I understand it, we serve different masters."

"Precisely why it might be fun."

"I will not be used as some boyish excuse for rebellion."

"You see what I mean? Difficult! I like it."

"You're a loon."

"And you're a silver swan sailing on liquid dreams."

Sophronia giggled. "Stop that. This is getting us nowhere."

"So may I court you?"

Sophronia looked over his shoulder, feeling dizzy. From the waltzing, of course. She stalled for time and then . . .

"Where's Dimity?"

Felix was thrown by the sudden switch in topic.

"And Pillover! Where's Pillover?"

Sophronia scanned the crowd frantically. There was the dandy who *had* been dancing with Dimity; he was now dancing with Agatha. The Plumleigh-Teignmott siblings were gone! Sophronia looked to the back of the crowd near the punch bowl. Lord Ambrose was also gone. Sidheag was still with her tall partner. Captain Niall lurked on the sidelines, his eyes on Lady Kingair with an odd expression in them. With no time to analyze any of it, Sophronia broke away from Felix.

"Are you leaving me in the middle of a dance *again*?" She'd done exactly the same thing to him the night they danced at Petunia's coming-out ball. He grabbed for her arm. "I'll stop being silly. I promise."

"This is not a cut, Felix. I must go fix something."

"Why is it always your problem to fix, Ria?"

"Because I see that there *is* a problem when no one else does."

With nothing more to say than that, Sophronia Angelina Temminnick did the rudest thing she had ever done in all her life: she left a high-ranking peer of the realm standing alone in the middle of a waltz. For the *second* time of their acquaintance. *Oh, dear,* she thought, *he might never forgive me.*

Sophronia was just in time. She saw the hem of Dimity's gown, a strikingly bold peach-and-brown pattern not unlike a sun-bleached tiger, disappear inside a private carriage outside the hotel. She could also hear the sound of muffled yelling.

The driver struck up the horses, but not before Sophronia hiked up her skirts, ran down after them, and leapt up to the back step, a place ordinarily occupied by footmen in livery. It was not a perch designed for a ball gown, nor were any meant to stand there when moving at speed, but Sophronia held on. *No one is kidnapping my Dimity!*

The carriage careened through the streets at a dangerous pace, slowing only when traffic demanded. After a relatively short distance, it drew to a halt on a quiet domestic avenue. Sophronia jumped down and to the side, turning her head away from the carriage and pretending to walk along the pavement as if out for a stroll. Alone. In a ball gown. The door to the carriage opened behind her. She could not turn without arousing suspicion, so she proceeded at an unhurried pace until she was around the far corner of the street. Once there, she inched up close to the last house and peeked back around, cursing a fashion that dictated young ladies wear pale colors and big puffed skirts. She was undeniably visible.

Her position afforded her the opportunity to watch the carriage draw around to wait, having disgorged its contents. Sophronia ruminated. *Lord Ambrose, who does he belong to? Is he a rove like Professor Braithwope or is this a hive house? How do I find out? I don't even know which part of London I'm in.* A number of fashionably dressed individuals came and went, as if it were visiting hours. The visitors were not dressed for dinner, and they did not stay long. Sophronia observed for some three-quarters of an hour, hoping for an indication of...something.

Eventually, a young man in full evening dress sauntered up to the house. He had a nondescript face, good-looking enough, with a clean, straight nose and no mustache. He took off his hat to salute whoever opened the door. In the light cast by the hallway, Sophronia recognized him. He was the man who'd tried to get the prototype from Monique and the Pickleman at Petunia's ball. The man from Westminster. Sophronia had thought him a government employee, but now it was clear that this man was a Westminster *Hive* drone and this was the hive house. Lord Ambrose must be a member as well. The hive wanted Dimity and Pillover. *Oh, dear, I did hope it was the Picklemen. Vampires complicate matters, being all supernatural and hard to sneak around.* Clearly, the vampires wanted to press matters with Dimity's parents. The Plumleigh-Teignmotts must be the only ones who knew how to make the guidance valves. The vampires wanted to either manufacture and sell the technology or destroy it.

Sophronia was wise enough not to take on a hive alone and without preparation. Dimity and Pillover were on their own until she could return with reinforcements. Sophronia could only hope that her two friends would be of no use to the vampires dead. *Oh, Dimity, please remember some of your training.*

She turned her attention to hiring transport, but the roadways were still—not a single hansom to be seen. Then a fly came barreling down the cross street, drawn by matched white geldings and driven by two dandies of the highest order. One might even have called them fops, their trousers were so loud and their collar points so high. Sophronia glanced away; she did not want to be thought a light skirt. She had no time for shenanigans.

To her horror, the fly drew up next to her.

"What ho, little miss!" yodeled one of the dandies. His hair was a lovely pale gold, his face almost iridescent in the moonlight. He wore an outfit of silver and royal blue, accented with pure white.

The other, a young man with ebony skin like Soap, although with none of Soap's streetside aura, looked to his companion. "My lord, we are very close to Westminster. Should we be stopping in their territory?" His outfit was all soft peaches and dove grays with cream, a perfect complement to the other's clear colors.

"For a brief moment, I think, Pilpo, dear. They are accustomed to my sport."

"But, my lord..."

The gold-haired dandy smiled at Sophronia, showing a hint of fang.

*I spend my whole life without vampires, and in the space of one year I've met far too many.*

"One of Mademoiselle Geraldine's girls, methinks," he said. "You have the *aura*."

Sophronia blinked up at him, shocked.

"My dear child, did you think you and yours were the only players?"

Sophronia narrowed her eyes in the direction of the hive house.

"And Westminster," the vampire added, confirming her suspicions.

Sophronia said, "And Bunson's, and the Picklemen, and the potentate, and now—who, my dear sir, are *you*? If you will excuse my asking directly."

"Oh, I'm not *important*. Would you like a lift, little *lavender bud*?"

Sophronia considered this. *Lavender bud?*

The vampire dandy said, "Normally, my *dear* dewdrop, I prefer not to interfere. It's so much more *fun* to observe. But even I'm loath to leave an innocent young lady alone and entirely without protection on the streets of gay London-town."

Sophronia thought on the matter. She might be getting herself into more trouble, accepting a lift from a strange vampire—well dressed though he might be. But he wasn't threatening, and Dimity and Pillover desperately needed her. Besides, this man was well informed. Perhaps he might engage in some lucrative conversation.

With a nod, she allowed herself to be helped in by the other dandy, who took up position on the footman's perch of the fly, allowing Sophronia to sit next to the driver. Said driver gave her a charming, if fanged, smile, and whipped the horse into a trot.

## HOW TO BE A DANDY

The foppish vampire was not very forthcoming, although he found Sophronia's attempts to extract information highly diverting.

"Are you acquainted with the members of that household?" was her first foray, alluding to the Westminster Hive as they sprang down the street.

He rebutted with, "The house on the corner? Not at *all*, sweet almond flower."

"No, the house in the middle. The one with the birches at the front."

"I know them by *reputation*, of course, but who doesn't?"

Sophronia raised her eyebrows at him. "Me. I don't."

"Oh, my dear sugarplum, aren't you *precious*."

"Westminster Hive. Lord Ambrose. That's what I've got so far. I don't suppose . . ." She trailed off hopefully. He seemed like such a nice jolly fellow.

The nice jolly fellow gave a nice jolly laugh. "Curious as a kitten. Aren't you, puss? No, dear, no. I think a lift is more than enough interference. As I said, I do try not to participate as a rule. Although, this is unusual hive behavior for so *early* in the Season. What *are* they about?"

Sophronia said, hoping for an exchange, "I think it's all to do with Mr. Giffard's new dirigible."

"Do you indeed? And how is poor Aloysius Braithwope?"

"Not well, last I heard."

"Ah, dear, that's only to be expected with such an unfortunate mustachio."

"You know him?"

"We *all* know one another, puss-puss."

"What do you want?" Sophronia was moved to exasperation.

"Me? Stockings and breeches to come back into fashion. I do so miss seeing a man's calves."

Sophronia swallowed down a startled giggle as the fly drew up in front of Walsingham House Hotel. "No, *vampires*. What do you vampires want?"

The blond fop looked at her, cocking his beautiful head to one side like a bird. "The same thing you want, my kitten."

*What do I want, right now? Information. Is that all the vampires are after? Information.*

Pilpo jumped down and offered her his hand. A sweet flash of a smile crossed his face.

Sophronia stepped down and turned back to look up into the fly.

"There's a difference between us, you realize?"

"Indeed? Oh, *please* enlighten me, kitten." The vampire's blue eyes sparkled in excitement.

"I only want information. You people want to control it."

The blond threw his head back and laughed. "So wise for one so young. Most diverting! I must remember you, *little puss-puss*. Normally, I don't bother with the fairer sex. I think I might make an exception in your case."

"Thank you for the compliment, but I'd really rather you didn't." Sophronia hadn't meant to catch his eye. The last thing she needed was a vampire interfering in her life.

"Now, now, don't close all your doors, kitten. When you are finished, remember me. I believe I might even take on the potentate for your indenture. Such sharp little claws as Geraldine's can provide will look lovely on you, and *only* I can make certain that they have diamond sparkles."

Sophronia said nothing to that. He was right, best not to close all doors. After all, she was only recently considering how expensive her chosen profession might be. Wealthy patrons were not easy to come by, and she had a feeling this one would at least not expect a connubial relationship.

She said only, "Thank you very much for the lift, kind sir."

"I am at your disposal, kitten."

He was away before she could ask his name or his consequence. Nor, she realized, had she been afforded the opportunity to give him hers. *I suppose he will know how to find me, if he wants.*

Sophronia trotted up the steps and back into the hotel, the odd encounter forgotten as she concentrated on the task at hand.

\*　　\*　　\*

The ball was still in full sway, which was odd to Sophronia. She had the feeling ages must have passed, but a lively reel vibrated the floorboards of the Frond, and the celebration had continued despite her. She spotted Lady Linette instantly. The music teacher wore a bright pea-green-and-pink gown, vivid among the pastels of the young ladies. She was in conference with the potentate and Captain Niall. They all had worried expressions on their faces, and Sophronia wondered if her absence had been noted.

She was making her way over to them when a hand grabbed her arm.

"Where have you been?" hissed Felix.

"Not now, Lord Mersey!"

"You cut me. On the dance floor. Again. Miss Temminnick, you owe me an explanation."

Frustrated, Sophronia merely said, "Come with me if you must. I only have time to say this once."

They pushed their way through the crowd, ending up in front of the group of teachers.

Sophronia curtsied. "Lady Linette, Captain Niall, and Mr. Potentate, sir, please excuse the interruption."

"Yes, Miss Temminnick?"

"Dimity and Pillover Plumleigh-Teignmott have been kidnapped by the Westminster vampire hive."

"Miss Temminnick, what a shocking accusation!" Lady Linette clasped her hand to her breast.

*Good technique*, thought Sophronia.

271

The potentate looked down at her out of sharp green eyes as if she were some kind of bug in his tea. "I highly doubt that. Why on earth would the hive involve itself? I have everything under control."

"Have you any evidence?" asked Captain Niall, looking less doubtful.

"Only my own eyes. I followed Lord Ambrose's carriage to the house itself."

"The *hive* house? You can't possibly know its location." The potentate would not believe a word of it.

"It wasn't difficult. I simply used the skills I have been taught. I know it's the hive because I recognized some of the members."

"Prove it!" demanded the potentate.

Quietly, cautious of being overheard, Sophronia described the hive house in detail, including the birches in front and the nondescript nature of the street. She did not recount her odd encounter with the fop vampire. Somehow she did not think this would help her cause.

"That proves nothing," said the potentate, "except that this child somehow knows what the Westminster Hive looks like."

"And how would she know that, if she hadn't visited it?" Felix wanted to know. He believed her. But then Sophronia was beginning to suspect that he would automatically believe the worst of any vampire.

The potentate looked down his long nose at the boy. "And who, may I ask, are *you*?"

"Golborne, sir, Lord Mersey."

"Picklemen's get? I should have known they'd be mixed up in

this." The potentate turned on Sophronia. "You working for them, little girl?"

Lady Linette stepped in at that. "My Lord Potentate! Miss Temminnick is only at the beginning of her training. She isn't *working* for anyone...yet!"

The potentate was unconvinced. Glancing over the crowd of dancers, he said, "Ah, look, there's Ambrose. He can sort this out."

Lord Ambrose was lurking at the edge of the crowd, looking as if he had never left. The potentate summoned him over with a rude crook of the finger. The other vampire responded, a pleasant expression on his handsome face.

Of course, Lord Ambrose denied the accusation. "The Plumleigh-Teignmott children, you say? I suspect the father will have removed them, Lady Linette. I understand he is back working with the Picklemen."

"No!" gasped Lady Linette. "He never. His wife would never countenance it!"

"Oh, yes, indeed. She's helping." The handsome vampire shook his head in mock regret. "Shrimpdittle has been most forthcoming. I excused myself to read this report on his interrogation." His lip curled. "He claims the Plumleigh-Teignmotts are intending mass production of the crystalline guidance valves for sale to the British market. The Picklemen want controlling concerns." He handed over a bit of rolled parchment paper. "I bet that upsets the government's plans, eh, Potentate?"

Sophronia glanced at Felix. The boy's face was inscrutable.

She realized that if the Picklemen were backing Dimity's

parents' research, then the Westminster Hive had been trying to stop them all along. They'd used Monique to try to steal the original prototype months ago, and when that didn't work, they'd started trying to kidnap Dimity and Pillover. *But my school and the potentate are also involved. Are they mere bystanders, simply trying to ensure that the technology works properly? Or are they trying to gain control of the valves for the Shadow Council and the British government?* The Picklemen stood to make a great deal of money off those valves and control who had access to them. Westminster Hive clearly didn't like that idea and obviously didn't trust the potentate to put a stop to it. So they were trying to get hold of the valve technology themselves. Even if vampires could never travel in the aetherosphere, Sophronia suspected they would love to control which humans could.

She opened her mouth to protest, to explain this, but Lady Linette shushed her firmly. Good manners forced Sophronia into disgruntled silence.

Lady Linette perused the contents of Shrimpdittle's confession. "I should think Mrs. Plumleigh-Teignmott would at least have notified me of the family's intent to remove the children from my supervision."

"You know scientists, easily distracted."

Lady Linette looked again at the paper. "Are they really sending Shrimpdittle into exile?"

Lord Ambrose nodded. "The continent, as I understand."

"Ah, well, I suppose he couldn't be allowed to teach anymore."

Sophronia felt an intense sensation of relief. At least Shrimpdittle wasn't to be imprisoned or hanged, simply consigned to the wilds of Switzerland. She glared at Lord Ambrose. *I could confront him directly, accuse him of the kidnapping, but they're bound to believe an adult over me. I've no real proof.*

*Blast good manners.* She made the attempt. "But I saw—"

"You were obviously mistaken," interrupted Lord Ambrose.

Sister Mattie entered the ball and came bustling over to them. "My dears, Professor Braithwope is awake and lucid. He is asking for you, My Lord Potentate."

Lady Linette nodded. "You'd best get along, then, my lord."

The potentate agreed. "Ambrose?"

"Oh, no, I'll remain here. A ball with such tempting morsels is so very diverting."

Lady Linette slapped his arm flirtatiously with her fan. "Now, now, keep your fangs to yourself, good sir."

Lord Ambrose bowed to her. "Of course, dear lady, but perhaps *you* would honor me with a dance?"

"La, sir, how charming."

He whirled her off onto the floor, both of them dancing expertly.

Sophronia realized she was on her own in mounting a rescue attempt. She began cataloging her options. *I require supplies and a change of clothes.* There was nothing for it; she would have to return to the airship. *Plus, I'll need the hive house's actual address.* She looked at Captain Niall. The werewolf was the only adult who might help her. *I'll wager he knows the location.* She started planning. *Sidheag would be useful as well.*

"Would you mind a little company on your drive back?" Sophronia looked with wide eyes at Sister Mattie. "I find I am rather bored with this ball."

Everyone looked at her as though they had forgotten her existence.

Sister Mattie said, "Are you certain, dear? It looks like quite the treat." Her tone was wistful.

Felix protested as well. "But I had two more dances with you."

"How kind you are, dear Lord Mersey, but another time? Perhaps you might escort me out?" Sophronia used her best wheedling tone.

Felix had no choice. As a gentleman, he could do nothing but offer her his arm. He did so with grace if not alacrity.

Sophronia added, "And I believe Lady Kingair would also like to depart."

Captain Niall, who was looking at Sophronia out of the corner of his eye, said, "I think I'll be going as well."

The potentate offered Sister Mattie his arm, and they pushed through the crowd. Captain Niall followed, grabbing at Sidheag's sleeve in a lightning-fast move.

Sidheag left off her position, lurking partnerless near a potted palm, and trailed along with only mild confusion. She was game for anything that removed her from a ball. Plus, as she had once said to Sophronia, "Life's always more interesting when I chum about with you."

"What's going on?" She craned her neck back and whispered to Sophronia.

"I'll explain when we're more secure." Sophronia glanced meaningfully at the potentate's back.

"Where's Dimity?" Sidheag asked.

"Otherwise occupied."

"Oh, dear."

"Exactly."

Sophronia turned to her escort and said in a low voice, "Lord Mersey, I know *you* believe my story." She batted her eyelashes at him purposefully. "I was thinking there might be others who would be . . . interested . . . in Dimity's current location."

Felix blinked at her.

*Lord save me*, thought Sophronia, *from boys without training.* She nudged him with her elbow. "You know. *Others.*"

"Oh, yes, I see. Well, perhaps after the ball Father might, or . . ." Felix trailed off, Sophronia's expression telling him she was profoundly disappointed. "Perhaps sooner," he amended his speech.

They reached the street where the potentate's carriage—a landau with footmen in full royal livery—stood waiting for them.

With the potentate, Sister Mattie, and Sidheag safely ensconced within, Captain Niall stood patiently waiting to hand Sophronia up. He was looking particularly well, especially by comparison to the werewolves from earlier that evening. Certainly his top hat was tied on, but he'd forgone the ubiquitous greatcoat for an impeccable black velvet cutaway jacket and matched trousers with a cream brocade waistcoat. His dark hair, longer than was fashionable, was brushed to silken, glossy waves. No wonder young ladies swooned. Felix was handsome in his brooding way, but next to Captain Niall he was boyish.

Sophronia leaned in and kissed Felix gently on the cheek, a reward for good behavior. "Thank you, Felix, for your understanding and your help." She lowered her eyelashes prettily.

"Ria, you must be the most confusing girl I've ever met. You know I'm mad for you?"

"How kind of you to say." Sophronia gave her hand to the werewolf and he assisted her inside.

"Good hunting?" commented Sidheag, watching Felix's retreating back as Sophronia settled in next to her.

"Son of a duke" was Sophronia's only comment.

The drive back to Hyde Park was fast, tense, and uncomfortable. The potentate spent most of the time lecturing Sophronia on bandying accusations about without proper foundation.

"Imagine a hive interfering in matters of state! Even Westminster wouldn't dare. You are a stupid, fanciful child. Accusing vampires willfully like that. You've been corrupted by association with that Golborne boy!"

Sister Mattie at first didn't understand what was happening and then tried to defend Sophronia. "But the embroidered cushions did suggest the hive objected. I mean, our intelligencer inside, she indicated that they were upset with Picklemen actions."

Sophronia perked up at that statement. *So the embroidery was code—as I thought—detailing the danger between Westminster and the Picklemen. A spy from Mademoiselle Geraldine's was trying to warn us from inside the hive. But when Madame Spetuna abandoned her post to infiltrate the flywaymen, there was no one to transport the cushions, and the warnings didn't make it in time.*

But the potentate dismissed this evidence. "Poppycock! I cannot believe they would act without at least consulting me!"

Eventually, Sister Mattie merely tried to mollify him with platitudes. "Please, My Lord Potentate, try to remember that a pumpkin divided against itself cannot gourd!"

Sidheag followed the whole conversation in increasing bemusement, having no idea what was going on. Captain Niall held his tongue, stiff and uncomfortable in a vampire's carriage. When they arrived back at the airship, the werewolf got out and skulked away into the night. Sophronia had no doubt he would wait for them groundside. He was no fool, Captain Niall.

Back on board, the potentate strode off to visit Professor Braithwope with one last sharp reprimand in Sophronia's direction.

"You keep your opinions to yourself, little girl!"

Sister Mattie looked at her, face wrinkled with worry. "I'll endeavor to keep him occupied, dears. But please remember, a lily cannot change its spots."

As soon as it was safe to speak, Sidheag turned to Sophronia in frustration.

"What on earth is going on?"

"I don't think much of our school's patron, I'll tell you that much," said Sophronia, glaring at the vampire's retreating back and sticking her tongue out at it childishly.

"Sophronia!"

"I'll explain while we change. We have a rescue to mount and a hive house to infiltrate."

"What?"

"Come on, please!"

"What are we changing into?" Sidheag asked as they hurried back to their rooms.

Sophronia thought about her encounter with the fashionable blond vampire. "Dandies. We need to look like dandies."

Sidheag pursed her lips. "I'm *not* cutting my hair."

They did their best with the disguises, dressing in a combination of Sidheag's trousers and their own lace under-blouses and velvet vests. Real dandies would have had better-fitting clothing, not to mention superior cravats. The two girls ended up looking like something that came from an underfunded circus.

"We are ridiculous." Sidheag adjusted her coat in the mirror. "And you don't have a jacket."

"Preshea has one of those new little short ones, you know, like the bullfighters of Spain." Sophronia went off on a raid, returning with a bright red-and-gold bolero of which Preshea was particularly proud. Sophronia put it on.

"God's teeth," said Sidheag succinctly.

They did look preposterous, but Sophronia felt that would throw people off if they were caught. "Here, wrap this blue scarf around your waist, and I'll do the same with Dimity's fringed yellow one, and we can say we have been attending a fancy dress ball."

Sidheag did as she was told. "What will Captain Niall think of us?"

"Does that matter, so long as he gets us there? I do hope we have lessons soon on how to memorize locations. I'm annoyed with myself for not knowing how to get back to the hive."

"Better to worry about how absurd we look! No one in their right mind would let us into their house. Wait, hive? What *hive?*"

Sophronia explained about Dimity and Pillover being kid-napped by Lord Ambrose and the Westminster Hive.

"I think the vampires want to force their parents to either stop making the guidance valves altogether or hand control of the technology over to the hive. Dimity's parents are reportedly working for the Picklemen, and the vampires don't trust Pickle-men. Nor do I. For that matter, I just don't trust any of them." While she talked, she stashed anything she could think of that might be useful about her person—smelling salts in the waist-coat pocket, sewing scissors down the front of her corset, rib-bon around her wrist, and a perfume-soaked handkerchief up one sleeve.

"I'm confused. Sabotage or not, this is clearly a technology vampires canna utilize."

"I think that's why they're panicking. They're trying to ensure this mode of travel is under their influence."

Sidheag understood at that. "Can't have the prey bouncing about through the aetherosphere all willy-nilly, now can they?"

"Sidheag, you think like a predator."

The Lady of Kingair glowed in pleasure. "Thank you very much, Sophronia. What a nice thing to say."

They were discussing whether to climb around the outside of the ship or save time by running the inside corridors but risk the mechanical alarm when Vieve showed up.

"What's going on?" demanded the scamp.

"Get us to engineering fast and I'll tell you," replied Sophronia.

"My pleasure." Vieve whipped out her obstructor.

As they negotiated the halls at a jog, blasting one mechanical after another, Sophronia panted out her story again.

Vieve believed her without question. "Makes far more sense for the vampires to want to influence Dimity's parents than old Ambrose's excuse. Can't understand why Lady Linette would believe him."

Sophronia said, "This school has a vampire patron and a vampire teacher. Lady Linette *wants* to believe him. She wants to believe the potentate has control over the hives and that they aren't kidnapping her students on a whim. I think Sister Mattie and Professor Braithwope, were he capable, are on our side. Captain Niall certainly is."

"He would be. Werewolves always suspect vampires." Vieve nodded gravely.

The sooties, after their conquest of the upper atmosphere, were mostly resting. A minimal crew kept the boilers at temperature—maintaining a steady position, heat for the residential sections, and power to the mechanicals.

The three girls dressed as boys clattered in and through the relative quiet without raising any suspicion. Even if two of them looked like an operatic take on bull-herding Spaniards.

Sophronia hoped Soap was also asleep; somehow she knew he'd be difficult if he found out what she was up to.

"Crikey, don't you two look as fancy as fleas' eyebrows!" said Soap, appearing behind her.

"Yes, well, it's necessary." Sophronia was short with her friend.

"Necessary? Those trousers are awful tight." Soap's eyes were wide. "Not that you don't fill them out right, miss." He lost his train of thought. "Oh, blast it."

Sophronia came to his rescue. "We need to be able to cast doubt on a third party, in case we're caught."

"Caught doing what, exactly?" Soap demanded.

Vieve, little blabbermouth, answered him brightly, "Infiltrating a hive house."

Soap's dark eyes went worried. "Miss, is that a good idea?"

Sophronia gave up keeping him out of it. "No. It's a dangerous, vampire-riddled mission, but they have kidnapped Dimity and Pillover."

"I'm coming," said Soap instantly.

"Now, Soap, you haven't the training." But Sophronia was already reconfiguring her plan to include him.

"And you aren't finished with yours. At least I've experienced life." The boy was already stripping out of his coal apron.

"Oh, very well. No time to argue. I'm worried about Dimity. She's good but only in short bursts. Plus, can you imagine her in a hive house? All that loose blood lying about."

Soap said, "Coming, Vieve?"

Vieve shook her head. "Off-ship adventuring is not for me anymore. I'd sooner stay behind and provide the gadgets."

Sophronia was relieved at that; she really would have had to put her foot down. At seventeen, Soap was grown and able to decide for himself. Vieve was too young to go breaking into vampire hives and too cheeky to take such things seriously.

The three went out the floor hatch, shimmying down the rope ladder.

"So," said Soap, "where exactly are we going, and how do we get there?"

"My questions exactly," said Captain Niall, coming up behind them out of the dark.

Sophronia looked at him expectantly. "Westminster Hive. Coming, sir?"

"Oh, *really*, young lady!" He had changed out of his evening dress to his customary greatcoat.

Sophronia blinked at him.

"Dressed like that?"

*Blink, blink, blink.*

"With a sootie and Lady Kingair?"

"Someone has to get Dimity and Pillover out, sir. And you can't do it alone. Now, can you?"

"Who said I—"

Sidheag interrupted. "He couldn't do it regardless. The vampires would know the moment a wolf entered their hive."

Sophronia made herself look expectant and wide-eyed. "But he can *get* us there. Sir, you *have* to help."

"I do?"

"You believe me."

"I do." The werewolf was defeated by such logic.

"And you know where it is, don't you?"

"I do." Captain Niall sighed. "I'm going to get in a great deal of trouble for this. Very well, hop on." With that, he changed form.

Werewolf change is an unpleasant thing to watch, and poor Soap had never seen it before. He yelped as the handsome captain went from being a fine specimen of manhood to a large, rangy wolf with a top hat tied to his head, squatting in a pool of fallen greatcoat.

Sophronia tried not to hear the way Captain Niall's bones broke and knit back together with crunching noises. She tried not to see the way the man's silky hair grew down and became fur, spreading like mold over his body.

Soap was quietly and efficiently sick behind a pile of cast-iron pilings. He bravely returned once the change was complete, although he was distinctly uncomfortable with the alteration. "Oh, miss, do we have to ride *that*?"

Sophronia, who had ridden a wolf only once before, pretended confidence. "It's actually a pleasant way to travel."

"I doubt that, miss."

"You can go in the middle."

If Soap felt his manliness in question over such an offer, he didn't say so.

Sophronia climbed up front, her legs tucked up high. She gripped Captain Niall's furry neck with her knees and his ruff with her hands. Soap climbed on after, wrapping both arms around her waist in a death grip. It was very intimate, especially with only a few layers of masculine clothing between them. However, Soap seemed too frightened to take advantage of the situation. Sidheag, accustomed to werewolf transport, took the rear, over the beast's haunches, the most difficult seat to maintain. She gripped Soap's waist in turn. The wolf was only just big enough, but he was certainly strong enough, and he took off at a pace more rapid than any horse could manage.

# THE 16TH TEST

## MISBEHAVING WITH PURPOSE

Captain Niall carried them directly to the hive. Sophronia recognized the neighborhood instantly. He was wise enough to go nowhere near the front door but let them off at a back alley near the kitchen entrance, where merchants delivered goods and servants came and went.

Sophronia marshaled her troops. "Soap, would you go in the back? We will need a warning in case of unexpected visitors. If anyone sees you, how about pretending you're there to clean the chimneys?"

"At this hour?"

"Best I can think up on short notice. Sidheag and I are going in the front."

"Barefaced?" Sidheag protested.

"Can you think of a better plan?"

"Who do we represent?" Sidheag asked.

"We're dandy drones of a local rove vampire. We've been

sent to find out what's going on. We heard they kidnapped children, and our master does not approve. It's worth a try."

Captain Niall, still in wolf form, looked very worried.

Sophronia, thinking herself quite daring at giving a teacher instructions, even if he did look a bit doglike, said, "If you could stay to assist the retreat, Captain? Or go get the authorities, if you think they would come. Your decision."

The werewolf sat back on his haunches with an air of decisiveness. He'd wait.

"He can't carry five of us," protested Sidheag. "I mean, if we are, by some miracle, successful in retrieving Dimity and Pillover."

The werewolf growled.

Sidheag understood wolf growls. "Fine, he *can* carry five of us, but five of us would not be able to fit on top of him."

Sophronia waved a dismissive hand. "We'll figure that out later. We really should be getting on."

The two girls left the alley and made their way down the street to the front door of the Westminster Hive.

Sophronia practiced her walk and her mannerisms, doing her best to be a man of fashion. Sidheag, who looked more like a man, also already walked like one. Sophronia thought they might have applied fake mustaches to good effect, but otherwise they weren't bad. *If only our clothes fit better.*

They strode up the steps and pulled the bell rope.

A handsome footman opened the door. "Yes?" His eyebrows raised up nearly into his hairline at the sight before him. "...Sirs?"

"We have come to pay a call," announced Sophronia, deepening her voice.

"Indeed. And who has sent you?"

Sophronia wiggled her fingers in dismissal. "Oh, *you* know."

The footman pursed his lips, eyeing their attire. "Lord Akeldama *will* have his little jokes."

Sophronia nodded, connecting the dandy vampire to the name. Professor Braithwope had mentioned that name in class recently. *What had he said? Oh, yes, that Lord Akeldama was frivolous but had standing.*

"Oh, yes, he does like jokes." She twirled about slightly.

The footman frowned. "Are you in your cups? She won't like that, you know. It hasn't been a successful attempt. She's out of humor."

Sophronia stopped twirling. "He wants to know what's going on."

"He always does. He's usually more subtle about it."

Sophronia only looked up at the ceiling of the hallway as if bored by the conversation.

"Are you a new drone?" the footman pressed.

Silence.

"I suppose you had best come in. Who shall I say has called?"

"Lord Dingleproops and Lord Mersey," said Sophronia.

"Sounds like him," said the footman.

He took them into the front parlor. "Wait here, if you please? She's almost done with her current."

Sophronia and Sidheag waited. The door was left slightly ajar. They watched in horror as two other footmen walked by carrying the comatose form of a young lady with thick honey-brown hair.

"Pity," one was saying. "She had such neat stitches."

The girl's neck was savaged, her hair matted with blood.

Sophronia put a hand to her own mouth in horror, thinking for one terrified moment that it was Dimity.

"She will keep trying for a new queen. I think she's lost the ability."

"Wouldn't let *her* hear you say that if I were you."

Sidheag grasped Sophronia supportively by the arm. "Not Dimity," she whispered.

"No, the dress is too somber." Sophronia felt like she could breathe again.

The hallway cleared. A moment later they heard a familiar voice say, "I should return right away! It is, after all, *my* ball. Thank the countess for me, would you please? Such a delightful lady. So sorry the metamorphosis failed. It's nice to know she has everything to hand. Or should I say, to fang?" A forced giggle.

Sophronia and Sidheag exchanged terrified glances. "Monique!"

They turned their backs to the open parlor door.

Monique, unfortunately, noticed that the vampire's next callers were two young men of fashion waiting in the front parlor.

"Well, *good evening*, gentlemen! I do hope your audience is as enjoyable as mine."

Sophronia pulled out her handkerchief. *Never be without one, Lady Linette always says. So wise.* She pretended a coughing fit into it and turned slightly to wave her free hand at Monique.

"Oh, dear, sir, are you unwell?" Monique smiled flirtatiously.

Sidheag, meanwhile, bent down to buff a bit of lint off her boot.

"Simply a touch of the consumption, miss," said Sophronia gruffly into her handkerchief.

"Oh, well, do take care." Monique looked as though she might enter the room to converse further, but the footman, standing behind her, cleared his throat.

"Oh, yes, of course *she* is waiting. Lovely to meet you, gentlemen. Oh, dear, I suppose we haven't met. I'm Monique de Pelouse." Monique was executing the confused-but-coy-and-charming maneuver.

Sophronia and Sidheag both bowed. Sidheag kept her head turned away. Sophronia kept her handkerchief pressed to the lower half of her face.

The footman said sharply, "Miss!"

Monique sparkled at them. "Well, any friend of the countess's is a friend of mine. I'm having a ball at this very moment at Walsingham House, if you gentlemen would like to join me there later? You'd be more than welcome."

Sophronia murmured an assent.

Monique clapped her hands. "Capital. Now, do pardon me?" She drifted away.

The footman returned after letting her out into the night.

Sophronia said, in a shocked tone, "Who was *that* forward bit of baggage?"

The footman was disapproving. "New drone, so green. My apologies, gentlemen. We thought witnessing metamorphosis would dampen her enthusiasm. The metamorphosis failed, and she's as bad as ever."

Sophronia and Sidheag exchanged startled looks. *Monique has found herself a new patron in the Westminster Hive already? Powerful connection. She must be involved in Dimity and Pillover's kidnapping.*

Sophronia nodded sympathetically to the footman. "Our condolences on the loss of the female drone."

"Poor girl. A very talented embroiderer, so fast. I've never seen one better or more obsessed with decorating throw pillows."

*Oh, no,* Sophronia thought, *the school's spy. The intelligencer who tried to warn us with embroidered cushions. Did the hive figure out she was a spy and kill her in the guise of metamorphosis?* She felt a cold sweat spring up all over her body and hoped vampires couldn't smell fear.

"It's what happens." The footman looked philosophical. "Haven't made a new queen in decades. Not likely to change with drones like that Miss Pelouse. She needs a good deal of refinement."

Sophronia said sagely, "They always do."

The footman gave her a look that suggested a man in a red bolero ought not to comment on anyone else's flaws.

Sophronia was defensive. "We came from a fancy dress ball, my good man."

He looked mollified.

"No time to change," added Sidheag.

Sophronia gave her a quelling look. That was more than enough. Gentlemen should not have to explain themselves to footmen! Even if they were all drones. The footman hadn't earned his rank yet; the dandies had.

The footman led them to the rear of the hive. The house

291

was remarkable, all beautiful artwork, modern furnishings, inventions of great worth, and priceless Persian rugs. The staff, gliding to and fro in expensive black-buttoned shoes and starched aprons, were all young and beautiful. The Westminster Hive, whatever else might be said of it, certainly had taste. Monique would fit right in, visually at least. Yet there was something about the place that troubled Sophronia. It felt like spoiled milk, only less smelly. All that plush carpeting muffled sound so that the servants moved noiselessly. And then there was the dead embroidering agent to consider. But it wasn't only the silence, or that gruesome body; there was something missing.

In the back parlor sat a beautiful, plump woman, who was the focus of a great deal of attention. To her left stood a tall, reedy man with a reluctant hairline and to her right... Dimity and Pillover. Dimity was stretched out in a dead faint on a velvet ottoman. Pillover, white-faced and trembling, was taking tea.

Sophronia realized what had been bothering her so much about the hive house: there were no tracks, no faint noises of background steam, and no mechanicals. No mechanicals *at all*. The staff was entirely human. Sophronia had never seen anything like it in all her life.

The footman announced them. "Lord Dingleproops and Lord Mersey to call, my lady."

Pillover gasped and stared at Sophronia and Sidheag. It was a small mistake, since his shock might be attributed to the egregiousness of their attire rather than previous acquaintance.

The plump woman could only be the Westminster Hive queen, Countess Nadasdy. She was impeccably dressed to the height of style. She had on a gown with a very large skirt and a very tight bodice, although she was a tad round for such an outfit. She looked, Sophronia felt, a little like a milkmaid from a dairy farm—fond of cheese. Her cheeks were rosy and her manners light and gay, but she only seemed frivolous; those cornflower-blue eyes saw everything.

"Good evening, gentlemen. Welcome." Her voice was warm and soft, very ladylike.

Sophronia and Sidheag bowed deeply.

"Good evening, Countess," said Sophronia. "Our master tenders his warmest regards. Our condolences on your recent"—she paused delicately—"mis-fang."

"Oh, thank you. And thank him for me, will you please? Pity he could not send more appropriately dressed messengers." The woman tittered at her own insult.

"We were nearest to your abode when he heard the news. He felt time was pressing and sent us on immediately. We were attending a fancy dress ball over yonder." Sophronia waggled a hand in an unspecified direction. "Please excuse our eccentricity."

"Yes?" said the countess. "And what is his lordship's vaunted news? I did not publicize my intent to bite. Failure is all too often the outcome this century." Her gentleman companion put a consoling hand on her shoulder. She shrugged him off.

"Ah, no, you are correct—he did not know of that. No, he understands you have visitors."

"Oh?"

Sophronia wandered over to the couch, took out the smelling salts from her waistcoat pocket, and administered them to Dimity. None of the vampires objected. Dimity revived only to squawk at Sophronia—suddenly there and so peculiarly dressed.

"Hush now, child," condescended Sophronia.

Dimity's eyes widened, but she remembered her training and hushed, sitting fully upright.

Sophronia returned to stand next to Sidheag, crossing her arms. "Should you be involving yourself to such an extent? Kidnapping is a tad rude, wouldn't you say?"

The countess moved to sit next to the revived Dimity and placed a white hand on the girl's arm. Dimity shivered and looked down at her lap.

"Such harsh vocabulary, Lord Dingleproops. We merely *borrowed* them for a little. Didn't we, dears? And we've been having a lovely time of it, haven't we? So educational. Not every mortal gets a chance to witness metamorphosis. Even an unsuccessful metamorphosis." The countess dabbed at her mouth with an embroidered handkerchief as if remembering the blood that had recently been there.

Dimity looked as if she might faint again.

At which moment the parlor door burst open and Soap, carrying all those things needed to clean a chimney and a good deal more besides, clattered inside. He was covered in even more soot than usual, shedding it as he walked.

The countess let out a small scream. "My carpets!"

Sophronia was instantly on her guard. Soap wouldn't make a fuss unless he wanted to warn them of something.

The sootie doffed his cap at the august personages. "Evening, all. I'm here for the chimneys. Said I was to start with this room, if that suits."

"No, that certainly does *not* suit," said the countess.

"But madam, skinny as a *pickled gherkin*, I am. I fits, I assure you."

*Oh, dear,* thought Sophronia, picking up on Soap's hint, *we've got Picklemen coming.*

Mild chaos ensued, with the countess's staff trying to hustle Soap out of the room, struggling to stop him from shedding further. Soap dodged them and clanged loudly. The countess issued increasingly strident instructions.

Sophronia and Sidheag took the opportunity to shift closer to Dimity and Pillover.

"What are you doing here?" mouthed Dimity at them.

Sophronia made a small shushing gesture.

Into the madness strode a tall, elderly gentleman in a top hat with a band of green about it. He was followed by three similarly dressed men, a short lady in somber grays carrying a reticule shaped like a metal sausage dog, and Felix Mersey.

Sophronia thought, *Now we're really in the soup.*

The handsome footman followed, looking harried. "I tried to stop them, Countess, but they insisted, and he *is* a duke."

The tall, reedy vampire placed himself before the countess protectively. "Duke Golborne!"

"Duke Hematol," replied the Pickleman.

*My goodness,* thought Sophronia, *Felix took my suggestion and involved his father, how remarkable. I may owe him another kiss.*

The short lady, who Sophronia realized was Madame Spetuna in a new disguise, put her reticule on the floor. The reticule puffed steam out its ears excitedly and trundled in Sophronia's direction, tail wagging back and forth.

The countess shrieked even louder. "Mechanimal! Get that repulsive thing out of my hive!"

Several of the staff left off chasing Soap and dove for Bumbersnoot, who scuttled away at a much greater speed than Sophronia had thought him capable of.

The countess began fanning herself vigorously with a gold lace fan. Then she squealed a third time, for Bumbersnoot bumped against her foot. A maid dove after him, upsetting a lamp with a stained-glass shade.

Duke Hematol reached out with supernatural reflexes and caught the lamp before it fell.

This display of otherworldly prowess upset the head Pickleman, Felix's father. He began to harangue the vampires, accusing them of all manner of dastardly deeds. The chief offense of which seemed to be trying to steal control of the crystalline guidance valve and its patents and production. Although they must have seen the body, no one cared about the girl who had been savaged. That, apparently, was ordinary vampire practice.

"We will not have Picklemen harnessing the aether and using it against us!" the Duke of Hematol said in defense of the vampire position. "Nor will we be ostracized from a technology that can change the course of human transport! We will not permit you to maintain sole control. Other possible applications for these valves are too dangerous." It was like a heated debate in the House of Lords.

Soap, shrugging off all attempts at dismissal, went over to the fireplace and began clattering up it, causing as much ruckus as possible—more, in fact, than one might expect.

Bumbersnoot charged about with Westminster drones in hot pursuit.

Sophronia gave Dimity the nod.

Dimity cast herself prostrate at the feet of the Picklemen, begging them for salvation from imminent vampire doom. She claimed all manner of mistreatment at the hands of the countess. The tea was lukewarm. The biscuits stale. The seat cushion lumpy. And a girl had been bitten to death right in front of her! She demanded she be rescued instantly and rounded out her complaints with a plaintive explanation that she was missing a ball!

Bumbersnoot trundled over Dimity's elegantly draped skirts, pausing to nibble at a large purple bow, before dodging the grasping hands of a footman.

Pillover began arguing with his sister. Protesting that, for being kidnapped, they had actually been treated fairly and the tea was excellent. Sophronia wasn't certain if he was aware of the plan, which currently consisted of causing as much pandemonium as possible, or if he simply had a brother's objection to a sister's fibs.

Felix had spent the past few minutes staring at Sophronia, his mouth agape. He looked like a fish. A handsome fish, but a fish nonetheless. However, Sophronia knew it was only a matter of time before he got his voice back and demanded to know why she was dressed like a circus dandy. She made frantic silencing motions at him.

The two dukes moved from debating to yelling. The Pickleman claimed that the vampires had no right to go around kidnapping children and forcing the hand of perfectly respectable scientists. The vampire protested that any technology that excluded the supernatural ought to be banned outright.

Meanwhile, Soap upended the entire coal scuttle onto the fireplace stoop with a tremendous crash.

Bumbersnoot scalded a chambermaid, who screamed.

The countess stood up, trembling in agitation. No doubt her well-run household had never before seen such chaos.

Sophronia began making gentlemanly noises about everyone turning potty, mostly to add to the kerfuffle. Sidheag joined her, both of them attempting to sound as upmarket and foppishly offended as possible.

"This is going too far," insisted Sidheag, waving a handkerchief about her face. "Coal dust, in a hive, can you believe it?"

Sophronia spoke through gritted teeth. "Agreed. It's like the Marquis of Inkuppy and that dyed-blue poodle he will insist on carrying everywhere. It can't be permitted."

"What's next, *green* champagne?"

"Or *leather* waistcoats?"

"Leather waistcoats! Dingle, you go too far!" Sidheag chortled, slapping Sophronia lightly on the arm. "Aren't you a *hoot*?"

The Pickleman duke turned sharp eyes from his vampire foe to the oddly dressed dandies. "And who, pray tell, are you?"

"Who we *are* is not important. Who we *represent* is the tick."

"Oh, and who might that be?"

Sophronia flashed her hand up into the air in a flamboyant gesture. "Who do you think?"

"Blast it. Is he also involved?"

"You know *he* doesn't like to involve himself. You may think of us as mere observers."

"Oh?"

Sophronia tilted her head coyly. "However, I believe we may have a solution to this madness. As a concerned third party, if we were remanded custody of the, um, borrowed property, perhaps you could all sort out the other aspects to your satisfaction, and our lord will return the children as needed."

"I thought Lord Akeldama didn't *like to involve himself.*" Both dukes looked suspicious.

Sophronia said, "He has an affection for children."

"Father," said Felix, tugging on the Pickleman's sleeve.

"Not now, boy!"

"But, sir—"

"Silence!"

"Yes, sir." Felix gave Sophronia a funny look.

Sophronia winked at him.

Strangely enough, the countess and the Picklemen actually considered Sophronia's offer.

One of the other Picklemen said, "How do we know those two drones aren't on your side, madam? Given that they are *still* working for a vampire. You would have a necessary alliance in place, after all."

The countess waved an airy hand. "Oh, Lord Akeldama is as autonomous as any rove can be."

"Certainly more than the potentate," added Sophronia, pushing her cause. That seemed the right thing to say.

Dimity started whining again, aiming to make herself

as unwelcome as possible. Pillover grumbled at her to stop whinging. They resumed bickering. The countess and the Pickleman duke ordered them to be silent. At the same time, Soap resumed banging around in the chimney. One of the footmen began trying to persuade him into a different room. Soap used all his wiry strength and stubbornness to protest.

Meanwhile, the rest of the household staff still chased Bumbersnoot. The mechanimal had taken refuge under a sofa and was resisting extraction by feather duster. Eventually, he singed the duster into obscurity, the room redolent with the smell of burned feathers. Sophronia gave a casual little whistle. He reemerged, upsetting a small marble statue that looked as if it might actually have come from ancient Rome, and headed toward Sophronia. He was diverted by a footman diving for him.

The mechanimal was steaming and hooting in excitement, and his little mechanical tail was going back and forth with great rapidity. Sophronia had never seen it move so quickly, which reminded her of something Vieve had said. *When his tail starts to wag as fast as a hummingbird's wings . . .*

*Oh, dear*, thought Sophronia. Madame Spetuna must have been running him practically everywhere over the last few days. Either that or Vieve's calculations were terribly off.

The dog's tail became a blur. *Ticktockticktock.*

She looked at Sidheag. "I think it's time we left."

Sidheag reached down and grabbed Pillover and Dimity up by the arms. Together the three of them backed toward Soap and the mound of chimney-cleaning tools.

The footman grabbed Bumbersnoot. Bumbersnoot spat out

a spiderlike object that was awfully familiar looking. It landed at the footman's feet, hissing ominously.

How much time had Vieve said they would have once the explosive was launched? Only a few minutes.

Soap tackled the footman, trying to wrestle Bumbersnoot away. The two fell and landed on top of the explosive spider. They rolled to one side, still very close.

Sophronia did the only thing she could think of. She tumbled forward in one of Lady Linette's rolls, grabbed the explosive, and hurled it at the queen of the Westminster Hive.

At the same time, Sidheag threw all of Soap's coal and equipment up into the air.

Soap whacked the footman upside the head with his coal scuttle, grabbed Bumbersnoot out of his grasp, and stood.

The spider exploded at the countess's feet. The room became nothing but steam, smoke, and coal dust.

By the time the chaos had cleared, the two dandies, the chimney sweep, the mechanimal, and both Plumleigh-Teignmott children had disappeared.


They had to move incredibly fast; vampires were much quicker than they could ever hope to be. Such vampires as these would be startled only for a moment. Sophronia was banking on them focusing on their queen and then getting caught up in the group of Picklemen and their own drones before they could give chase. She was also hoping Madame Spetuna might do something to help delay the enemy.

Sophronia's group burst out the front door of the hive house and ran down the street pell-mell. Dimity brought up the rear, as she was overburdened with a fluffy ball gown and a recent faint.

Captain Niall, still a wolf, bounded toward them. His attached top hat tilted coquettishly.

"Please, get Dimity and Pillover to safety," said Sophronia to the werewolf. "Sidheag, you, too. No point in all of us getting into trouble."

Without protest, the three climbed up onto Captain Niall's furry back. Behind them, a host of people poured forth from the hive, the likes of which had never been seen in the neighborhood before. The group included Picklemen, disheveled and covered in soot; Madame Spetuna, who seemed to be doing her best to trip everyone up; the Duke of Hematol, a vampire without hat or jacket; and a goodly collection of frantic drones. The queen herself, of course, could not leave the hive.

Captain Niall should have sprung away at that juncture, but he did not. He growled at Sophronia and Soap, who stood alone on the pavement. Soap clutched Bumbersnoot in his arms.

Sidheag explained the werewolf's behavior. "He won't leave anyone behind. It's not the military way."

"We don't fit!" protested Sophronia.

"I've an idea," said Dimity, hopping back off and pulling down her petticoat right there in a public street. *She's come a long way, has Dimity*, thought Sophronia proudly.

Dimity handed the stiff horsehair garment to Sophronia. "Use this as a sling." She climbed back on.

With a shrug, Sophronia and Soap sat down in the street on top of the skirt. Embarrassed by her own temerity, Sophronia curled about her tall friend, Bumbersnoot between them, wrapping up in the big purple petticoat like a cocoon.

Soap said, "I'll get you all over with soot, miss," clearly mortified by such intimacy.

"That's all right, Soap. It's Preshea's jacket and Sidheag's clothes."

Captain Niall gathered up the edges in his teeth and levered. They were only a hairbreadth above the ground, but it was enough.

Thus burdened, the werewolf leapt away, looking more ridiculous than he ever had or ever would again in all his long life.

Duke Hematol, being a vampire, might have caught up to them. But fair sportsmanship must be considered. Technically, they had gotten away, right and proper. Plus, the duke was not the kind of man to go running after anyone through the streets of London without his coat and hat. Lord Ambrose might have followed, but he was still at Monique's ball. If Hematol had given chase, Captain Niall would have been required to fight him, and that would have been far too messy. Why involve the werewolves in such a shameful business? It was, in the end, impolite to borrow another man's children. So the Duke of Hematol returned to his queen empty-handed.

Consequently, the overburdened werewolf attained the safety of Mademoiselle Geraldine's without incident. His passengers tumbled off his back, or out of the petticoat sling, and then climbed up the rope ladder with a collective sense of giddy freedom.

"I canna believe that worked," said Sidheag, her Scottish accent broadened by shock.

"Do you two have any idea how ridiculous you look?" said Dimity, still appalled by the dandy outfits.

"That was jolly," said Soap, grinning widely and hoisting Dimity's purple petticoat over one shoulder.

Vieve was waiting for them. "What happened? Tell me all!"

"Well," said Dimity, "where to start? I was held hostage by a vampire queen!" She and Pillover and Sidheag all began talking at once and on top of one another, detailing the events of the last few hours.

Sophronia stood silent, clutching her mechanimal reflexively to her breast.

Soap shuffled over to her. "Are you well, miss?"

Sophronia was embarrassed to find herself shaking.

"Oh, now, miss." Soap put his arm about her, awkwardly patting her back. As if she hadn't just spent a sling ride wrapped about him like a streetside doxy. "There, there."

Sophronia turned her attention on Bumbersnoot. She was enjoying Soap's comforting embrace too much for her own peace of mind. She'd liked it in the sling, too. He did have very nice muscles. And he smelled good under all that soot. To distract herself, she mock chided the mechanimal. "Bumbersnoot, you horrible creature! Premature exploding is not done!"

*Tick-tock, tick-tock* went Bumbersnoot's tail, back to normal speed.

"Oh, now, miss, he did his best," Soap joined in.

"Thank you for rescuing him, by the way."

"Thank him with a kiss," suggested Sidheag, coming over. She had left the storytelling to Dimity and Pillover and was watching Sophronia and Soap through narrowed yellow eyes.

Sophronia tried to back out of Soap's embrace, but his arm tightened. She looked up in confusion. His laughing brown eyes were unusually serious.

"Go on," encouraged Sidheag.

Sophronia stood up on tiptoe, intending to peck him on the cheek.

Soap leaned in, grabbing her chin gently, and kissed her. A proper kiss, on the lips.

Sophronia blinked and sputtered. His lips were very soft.

Sidheag said, "Excellent."

"Good night, miss," said Soap, and before Sophronia could recover her faculties, he wisely scampered off. This left Sophronia with one hand pressed to tingling lips and no plan, for once in her life.

Eventually, she recovered and glared at Sidheag. "Why do you encourage him? You know it's not possible."

"What's not possible?"

"A sootie and an Uptop."

"Now, Sophronia, don't be snobbish."

Sophronia sighed. "He's a good friend, Sidheag. I don't want to ruin that. I don't think of him in that way."

"Are you certain?"

"You're as bad as he is."

"Perhaps I too have designs above my station."

Which was a terribly enigmatic thing for Sidheag to say.

After all, she was the Lady of Kingair, wealthy and aristocratic. Very few were above her station.

Dimity came bouncing over. "My goodness, what an exciting evening. Do you think we still have time to catch the last of Monique's ball?"

"Oh, Dimity, really!" said Sophronia and Sidheag in unison.

onique de Pelouse never returned to Mademoiselle
Geraldine's Finishing Academy for Young Ladies of
Quality. Her coming-out ball was pronounced a resounding success by those who cared to pronounce such
things, and she took her place in society that spring. She was
expected to make a very advantageous match, although there
was a niggling rumor about her preference for Westminster
vampires. No suitors gave it much credence.

Sidheag and Agatha were taken off probation. No explanation was given, and Sophronia was left with the distinct sensation that they had been less circumspect about the monitoring
of Monique than they originally thought. She suspected that
Monique's working for Westminster and the potentate's blatant
refusal to believe that the hive was involved was considered
embarrassing by the school. Sister Mattie probably argued in
their favor. Sophronia also understood what lesson she was to

have learned from her ostracism. *My strength as an intelligencer is in my friends.* But she wasn't certain whether she was to take that as a need for more independence or less.

She tried several times to visit Professor Braithwope but was forbidden entry. "Enough" was Professor Lefoux's curt comment the fifth time. Sophronia tried to pass along a homemade card and even snuck onto Sister Mattie's balcony to pick him a bunch of foxgloves, but no contact was allowed. She wasn't certain if this was because he was now insane and dangerous to her or if the teachers had some inkling of her involvement with Shrimpdittle and figured she was dangerous to him. Lessons were dull without his inquisitive mustache. She developed an odd sensation behind her eyeballs, like the press of tears, but no tears came. The burn of guilt, she supposed. Something new and unpleasant to learn to live with. She plucked at her meals and began to think much longer and harder about consequences as well as actions.

Genevieve Lefoux disappeared from Mademoiselle Geraldine's before the airship reached Dartmoor. Professor Lefoux was entirely untroubled by her niece's absence and began to receive letters, a few months later, from a previously unheard-of nephew, Gaspar Lefoux, who had been accepted into Bunson's.

"Distant relation, you know. I had no idea he had evil-genius ambitions. Of course, I am delighted he has found himself a place. Who wouldn't be?" Sophronia overheard her say to Sister Mattie.

"Well, Bunson's is in bed with the Picklemen," protested the nun. "Even more so now. They won the contract to produce the crystalline guidance valves, did you hear? The potentate is introducing legislation in opposition, but it won't pass."

"That is a worry. Well, my nephew knows his own mind. He'll keep to the proper order."

"You'd better be careful, or the Octopus will have him," replied Sister Mattie.

Sophronia wondered if Vieve might be doing a little spying for her aunt while she acquired an education. *It'd be a good thing, a scout at Bunson's.* Her musings were interrupted.

"Sophronia, get a move on, please. We're late for breakfast!"

"Oh, yes, Dimity, of course."

"Post is in, did you hear?" Dimity bustled up alongside her and took her arm.

"Mmmmm?"

They rounded the corner to the great dining hall. Everything was back to normal; the girls were all seated at their various tables, looking neat and tidy and ready for lessons. London and all its charms were now far behind them.

Sophronia and Dimity made their way to their table. Like Monique, several of the older girls had been left behind in London, off to find husbands. Their beaux were carefully selected, their instructions clear, and their new lives as intelligencers begun. And two new debuts sat wide-eyed at their dining table, staring with awe at Preshea. Preshea who, like some evil monster of Greek mythology, had sprung fully formed into Monique's shoes. Literally, as she'd been gifted with the older girl's peach kid boots.

Dimity took her customary seat. "Oh, look, Sophronia, you've got letters. How exciting! Who from?"

Sophronia opened the first one. "Goodness gracious, Felix Mersey."

"Oh, what does he say? Is it a declaration?"

Sophronia considered the brief but pleasant paragraph. "No. Compliments and excessively charming inquiries. But blessedly there's no mention of me dressing as a dandy."

"A courting letter! How exciting."

"Mmm. You know, I think he thinks I favor the Picklemen now. Vampires, after all, kidnapped you."

"Well, don't we? It wasn't exactly comfortable for me." Dimity had a gift for understatement. "And they did kill that poor girl." She shuddered with remembered horror.

Sophronia put a hand on her friend's arm in sympathy. "I'm more in favor than I was, but why did the hive risk so much to stop them? There's something more afoot."

"Will you ever stop seeing conspiracies?"

"When others stop concocting them, I suppose."

Dimity sighed. "So it goes. Now, what's in the other letter?"

This one was even shorter than the first, a few flowery lines and an elegant signature. "Lord Akeldama pays his respects. Well, gracious me."

Dimity was confused. "Who's he? Is he also courting you?"

"In a way, I think he may be." Sophronia gave the letter to Bumbersnoot to burn. Safer that way.

# The End

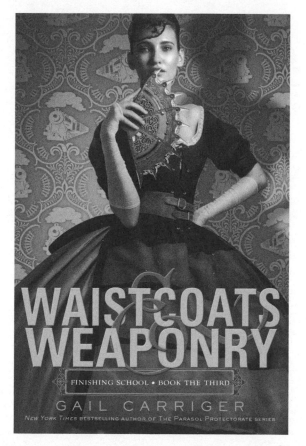

Gather your poison, steel-tipped quill, and the rest of your school supplies and join Mademoiselle Geraldine's proper young killing machines in the third rousing installment of the *New York Times* bestselling Finishing School series. Turn the page for a top-secret peek that you won't find anywhere else!

Available November 2014
however books are sold.

eduction in its purest form is a never-ending acquisition of knowledge about another individual. Every male is a new challenge, every occasion warrants a different approach. Take the greatest of care when applying these techniques, for they can be more dangerous than actual weaponry."

The girls all straightened. Lady Linette's lessons were always interesting, but seduction was supposed to be the best. What young lady didn't want to know how to manipulate a man? This was what finishing school was all about!

"You already have eyelash fluttering and flirting with fan and parasol, now let us consider holding a man's gaze with intent and purpose. This can be perceived as a bold stance, an outright challenge, or an unspoken offer. Let me demonstrate." Lady Linette came before each of them and with a few micromovements of lashes and lids demonstrated the differences among the three gazes. Each girl tried each gaze in return, feeling awkward, and then practiced on a partner for several minutes, feeling even more awkward. Periodically, fits of giggles interrupted the concentrated staring.

Eventually Dimity said, "Lady Linette, I don't mean to be ignorant, but what, exactly, is the *unspoken offer*? I mean to say, how do I know if I don't know, as it were?"

"Ah, yes, seduction. Have you read some of those horrid Gothics floating about? Oh, now, don't be coy, I've seen copies of *The Monk* passing from hand to hand. It's not forbidden, not at *this* school. Such an offer can encompass all things that men, as a general rule, require of women—from a kiss on the hand to one on the neck to the lips and beyond."

Dimity's eyes went owlish. "There's a *beyond*?"

"Don't interrupt, Miss Plumleigh-Teignmott. Where was I? Oh, yes. Then there is touching. A man may try to put his hands anywhere upon you, if you let him. A gentleman, of course, will ask first, but he will still try."

"Anywhere?" squeaked Dimity.

"Anywhere," said Lady Linette darkly.

"Oh, my."

Sophronia giggled at Dimity's awe. She herself was equipped with older brothers, several of whom attended university. Even before finishing school she had enjoyed eavesdropping on her family. As a result of indiscreet conversations between said brothers, she was rather more familiar with the intentions of young gentlemen than she ought to be. Apparently, gentlemen not only liked to kiss and touch women everywhere, they did that and more, on a regular basis, and mostly not with ladies at all, but with women of less genteel breeding. Some gentlemen, her brothers had whispered, even did it with each other. Although this was considered quite uncouth, Sophronia gathered, once one left Eton.

"Is that what the longing look is offering?" Dimity wanted to know.

"Generally speaking, yes. It is an invitation."

"Oh, dear, rather powerful, isn't it?"

Sophronia suspected Dimity would never look a man in the face again, for fear of issuing invitations.

"This is why you must master the differences among the three, not to mention the nature and length of the look itself. Facial expressions, my dears, can be thought of as part of one's toilette. In fact, clothing can also transmit messages. Tight stays, for example, offer up to the gentleman the slenderness of one's waist. Wouldn't he like to put his hands about it? A low décolletage suggests that he might like to touch, just there."

All the girls gasped. A few who were wearing dresses with low necklines surreptitiously tried to tug them up.

Sophronia found herself thinking of Felix Mersey. The young viscount had taken rather a shine to her, almost a year ago now, and they maintained a cautiously civil correspondence. The kind of correspondence no parent would sniff at. Although Sophronia's mother might have had the vapors if she'd known her daughter was receiving missives from a duke's son. Vapors of joy, mind you. Once or twice Sophronia had, rather desperately, searched between Felix's brief lines of courteous discourse for something more. But Lord Mersey either hadn't it in him to pen words of love, or had lost his taste for Sophronia after her Westminster Hive infiltration. In which case, his letters were mere formality from a gentleman who would not be so rude as to break off a courtship via the written word. Sophronia suspected the latter. After all, it would shake any gentleman's regard to find the object of his affection dressed as a male dandy and cavorting about with a chimney sweep.

Not that Sophronia was at all sure she wanted such attentions from Lord Mersey. His father was a Pickleman. She had come to like some of the supernatural set, all of whom, she knew in her heart, the Picklemen would happily see dead. As much as she admired Felix's slouch and overconfident flirtations, how could she reconcile his politics with her dislike of his father's secret society?

Nevertheless, Sophronia found herself daydreaming about the upcoming masquerade. She'd written to Felix of the momentous occasion, more for something to say than in the hope that anything should come of it. But, of course, he'd managed to wangle himself an invitation—after all, he was training to be an evil genius and his father *was* a duke. *If I wear a low-cut gown,* she wondered, *will Felix want to touch my décolletage? And do I want to lure him in because I think I may have lost him? Or do I want him for himself? He does have very nice eyes. And his waistcoat is always well fitted.*

Sophronia cocked her head, considering. *And would I want him to kiss me and more?* Her pulse raced and she had to consciously slow her breathing so Lady Linette would not notice.

*It's amazing that there are such possibilities inherent in just a long-ing look. Men really are weak willed.*

Lady Linette stopped the looks and returned to instruction. "What were we discussing?"

"Um, touching," said Preshea, in an unusually meek tone.

"Oh, yes. He may also wish to *kiss* there."

"What, the *décolletage?*" Dimity squeaked.

"Quite often."

Sophronia, thinking of her brothers' lewd talk, asked, "And elsewhere?"

Lady Linette smiled. "Well, yes, the very best ones like to kiss all over."

Most of the girls inhaled in shock, and then began asking questions all at once. What did it feel like? Was it nice or was it damp? After touching and kissing, what happened? And could this really all start with simply staring directly into a man's face at a ball?

Agatha looked as if she would like to faint. Dimity's cheeks were rosy with embarrassment, but she was utterly enthralled. Sophronia hated to admit it, but so was she.

Lady Linette held up a hand as the wave of curiosity crashed over her. Had she been a more sensitive individual, like Sister Mattie, she might have been embarrassed by the unladylike enthusiasm. But Lady Linette was an expert in manipulation, and if knowledge of connubial relations would arm her girls better in how to infiltrate society, then she would deliver unto them the necessary.

"Calm down, ladies, do. Let us practice a few more initial

seduction techniques, and discuss more on the consequences later. We are all a little overwrought at the moment. Suffice it to say that you must remember all the rules of polite society. No more than two dances with the same gentleman. No longer than the space of a dance and a half hour in one man's company. Do not walk out with a male alone, especially not to the conservatory, unless you are related. The goal is always to keep yourself safe from ruin or accusations thereof. After you have mastered the initial looks, we will move on to the seduction itself, and the boundaries that you must keep in place to protect your reputation. I will discuss how to employ canoodles and of which variety, without being caught. We may even study some light anatomy. Anything more than that, I hope you all understand, is reserved for the marriage bed. It is your mother's responsibility to explain such details of that situation to you as she sees fit."

An audible sigh of disappointment met this statement.

The girls then spent a most enjoyable hour practicing longing looks without any true understanding of what might result. It wasn't all that different from the entirety of their education at the academy. In a strange way, it was like practicing to kill someone with a bladed fan when one had yet to experience any actual act of assassination. Sophronia found herself more worried about how to respond to an imagined Felix kiss—the amount of pressure, what if there was excess saliva, where to put one's hands?—than she was about dealing out death. Although the concerns were oddly similar—amount of pressure, what if there was excess blood, how to keep one's gloves clean?

Of course, Sophronia had kissed Soap. Or more precisely,

Soap had kissed her. Which had managed to be both comforting and unsettling. She didn't like to think about her friend in *that* way. Although, when she let herself, Sophronia was all too apt to ruminate upon Soap's kiss. It had been a very nice kiss. And she hadn't worried about pressure or saliva or her hands; Soap had taken care of all of it. He was like that. Felix would be different. So very publicly suitable, a duke's son, yet so very politically unsuitable, *that* duke's son. Sophronia admitted to titillation; Felix was a challenge.

Sophronia shook off thoughts of both boys, which wasn't easy when practicing seduction. Thinking of Soap, she found, turned her longing gaze into one of frustration and puzzlement. And thinking of Felix made Dimity, her partner, come over very fidgety.

"Sophronia, don't look at me like that!"

"Like what?"

"All wistful, it makes me uncomfortable."

"Isn't that the point?"

"I don't know, is it? Lady Linette, please come assess Sophronia's look. I think she's executing it wrong."

Lady Linette duly came over and Sophronia duly looked at her and thought of Felix.

Lady Linette blinked back at her, impassive. "No, I think that is rather good. Perhaps a bit too much of an offer, Miss Temminnick. Can you tone it down slightly?"

Sophronia tried to think of both Felix and Soap at once.

"Oh, dear me, no, dear. No. Better the first time. Keep practicing."

Sophronia tried again.

Preshea said, "Ooooh, Sophronia, who are you thinking about?" Exchanging smug glances with a few of her cronies, she added, "I wager we can guess."

When Sophronia did not answer, Preshea added, "And how is our dear Lord Mersey?" There was an edge of bitterness to the sly question. She had rather fancied the young viscount for herself. Miss Preshea Buss was so pretty, she resented that he seemed so concentrated on plain, brown Sophronia.

Sophronia replied, blandly, "He's well, thank you for asking. Should I tender your regards?" The implication being, of course, that she had the right of correspondence when Preshea did not.

Preshea tossed her glossy black curls. "No, thank you. Besides, you'll see him before another letter gets through."

"Indeed I will, at my brother's soiree." Sophronia's tone was deceptively mild. "With ample time for conversation, as he has already requested the dinner dance."

At which every girl in the room glanced at her with envy. Sophronia hadn't meant to antagonize the whole class. She'd only meant to use the social cachet to quiet Preshea.

"Ladies, a little less gossip, a little more longing looks!" reprimanded their teacher. "Sophronia, you might consider your choice of escort with better care in the future. Lord Mersey is not on the agenda for a marriage of infiltration, and Picklemen do not make good patrons." Sophronia was duly chastised.

The others got back to it, giggling softly among themselves.

Dimity asked Sophronia, "Did he really ask you for the dinner?"

"No, but he will."

"Are you sure? I thought you were afraid you'd lost him."

Sophronia fanned out her gloved hands in a gesture of dismissal. "Perhaps, but not to Preshea, I haven't! Besides, he's still interested enough to come to my family's masquerade. Although that could be because as a gentleman he can only politely break off with me in person."

Dimity nodded her understanding. "If you learn these seduction lessons well, you might be able to keep him. Despite Lady Linette's opinion, I think he's a delicious prospect. For fun, if nothing else. I should like to see you try."

Sophronia firmed up her spine. "You're right! Let's practice."

They tried diligently for the next twenty minutes. Sophronia wished for Sidheag. She was very good on the subject of understanding the male psyche, having grown up in a werewolf pack, all of them soldiers, not to mention visits with the rest of the regiment regularly. Her knowledge was far more complete than Sophronia's bits of gleaned gossip from indiscreet brothers.

At the end of the lesson, Dimity and Agatha scuttled off, eager to return to their private chambers, hoping that Sidheag would be waiting there, pigeon crisis averted. Dimity carried Sophronia's hurlie safely stashed in her reticule, out of Lady Linette's clutches.

That good lady rarely forgot anything. "Well, Miss Temminnick, give it to me."

"Lady Linette?"

"The unregistered wrist claw thing you used to save yourself earlier this evening."

Sophronia pulled back her sleeves, showing the bandage on one side and the complete absence of the hurlie on the other. "I'm afraid I lost it in that very scrabble. You see, I had to leave it behind, hooked on, in order to get through the hatch."

Lady Linette was skeptical.

Sophronia stood quietly, no elaboration that might give away the lie, no excess blinking that might betray a direct falsehood. She was applying, with great expertise, every one of the lessons that Lady Linette herself had taught her.

"Sometimes, Miss Temminnick, I worry that we are training you *too* well."

"Is that possible, Lady Linette?"

"I don't know. I suppose in the end it will ride on where your loyalties lie."

"I suppose it will."

"Where *do* they lie, Miss Temminnick? You are what, sixteen now? Old enough to marry. Old enough to leave this school, should your parents wish it."

"I haven't learned everything yet."

"Nor have you finished properly. That is not the point."

"What is the point?"

"You are old enough to know your own mind. Whose patronage will you undertake? Queen and country, supernatural, Picklemen? Will you follow your training in the pursuit of our ends, or those of your beau?"

"And what of my own wishes?"

Lady Linette was not so foolish as to answer that. "Or the vampire who sends you gifts?"

"Reading my mail, Lady Linette? How gauche. I guess the

answer to your question is, I don't know yet." Sophronia felt emboldened. "I like this school but not the potentate, although working for queen and country seems no bad thing."

"The one is tied to the other, I'm afraid." Lady Linette seemed genuinely contrite, either because of the potentate himself—who did have a regrettable personality—or the fact that Queen Victoria's government had so fully integrated the supernatural element.

"That is the difficulty, isn't it? Right now my vampire friend's gifts, I must own, are attractive. Although not my vampire friend himself," Sophronia replied.

Lady Linette was looking at Sophronia with more respect than she had ever shown before. "He is not so bad a choice. We would be sad to lose you, but he could absolutely afford your indenture. Although he is a vampire; he might want something extra for it."

Sophronia felt almost like an equal. What, she wondered, had just happened in that class to cause this shift in her own social standing with her teacher? Whatever it was, she hoped to capitalize on it. She rather enjoyed the novelty of garnering respect from an adult. So she accessed her training and responded as it dictated.

"When I have made up my mind, Lady Linette, you'll be the first to know." *Well, after Dimity, Agatha, Sidheag, and Soap. And Bumbersnoot. Bumbersnoot will have to be included in any of my future plans.*

"Very considered response, Miss Temminnick. A word of warning: you can't change him, Miss Temminnick."

"Who? My vampire friend or my Pickleman beau?"

"Yes." Then, in one of her rapid switches of topic, designed—they had all learned—to unsettle an opponent, Lady Linette said, "Where is Lady Kingair, Miss Temminnick?"

"Unwell," said Sophronia, instinctually covering for her friend's absence.

"Oh, indeed, and what form of illness has afflicted her? She's customarily so hardy."

*When fibbing, always stick as close to the truth as possible.* "Of the sentimental variety. She had a letter that quite overset her."

Lady Linette's expression changed. So much so that Sophronia wondered if she knew the contents of Sidheag's letter. Had she intercepted a private pigeon before it reached its intended target? Highly illegal, of course, worse than reading Lord Akeldama's notes, but Lady Linette was an intelligencer. She did more illegal things before tea each day than most people did in a lifetime.

The teacher said, "Understandable sentiment, I suppose. But I expect to see her at supper, otherwise I will send matron. Perhaps she is in need of laudanum to settle her nerves."

"Very good, Lady Linette. I will let her know."

With which Sophronia escaped, gliding down the passageway as quickly as her skirts would allow.

Sidheag had not returned, not that they could conceive of a way for her to do so without being found out. The school was, after all, floating midair and very high up. In deference to the presence of Preshea; her new chamber-mate, Frenetta; and a gaggle of other girls, the three friends retreated to Sophronia and Dimity's room. Bumbersnoot was delighted to see them. The little mechanimal trundled about tooting smoke out his ears and puffing steam from below his carapace. His tail tick-tocked back and forth and Agatha, despite Sophronia's admonishments not to spoil him, fed the metal dog torn scraps of a brown paper bag that had once held sweets.

"What will we do if she is out all night, alone, with a were-wolf?" Dimity was upset by the very idea.

"He's a teacher, surely that counts for something?" protested Agatha.

"He's not a relative. If word gets out, her reputation will be in ruins." Dimity was probably correct in this assumption. "Didn't we just learn that a young lady should never be alone with a gentleman for any length of time? Do the other teachers know she is with him?"

Sophronia said, "I don't think so. Lady Linette just asked me where she was."

Dimity swallowed. "That is *not* good."

"Worse, she only has until supper to reappear. Matron's coming by to check."

"Then what will we do? Pillows in the bed won't work on matron. None of us looks enough like Sidheag to pull a wig-and-switch, either." Dimity wasn't the best intelligencer, but some of the training had stuck.

Sophronia was out of options. "We have to hope she returns in time. Nothing else for it." She sat down on her bed with a thump.

Dimity said out loud what they had all three been secretly wondering: "Do you think Lord Maccon has been successfully challenged?" It was a most delicate way of putting it. Lord Maccon was Sidheag's great-great-great-grandfather, in truth the only father she had. He was also Alpha of the Kingair Pack, and Alphas had to fight for their position constantly. He was supposed to be the second-most-powerful werewolf in all of Britain, but new werewolves did happen, and loners, those unattached to a pack like Captain Niall, could be strong. If one had challenged Lord Maccon and won, it meant the Laird of Kingair was dead.

Sophronia said, "I don't like to think it, but it would explain Sidheag's behavior."

Agatha, who knew Sidheag better than anyone, began to cry.

"Hush, now, we don't *know* that's what happened," Sophronia tutted at her. "It could just be war. Queen Victoria is always sending her werewolves to fight on the front lines somewhere foreign."

Bumbersnoot butted up against one of Agatha's slippered feet, his tail wagging a little less, his floppy leather ears wiggling sympathetically.

Agatha blubbered, "But she does love him so. I know she talks gruff, but he's her one and only Gramps. If he's been hurt or killed..." Great fat tears trickled down her round, freckled face.

"Now, now, Agatha, where's your handkerchief? You'll come over all blotchy, and Professor Lefoux will notice in our next class. Can't have that." Sophronia bustled about collecting one of her spares.

Agatha tried to recover her emotions. She was terrified of Professor Lefoux. Professor Lefoux had no respect for finer feelings, even when they were being applied with purpose. Gadgets, felt Professor Lefoux, solved any problem.

Agatha disposed of one damp handkerchief, and by the time she'd finished with another, her sobs had subsided.

"Good girl," said Sophronia.

Dimity said, "Sophronia's right. We don't know the real truth of any of it."

Sophronia added, "If Sidheag doesn't return, our only hope is that Soap has uncovered something of merit."

Dimity and Agatha looked uncomfortable. They knew it meant Sophronia was sneaking out later that night on one of her clandestine visits to engineering. They also knew it meant Sophronia had no means of protecting Sidheag's reputation, because if she had, she would be doing that instead.

Matron would come and Sidheag would not be there.

So it turned out to be.

# THE PARASOL PROTECTORATE

## BY GAIL CARRIGER

## A COMEDY OF MANNERS SET IN VICTORIAN LONDON
## FULL OF WEREWOLVES, VAMPIRES, DIRIGIBLES, AND TEA-DRINKING.

Alexia Tarabotti is laboring under a great many social tribulations. First, she has no soul. Second, she's a spinster whose father is both Italian and dead. Third, she was rudely attacked by a vampire, breaking all standards of social etiquette.

Where to go from there? From bad to worse apparently, for Alexia accidentally kills the vampire—and then the appalling Lord Maccon (loud, messy, gorgeous, and werewolf) is sent by Queen Victoria to investigate.

With unexpected vampires appearing and expected vampires disappearing, everyone seems to believe Alexia is responsible. Can she figure out what is actually happening to London's high society? Will her soulless ability to negate supernatural powers prove useful or just plain embarrassing? Finally, who is the real enemy, and do they have treacle tart?

"WICKEDLY FUNNY." —Angie Fox, *New York Times* Bestselling Author

"*SOULLESS* HAS ALL THE DELICATE CHARM OF A VICTORIAN PARASOL,
AND ALL THE WICKED FORCE OF A VICTORIAN PARASOL SECRETLY
WEIGHTED WITH BRASS SHOT AND EXPERTLY WIELDED. RAVISHING."
—Lev Grossman, *New York Times* bestselling author of *The Magicians*

"CARRIGER DEBUTS BRILLIANTLY WITH A BLEND OF VICTORIAN ROMANCE,
SCREWBALL COMEDY OF MANNERS AND ALTERNATE HISTORY. . . . THIS
INTOXICATINGLY WITTY PARODY WILL APPEAL TO A WIDE CROSS-SECTION
OF ROMANCE, FANTASY AND STEAMPUNK FANS." —*Publishers Weekly* (Starred Review)